||| ||| W9-AAG-379

Jealousy

Linda Brickhouse

http://www.melodramapublishing.com

If this book was purchased without a cover you should be aware that this may have been stolen or reported to the publisher as "unsold or destroyed." Neither the author nor the publisher has received payment for the sale of this "stripped book."

Jealousy
Copyright © 2007 by Linda Brickhouse

All rights reserved. Printed in the United States of America. No part of this book may be used or reproduced, stored in a retrieval system, or transmitted by any means, electronic, mechanical, photocopying, recording, or otherwise, without written permission from the publisher. Although every precaution has been taken in the preparation of this book, the publisher and author assume no responsibility for errors or omissions.

For information address:
Melodrama Publishing
P. O. Box 522
Bellport, New York 11713-0522

Web address: www.melodramapublishing.com
e-mail: melodramapub@aol.com

Library of Congress Control Number: 2007926646
ISBN 1-934157-07-4
First Edition

This novel is a work of fiction. Any resemblances to actual events, real people, living or dead, organizations, establishments, locales are products of the author's imagination. Other names, characters, places, and incidents are used fictitiously.

10 9 8 7 6 5 4 3 2 1
First Paperback Edition

Jealousy

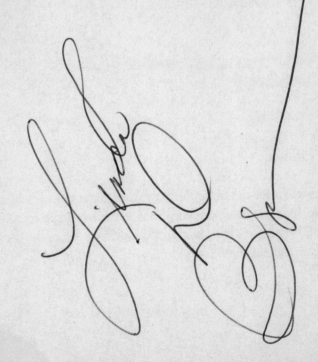

Acknowledgements:

I stood in the middle of a storm wondering where to go for shelter and seconds before the wind and rains hoisted me away you claimed me your child. Thank you Lord for always rescuing me from every storm and suddenly I feel the warm rays of the sun.

There is no mother greater than my own. I thank you Margaret for your grace and only hope I earned your love.

Daddy, thank you for the wind that hit me in the face, and the force that pushed me forward. I'm here!!!

So many people come into our lives for so many different reason and I appreciate every one that have contributed to me being the woman I am:

My son's have given me love that was unimaginable and I pray that I have made them proud.

To Russell, kinship is more than blood thank you for being the greatest brother I'll ever have.

To my Creative Exec, and Correspondence person I love you all like a fat girl looooovvve .... but you know this big girl likes shoes. (Sonia, and Derrick)

My family that I have cried with, saved lives with and just had a good time with I couldn't have dreamed this big without you so, thank you.

To my publisher Melodrama, I know I have said it more times than I could count but thank you so much for all your support.

THE CHARACTERS IN THIS BOOK ARE NOT YOU..... NOPE NOT YOU EITHER...... I LOVE YOU ENOUGH NOT TO TELL THE WORLD HOW CRAZY YOU ARE ....

With Love,

Linda

1

The Betrayal

Chaka realized the horrible mistake he made almost too late. Standing next to the luxury silver colored vehicle, he smiled at the two brothers approaching. Nothing about the way they walked or looked suggested malice as they greeted him. Intertwined in the brotherly embrace he felt the butt of a gun. He gave it no thought. In the streets, they were prepared for battle. Today was no different. As he turned to greet the next man, the hairs on the back of his forearm stood on end. Immediately he disregarded the feeling believing the two men before him were loyal and trusted. They were more than friends they were family. Over the years, the trio shared meals, money and life lessons. He would never have suspected they were going to betray him.

A confused look stretched across Chaka's face as he felt the barrel of the gun in his stomach. Immediately a cold sweat appeared as he realized this wasn't a joke. Reality kicked in as he reached for his own weapon but remembered it was underneath the driver's seat. Panic took control as he struggled to pull his hand away. Afraid to look down, he stared in the perpetrators eyes, hoping for an answer.

"How could they do this to me?" He whispered.

The sound of the shot made him shake. Next, he felt the fire spread and radiate to the soles of his feet. Tears slid, as he realized that they were there to kill him. The ground seemed to rise and meet him as he laid flat out on the black tar. Chaka didn't have a chance to think about the wrongs he done. He was in too much pain. In his peripheral, he saw Quinton on the corner. For a split second, Chaka believed he would live. The moment ended just as quickly. Quinton stood there, immobile without acknowledging that he understood what had just happened.

He attempted to catch his breath so he could speak, but nothing worked. His brain was screaming but nothing came out of his mouth. In a pointless effort, he tried to stop the blood by putting his hand on the large whole in his body. Instead of stopping, a warm gush of blood flowed around his fingers. The last sound he heard was gunshots in the distance as he took his last breath.

Quinton finally processed the events that unfolded. The fog lifted as he unsuccessfully tried to retaliate. His instincts kicked in too late, as he aimed the nine-millimeter semi-automatic glock and fired. The taller of the men zigged and zagged on the dead end street until he was able to hide in the cut out of the church. Chaka's killer was stuck in the middle of the street, as the first shot barely missed him. Quickly, the man got his bearings and returned fire without aiming. Neither shot hit its target. The 6'2" black man standing in the middle of the street didn't give thought to his safety as he stormed towards his fleeting target. Firing one shot after the next he cursed silently. Out of bullets, he reached for another clip and realized he was empty. Broken, he watched as the two men climbed the low wall and disappeared into the park.

The whites of his eyes were blood shot red. He stood there unsure of his next move. The sounds of the sirens broke his confusion. He jumped into his truck and sped away.

Leaving Chaka on the ground left him feeling guilty and enraged.

2

The Rage

Quinton hit the heavy oak door with such force, the glass windows rattled. The thunderous sound scared the women in the living room. Anissa leaped from the couch heading to the door as it flew open. Eve ran behind her to find out what was going on. Stunned silent by his appearance, Eve found her voice first.

"What the fuck happened?" she screamed.

He couldn't respond. The words had disappeared between his head and his mouth. The split second that he stood there, Anissa watched him. She searched for any signs that he might be hurt. Accepting he wasn't physically scarred she looked him over again, slower from head to toe. His eyes, never met hers as she began to speak. He pushed past her. Storming up the steps two at a time, he entered their bedroom.

Mentally he cataloged his next movements. Standing there in his underwear he frantically snatched one item after another from his dresser drawers.

The smell of something burning followed in his path. Anissa immediately recognized the scent and knew Quinton had fired a gun. Something terrible happened, whatever it was had him shook. Standing there afraid to move she pictured him coming through the door. She calculated everything about him that was wrong in the few seconds she saw him. Nervously she ticked off one item after another in her head. She didn't want Eve to realize what she was doing. It could only cause more drama. The feeling of panic welled up as she stood there waiting for answers.

His normally smooth chocolate skin was ashy. His easy manners were replaced by an unleashed rage. Sweat poured into his eyes and his lips were parched and white. The next thought paralyzed her.

Where was Chaka?

Afraid to speak aloud, she turned to Eve and waited. At the very moment Anissa thought it, Eve spoke the words.

"Where is Chaka," she asked softly.

They stared at one another. The shrill of the telephone's ring was going crazy in the background. Terrified and too afraid to move they waited. Q was tearing down the stairs when the noise finally stopped. He didn't slow his pace or acknowledge either of the women at the bottom of the steps waiting for him. Rounding the corner, he stormed to the basement.

At sixteen, he developed an unhealthy curiosity about handguns, and was quickly into all the accessories. Beneath, the staircase in the basement was a hidden metal ventilated vault especially designed for storing weapons and other toys he loved to play with. Nothing was too small and the price was no object but like any thing, he had his favorites. It only took him a blink of his lashes before he made his choice. The X-Harness shoulder holster would fit just right for the occasion. His twin Smith and Wesson .357 Sig were next on his agenda. Quickly, he placed the guns in the designated slots and recited the characteristic that made these beauties his favorites. The stainless steel chassis system, the reversible magazine catch, the interchangeable grip, and the dual slide stop were only part of their charisma. Quinton was using every trick he knew to keep his sanity. If reciting the Lord's Prayer was going to help, he would try it next. Finally he got around to his ammunition. Inside the cargo pants, he loaded up clips as if he were going to Desert Storm.

His phone vibrated. Instead of bothering with the annoyance, he threw it across the room and slammed the vault. Standing in the dim-lit room, he reloaded and stormed up the steps.

Although, it seemed longer Quinton had only been in the house twelve minutes. As quickly as he had come, he was ready to leave. Standing in the doorway, he fit the description of an ordinary perpetrator. Black man, dressed in black and armed. The deranged look completed the image of man on a mission. Anissa could not stop the tears as she watched him prepare to leave. She wanted to beg him to stay but she knew he had to go. Biting her cheeks, she allowed him to move by her questioning eyes.

Eve however, blocked his path and cranked her neck with the force of a bulldozer.

She needed to know where Chaka was and why hadn't he come home yet. The look on Quinton's face stopped Eve from talking. Fearful of the answer, she swallowed the question.

Without looking at Eve or Anissa, he answered. The strength in his voice was a facade.

"They got at Chaka. Right now, I don't have time to tell you all the details. When

"Jake" (the slang used to describe police in New York) brings his punk ass here just act like you don't know shit."

He turned, looked at both women, as if it would be his last. He retraced his steps to Anissa. Standing on her tiptoes, she leaned into him wanting to smell him, kiss him, and hold him. The kiss was the softest, most loving touch they shared in a long time. She held on not wanting to let go.

The door slammed against the wall as he stalked out into the cold.

Buck was stumbling in the dark, when he heard his phone. Sasha called him with the news.

"They found Chaka on Furman Street and the dead-end. He's been shot. The cops are everywhere; you had better get over there now."

She whimpered while trying to understand why this happened to such a good person.

Buck didn't waste words when he was sleepy. The noise in his head subsided as he yelled into the phone.

"Who the fucks been shot?" He asked when he got his head together.

Carefully, she chose each word praying he wouldn't go off. Closing her eyes against the rage, she waited.

The usual big cuddly teddy bear she had fallen for was now behaving like a starving grizzly bear. Nothing she attempted to say reached him after he heard someone shot Chaka. Pacing back and forth, he reasoned with himself. The frustration and confusion forced him to over heat.

"I'll call you later," he snapped and disconnected the line.

Alone in the Monte Carlo he felt the rage moving in him. It started like a mild misty rain and turned into a level-two disaster without warning. He became a maniac behind the wheel - taking lights and barely looking out for on coming traffic. At the first curve, he honked until cars moved out of his way. When his bully tactic didn't work, he drove on the narrow shoulders. A couple times, he just cut drivers off forcing them to slam on their brakes.

Jackie Robinson Parkway was an amateur racecar driver's dream, but to a regular "Joe or Jane" it was a nightmare. Blind spots that lead to open lanes, narrow dips, and dangerous curves compressed the race-track style parkway. However, Buck didn't give a damn about the other driver's safety. He wanted to get to Brooklyn. Now.

Twenty minutes later, he was pulling up in front of Chaka's home. Barely turning off the ignition, he leaped from the vehicle. A car nearly side swiped him as he darted out into traffic. Too, angry to notice or care, he rushed on. His shirt flapped in the wind as he banged on the door.

There it was again, Anissa noted: the wild-eyed evil look and the mechanical movements. Buck brushed by her as he entered the foyer. Before, he could ask her anything she questioned him.

"What the hell happened? Tell me everything is going to be okay," she pleaded.

Buck stood still as it registered that it must be true. Someone shot his friend. Neither Anissa nor Sasha said if he was alive. The thought weighed heavy as he waited for Anissa to tell him something useful.

"Where's Quinton Anissa," he demanded.

Anissa looked at him strange, before she said a word.

"He left here about forty minutes ago. I thought he, you, and Chaka were together," she said. Her hands shook as she tried to understand.

"Where were you Buck?" she asked quietly.

Accepting he didn't have any answers wasn't easy but Anissa watched him as he ran to his car.

Buck felt the rage and anxiety build as he exited the door in search of Quinton. The questions kept coming. However, there was not a soul to fill in the blanks. He contemplated his next stop before he gave up and went to find the answers. Buck was an impulsive man and thinking wasn't the strongest thing he did. Through the years, he had taken his role as the muscle of the crew seriously. Today, he had failed to protect his friends. They were both somewhere and at least one of them was hurt.

"Shit," he cursed as he decided he had to do something.

Over the years, the crew made an enemy or two but mostly it was mild beefs that didn't warrant any gunplay. Quickly he decided an outsider had too much to lose if they went against Baker Boys 5. The only person he believed could be responsible for shooting Chaka. It had to be that snake-faking ass Earl. Thinking the lames' name left a nasty taste in Buck's mouth. Before he could control the impulse, he spit on the sidewalk with as much venom as he felt for his enemy.

Buck had done enough dirt to know that a weakling found courage at least once in his life. Earl must have found some courage, he reasoned. As if hearing the words aloud made them true, he spoke.

"I should have killed you a long time ago but motherfucker your days are numbered." Slamming his hand on the steering wheel, he allowed the fury to take over. Wrong move he decided too late, it scared him how much hatred he harbored in his heart.

He feared a great many things in his life but Buck had always stepped up to his fears like a warrior. For the first time, his fears made him stand still. He knew if he saw Earl before he had found a way to deal with his anger, he would kill him.

In the middle of the street, Buck imagined himself wrapping Earl's dreads around his neck until he strangled to death. He envisioned his beady eyes bulging and his tongue hanging from his mouth as he desperately struggled for his next breath.

3

Overjoyed at someone else's misery

The smoke rose high above the dread's head as he exhaled. His cold beady eyes were slits as he fully enjoyed the rhythm of the steel drums and melodic sounds of old school rockers. The heavy-laced Jamaican chat washed over the lanky man-child, as he appeared to be celebrating the death of his only nemesis in the world. Swaying to the beats, he thought about Chaka Dubois. He remembered the days of hanging out on the steps dreaming about when they were rich. He remembered wanting to fit in so desperately he trusted every word Chaka said. Only to later, find out he'd been used.

Chaka seemed to have the answers to everything and Earl was stumbling around trying to figure out most things. Especially, since his father had gotten locked up for possession of more than 1000 pounds of weed. Earl needed a friend.

The Baker Boys 5, Chaka called his crew. They did everything together from selling cookies to classmate, to partying and selling weed. Accepting their friendship he thought was a blessing.

In his relaxed haze, Earl giggled to himself as thought about better times. The crew changed him from the weird dressing outsider with a heavy accent to a street hustler in less then a year. With Chaka's influence, he took over his father's illegal business and they began getting money together. It was only natural that he trusted the crew with his life and they took him in and trusted him with some things. Chaka never really shared his motives although by the time Earl figured it out he was ousted from the group.

Now that Chaka was dead, he hoped to embrace the original remaining members of the Baker Boys 5 and the extension of their success the Dirty Dozen. However, he wasn't opposed to a hostile takeover. This was his chance and he wouldn't allow fucked up emotions to get in his way. Too long, he accepted the shadows and lurked about trying get along while the crewmembers flourished. They flaunted their success while Earl struggled to get just a little more than enough. He was tired of being the outcast thrown out of the kingdom. A kingdom he believed he helped build. Slowly the resentment took over the easy mode he had earlier. He wanted to forget he'd ever given Chaka a second thought. Looking around he decided with out the Baker Boys 5 he had managed to do well. Counting his blessing, he lit another spliff and waited for the high.

The earthly scent of weed had him on an ultimate climb. The gates opened as the flame burned. Earl willingly allowed his mind to wander back through his teenage years.

If only half the men claiming the Dirty Dozen knew, that Earl was one of the founders that helped to plant the seed. They might not have believed half of Chaka's bullshit but the truth was that this was a well-hidden fact. Even the fact that they were once friends didn't exist for most, unless it was to describe Earl's so-called betrayal. However, Chaka's wrongdoings were well covered despite all the bullshit. He had not forgotten the threats, the snitching, and the lies that made them enemies and destroyed Earl's sense of loyalty for the crew. There was no possible way Buck or Quinton would accept that he had nothing to do with Chaka death. Telling them the truth about Chaka didn't matter then. And it surely would make a bit of difference now. He intended to use their anger to suit his needs. He would do to Chaka's crew exactly what Chaka had done to him.

The name the Dirty Dozen was an extension of the original Baker Boys 5. The concept was the same. The moniker was a rip-off from the original movie scripted by Lukas Heller and Nunnally Johnson. Chaka yelled excitedly in the basement at the end of the movie.

'It's basically a suicide mission in them streets hustling. But the truth is our training starts at birth. We live behind the enemy lines and the promise is the chance at having money, material things, and a temporary sense of freedom.'

Understanding the excitement, Earl quickly caught the wave adding his two cents. He declared they could probably form their own Dirty Dozen by invading other states.

Earl believed he should have been more amped up about Chaka's death. Instead, he was feeling nostalgic and empathy for the family he left behind. Bitterly, he cursed. Chaka didn't deserve any of the emotion he wasted. However, there he was still showing solidarity to the man that marked him a snitch in the earlier years. He carried on by himself until he felt the memories slipping past the barriers.

It was a cool day; the wind was whipping trash around as the four men stood just outside the fence of Ocean Hill projects, waiting for a few senior citizens to go by. Chaka and Earl were side by side while Quinton and Buck faced them. Nervously, Earl handed Buck the nylon knapsack. Short of dropping the bag and running, he waited for the chaos.

A panel van sped up onto the sidewalk where the boys were standing. Doors flew open and "Jake" seemed to be on their asses. Earl took off past two police men in the rear of the truck. Chaka tried to run into the street and was clothes-lined by a huge forearm of another officer. Meanwhile Quinton stood still, throwing up his hands in surrender. Buck took off running holding the bag. Before the cops could get close, he leaped over the black Iron Gates and slid past the wooden benches, and concrete tables Earl watched the mess unfold from the parking lot between two cars. The bag weighed Buck down a bit but he adjusted it while in flight. Someone was coming out of

309 McDougal. Straight was the quickest way to any point. The decision proved to be a huge mistake. Instead of heading straight to the back door and continuing out to Broadway, Buck lost his bearings

BUCK THOUGHS:

Taking the steps two at a time, Buck went up the stairs. By the third floor, he heard the static filled radios as the T n T gave chase. Damned he thought as he debated with himself. Suddenly the light went on and he exited the A stairwell doubling back to the B side. Quietly he opened the door and began a slow descend. Someone had put one of the officers on to his path because as Buck got to the first floor and deliberately used his body to open the door he met the barrel of the officers service revolver. The shit-face grin on the cop's face left Buck disgusted.

The officer slammed him against the pale concrete wall. Just at impact, Buck felt his knees come out from beneath him. Jake had kicked him in the back of his knees forcing him forward on all fours. Sheer momentum and the heavy forearm to the back of his head left Buck lying on the dirty floor.

In disbelief Chaka, Quinton, and Earl watched as the cops pushed Buck towards the van. The trio sat on the freezing curb in handcuffs waiting for another paddy wagon.

Earl couldn't believe he hadn't been paying attention and allowed an officer to creep up on his hiding spot. Fear almost made him shit on himself as he heard the cuffs clink against the lock. The idea that he was even in the middle of this caused Earl to rethink the reason he was there in the first place. He couldn't go to jail that was a fact and he vowed he would do everything in his power to stay out of the system. Chaka kept giving Earl dirty looks during the entire ordeal. It didn't take Quinton long to figure out Chaka believed Earl set them up. However, no one ever asked Earl anything. They went about the proceedings waiting for their parents to arrive.

Buck was in a cell separate from the rest of the crew. Ms. Sadie came down to the precinct and took Chaka home. Quinton's father Mr. Saunders showed up with a belt for his child. Meanwhile, Earl went untouched, no parent called, and he walked without a desk appearance.

4

The Funeral service

No matter how many times Quinton rehearsed the words he couldn't believe they were true. This was Chaka's going home service. Something was definitely wrong with the sound of those words.

Standing in the mirror, he refused to look at his face. The confidence and assertiveness of the well-rounded man was buried deep beneath his sorrow and shame. He didn't want to see the pain in his pitiful eyes or the tears that clouded his vision. As if on autopilot, he moved about in a daze. Obligation helped him to don the suit Anissa laid out for him. Regret made him want to stay home. The pain he felt at losing his best friend and partner was greater than anything he had ever experienced.

Confused and exhausted Quinton accepted his grief. He failed. Chaka should not have died that day. He wished he had gotten there sooner, or pulled out his gat faster. Maybe, he reasoned, he could have saved him from the horror. The tears flowed, yet again, as he imagined Chaka lying there on the ground with blood covering his chest. He re-lived every second that it took him to respond to the fact that a shot rang in the distance. It took him another few seconds to watch Chaka's body fall. Finally, he reacted but it was all in vain. The killers got away. The thought almost paralyzed Quinton as he felt the dry lump in his throat. Followed by the rapid pound of his heart and nervous feeling in the pit of his stomach, he needed to lie down.

"Fuck this," he hissed snatching at his necktie. Anissa watched her heart-broken man. Slowly she entered the room offering the tenderness of a loving touch. She picked up the tie and walked to him. Quinton didn't bother to protest. She was determined to help him get through the day. All he really wanted was be alone.

He sat motionless on the bed, allowing her to fix his clothes. She spoke softly, "Babe, it's going to be okay. If you don't want to do the eulogy don't worry about it. We'll find a way around it."

Anissa's voice annoyed him. He wanted her to shut up; he had to save face. She was trying to make things easy. He had to face the pain, especially since he failed when it mattered most. The least he could do was stand up for his boy in death. The emotion Quinton was carrying had him in a tale spin. He wondered how she would feel if she knew, exactly what he done. He vowed to put this past him.

The agony of the day moved in slow motion. Faces of mourners blurred before him as they each offered heart felt sympathy and condolences. All Quinton could see was his own pain. Glancing around the church, he searched for the only faces that could understand his pain. Buck was in the rear of the sanctuary away from the crowd. The twins - Danny and Dave - were standing near the closed casket, silently trying to understand how this could have happened.

All four men huddled together in clutch as they observed mourners in the pews. Looking for any clues that one of them may have been responsible for the murder.

Eve sat next to Anissa and refused to move. She looked straight ahead and barely acknowledged anyone in the room. She didn't try to understand why so many women whimpered over her lover. The thought only infuriated her sitting there listening to them bawling and showing out. Her emotions were all over the place. Although, she loved Chaka she wondered if her search for more stopped her from grieving. Angry she couldn't accept he would never experience the feeling of loving him completely. While everyone else was grieving Eve fought with her own emotions.

"How can I claim to love him but never really fell in love," she whispered.

Anissa tried to acknowledge Eve had spoken but wasn't sure. She leaned closer to her hoping she would repeat whatever she had whispered.

"Huh, what did you say?" Anissa questioned.

Eve shook herself knowing she couldn't let anyone know her true feelings. Glaring at Anissa, she responded.

"Nothing."

Instead, she glanced around the church until she was able to deal with the stresses that plagued Chaka's funeral.

Out by the corner Eve spied the elegant dark skinned woman entering the church. Immediately, she felt a chill. This woman was different from the others. Her walk screamed confidence despite the occasion. The tears were genuine but it was her clothes that Eve paid attention too. She was dressed like a widower - not overly done - but tasteful in a simple black sheath and matching jacket. She wore a pillbox hat with an attached veil. Her shoes matched the classy ensemble to a tee. The slant-eyed sister, with long jet-black hair, slim build was balancing on at least three and half inches of classic closed-toe heel. There wasn't a missed step in her walk or drop of her head as she removed the oversized designer frames. Eve decided she wasn't exceptionally pretty but she was respectful. She was drawn to the way she stood out in the crowded church.

Eve was jealous but she didn't understand why. Reasoning with herself, she accepted most of the women in the room would have traded places with her any day. So why was she sitting there envious over this stranger. The feeling definitely was inappropriate at a funeral. More importantly, she was Chaka's woman –now was the time to behave like it. She chastised herself but could not stop the feeling. Intrigued she watched.

The woman walked straight to Buck and greeted him with a hug. The duo's embrace could have so many meanings but Eve decided she was another one of his fans, coming to support him in his time of need. Surprisingly, Buck's face lost the angry scowl as he held the hand of his guest, leading her to the second row.

Eve again felt a tingling in her core as she witnessed Buck's demeanor change. He was comforting her, instead of the other way around. Quinton also seemed to offer her a sense of comfort in his brief nod. The feeling of envy resurfaced as she realized neither Buck nor Quinton had offered her so much compassion. The last few days, they behaved as if it were her fault Chaka was gone. Eve was outraged and the anger began to rise slowly yet controlled.

At the last viewing, Eve eyed the strange woman suspiciously; suddenly she wanted to know who she was.

Anissa almost lost her resolve as Quinton stood to read the eulogy for Chaka. The sorrow and the anguish were wrenching as he struggled to control his emotions. She sat up and tried to will her strength to help Quinton through these moments. She refused to hide her face or take her eyes from him. In a clear strong voice, he began reading the words.

Something happened. He balled up the paper. Lowering his head, he found the words in his heart.

"Saying I'm going to miss him doesn't begin to tell our story. In two lifetimes I couldn't have asked for a better friend."

His emotions threatened to get the better of him but he continued. Taking a deep breath, he bravely allowed the words to flow.

"No man could suffer a greater lost than the one I have to live with today." Finally, the dam had broken and the tears flooded his face.

"I could stand here and tell you all about our fallen brother but every one of you know exactly what he means to you. Go away with your memories of him not someone else's written down on a paper."

For a few seconds longer he stood looking at the portrait of his friend before he retraced his steps into Anissa's arms. Anissa could not have been more proud of Q. He had done exactly what he set out to do all day. Sitting next to her she massaged his back and prayed they could hold it together until the service ended.

Everyone was having a difficult time dealing with Chaka's death. The nameless faces of mourners shook their heads or hid their tears as they listened to the pastors' message.

Buck's temper flared as he listened to Quinton break down during the eulogy. Sitting in the pew, he lost all control. Instead of crying out, he stormed from the church. He wanted to hunt down Earl and kill him. Stomping back and forth Buck thought about the deaths of friends and family. He cried over the loss of his grandmother after her long bout with cancer. He thought about the loss of Angela the girl that taught him the meaning of love. His thoughts roamed over countless faces and he raged the moment he thought about Chaka. Angry he wondered why loving someone always meant losing him or her. The only thing that would give him peace he decided would be to kill Earl. Again, he envisioned himself choking Earl until his body went limp.

Passersby's openly stared at the imposing six-foot man storming back and forth talking aloud and swatting at an imaginary figure. Nothing was more heartbreaking than watching the gentle giant transform into the haunted beast that seemed to be going mad.

Dave and Danny showed little emotion. Despite their feelings of helplessness, they were committed to the next step. Repeatedly the two scanned the room, gazing over familiar faces and trying to place a few of the not-so-familiar ones. Dave was searching for anything that might lead to a clue. Danny was searching for Earl. The twins had rationalized the whole scenario days ago and the conclusion could not have been clearer. They made a huge mistake in allowing Earl to live.

The idea of Chaka's murderer being his enemy was expected. Accepting the culprit was someone they once called a friend was devastating. Over the years even in their differences Chaka refused to go after Earl. He protected him from the death he deserved. However, Earl's repayment for the protection was to kill his protector. As frustrated as they were they couldn't walk away. Earl had made too many threats to let him live while Chaka was dead. He would die but not before they had armed themselves right. There could be no chance that his death would send anyone of them to jail. They had suffered that fate once before and

Buck hadn't really recovered yet. Moreover, they were not going to experience another loss like today.

Quinton's confusion coupled with Buck's murderous attitude was beyond dangerous. Dave and Danny's convictions to the situation were unshakable. Walking away meant allowing Earl to live. Standing strong meant raising hell and fuck the rest.

The Baker Boys 5 were dealing with a traumatic loss; a personal loss. The Dirty Dozen were loosing a figurehead but none of those dudes knew they were all suspects. The foursome looking for blood was more explosive than a nitro blast.

5

Introducing the Dirty Dozen

Success had never been an accident. It was a chore and the original Baker Boys 5 had done things for them that greater men couldn't imagine. Since their quest to be millionaires, they branched out over eleven other states throughout the US. (New Jersey, Connecticut, Philadelphia, DC, Virginia, the Carolinas, Florida, Georgia, Texas, and Louisiana-the newest to the fold.)

Every man representing the Dirty Dozen in one of those states was a native New Yorker. The plan was simply to succeed at all accounts. No man was on his own even if he was his own man. He had eleven other counterparts to help him in any endeavor. However, the initial product was drugs. Nothing they wanted could happen with out capitol and these soldiers understood fast money was the forbidden untamable desire to get high. They exploited it, and used the studies of old American gangster to make the transition less painful. Chaka loved to debate about the gangsters from the twenties that were now respected families in the new America. He thought it was ironic that prohibition had made these men multi-millionaires and the money had turned them into respectable men. He used that knowledge and the thoughts of each man in his circle to better run the vision.

It was the dream turned reality that Earl and Chaka started but only Chaka received the fruits from the tree they planted together. Their quality of life changed and their personal wants became a united front against any outside entity. They also became well-breed business men that had real estate in every one of the places they hustled. Strip-clubs, mini-malls, and minor recording studios were among the list of business these men held down. The most recent corporation was a golf course designed for building strong protégés. The target was young urban children whose parents couldn't afford or even image golfing as a sport.

At almost every function, the Dirty Dozen debated amongst themselves. All wanting to out do the other but they protected the foundation of their investments. There was a time when two members of the crew tried to collapse the tower. The attack was quick and severe. Chaka believed that no man could hide his true character for long. He used their loyalty to keep them balanced. If a man showed any signs of weakness in his ability to be loyal, he watched from the distance. He waited for the fuck up and then he replaced the limb with out thought. The conglomerate had only allowed one man walkaway with his life. That was Earl.

The last ride compressed a slew of fully restored classic vehicles. From Cadillac's El Dorado's, Lincolns, Buicks, Monte Carlo's and there was one 1955 ford- crown Victoria that lead the pack. It was the first car Danny every owned thanks to Chaka's weird sense of nostalgia.

Chaka had given each one of the men in the Dirty Dozen a beat-up used hoopty to symbolize the state of mind they were leaving behind. We were all beat-up by society and left to rot but beneath the rust and a flat tire were a beautiful body. He explained that how he viewed their struggle. The process in remodeling the car was about pride and commitment.

The commitment showed in all the vehicles that trekked from the church to the cemetery. Their pride lay buried behind the sorrow of losing a friend, a mentor, and a great business partner. Side by side the Dirty Dozen flanked the open grave, however, each member was alone with his grief.

The last Amen echoed as mourners threw roses atop the casket. No one moved it seemed there was something more to say. This couldn't be the only way to remember someone as loyal, and smart as the man that turned boys into millionaires. However, it was over.

Quinton quickly looked around and realized Petra had gone. He suddenly felt drawn across the street. There she was an ebony woman with sad eyes and a broken heart standing near the rear of the truck observing the last rituals of the service. She too mourned Chaka's passing. She also accepted that she would love him far beyond his grave and probably for the rest of her life.

Pitifully, Petra wondered how she had become his secret while Eve became his woman. Some how, she had allowed him to push her in the shadows, when he loved her first.

The bitter taste of jealousy and deceit made Petra angry, but her fear of losing him kept her quiet. She needed Chaka and she vowed to accept his love at all cost. Now she realized she had sacrificed her own self-love and worth for the illusion of a loving relationship.

Petra was loosing the battle, controlling her anger was more difficult with each second that ticked away. In the church, she spied Eve looking at her but she refused to acknowledge it. She noticed that her face twisted up as if seeing her was gross. However, today wasn't about Eve or her she quietly convinced herself. This was Chaka's funeral and she wouldn't do anything to disrespect the memory of her children's father. One day soon, she imaged her and Ms. Eve would get the opportunity to see each other. Petra stood defiantly knowing there wasn't a soul alive or dead that could deny the love she shared with Chaka. He had invested everything in their relationship. As quickly as she allowed the defiance to surface, she calmed herself. She didn't want to be angry with Chaka after today she wanted to only remember the good things she loved about him. Petra had grown use to the way he smiled when he was happy. She loved the way he held her close while they slept. She couldn't have wished for a better father for their children. More importantly, he was her shoulder to cry on and her friend. When the world felt like it was on her shoulder, he held her up. He encouraged her to continue when her family claimed it was a waste of time. She wanted to host the parties he and his friends gave. She wanted to be a part of the life he kept a secret. She learned to encourage him from the other side.

Caught in the moment she imagined Chaka's face the very first time they met. Almost tripping over her feet, she stared in the face of the "clear skin" boy. She couldn't decide if it was his big expressive eyes that held her captive or his jet black wavy hair. All she knew was he was fine. Sasha yanked her across the street and began the introductions.

"Chaka this is my study buddy Petra," she said with the biggest grin on her face.

Instead of speaking right away, he stared at Petra. Instantly, she felt self-conscious, and began straightening out her clothes. Finally, he responded to Sasha.

"Hey, nice to meet you," he said extending his hand.

Petra nodded but didn't extend her hand out of fear she would do something dumb. Sasha pinched her friend hoping to get her into the date but the pinch didn't help anything. Petra only yelled out.

"Ouch! Oh nice to meet you too," she said after recovering.

The date was clumsy for Petra. It was her first since she began school and Chaka being American made her a bit uncomfortable. This was one time in her life she wished she didn't have an accent. She wished she knew all the right words to say at the right time. Sasha was always telling Petra that no one noticed the way she talked.

"P, no one notices your accent because you rarely say anything," she chastised. Petra would only smile and try to imitate Sasha without the slight singsong to her voice. It always failed.

Chaka recognized the slight intone and encouraged her to speak. He asked her question after question about her studies, the island she was from, and the life she wanted when it was over. It took him years to admit he wasn't listening to her comments. He was attracted to the way she gestured with her body. He was in love with the sound of her voice. It was different, soft and confident. He was trapped in the sound as she talked animatedly about her home or her dreams.

The date was almost a disaster. Conscious of every move she made, she nervously dropped her fork. Twice she almost knocked over a glass of water. Sasha and Buck sat across from the couple observing everything, separately wondering if their first date was so weird. To make Petra feel comfortable Chaka pretended not to notice. The moment faded as reality set in.

The sad fact was he had made his choice and she hadn't been chosen. No amount of wishing, hoping, or praying could change that fact. She was the mother of his children and that was all she would forever be. Drowning in her thoughts, she wondered who would offer her condolences and share memories with her--the outsider. No one was the only answer that fit.

Years ago, she lost the fight and surrender to his will. Living without was not an option, as a result she accepted his reasons for being with Eve. Nothing she could do would make him leave her.

Her tears made him angry and her silence moved him out the door completely. Desperate to hold on to him, she allowed his wants to supersede her need. She prepared meals, washed clothes, and did whatever he asked of her. She was the example of a good West Indian girl, raised to take care of her home and cater to her man. Nevertheless, she wanted more. Deep down she should have demanded more but any part of him was better than not having him at all.

Chaka accepted her excitement and passion but he loved her courage. She had come to this country in search of the dream. He vowed nothing he did would stop her from achieving it. Falling in love with the ambitious, sassy scholar that trusted him with her life was the only unselfish thing he'd done. However, he never figured out how to be the man she needed. His excuse was always the same. Between circumstances and poor decisions, he wondered if he could ever be the man she wanted.

Being with Eve was the opposite of being with Petra. Petra wanted to cater to his needs and she did that. It was her sincerity and nurturing soul that made him stronger. When he was ill, Petra stayed with him until he was well. She chastised him when he worried about things he couldn't change. She was everything he wanted in a woman but he feared he would mess it up if he tried to be more than what they were to each other. Watching her with Chanice, (their daughter) combing her hair, or teaching her to jump rope confirmed he had chosen the right woman to bear his children. Some days he wished he could leave the streets behind. However, they were the only thing he did well.

On the other side of town, Eve didn't give a damn about his needs because she wanted her way. Her material-girl mentality and hellcat attitude were easier to comply with than trying to be something he didn't completely understanding. When Chaka began fooling around with Eve it was something to do he reasoned. Nevertheless, he was forced to admit nothing in his life happened by accident. Eve was his nemesis' girl and anything he could do to cause Earl pain was a bonus. The one thing he didn't count on was wanting the chaos, drama and dysfunction Eve brought to his life.

Like every one else in his life she served a purpose. She made him look better every time she left the house. Chaka was smart and he knew appearance made men seem greater. A beautiful woman on his arm, a clean ride, and million-dollar attitude could change lives. Image was about eighty percent of the business he was in and she spent his money well on maintaining the farce. The stress of his life was getting to Chaka as he pushed against the floor. Shutting out thought, he inhaled deeply and began the slow rhythm. Lowering his body, he felt each muscle in his arms at work. The tension in his shoulders begged for rest. Determined he continued. Fighting the distractions of fatigue, and gravity he welcomed the strain. Breathing in and out, as sweat rolled from his body, he imaged Eve's long legs wrapped around his back. The vision almost crippled him. Water rained from his hair as he physically tried shaking the thought from his mind.

Someone moving around on the floor above him forced him to listen. Without warning, the lights were on the person who was stomping down the stairs toward him. "Damn," he whispered, angry that he hadn't locked the door. Quiet was all he wanted. He needed to be alone with his thoughts. Finally, he saw her honey-kissed legs coming to him.

Eve stood inches from Chaka's reach. She smiled. Practically naked she waited for a response. Curiously, he acknowledged her standing there in her "fuck me" pumps, a silk bathrobe, and a see-through bra and panty set. The heat began slow and turned into a raging inferno. His penis pointed north as Eve slid to her knees. She crawled to him. Being sexy was a state of mind but the beautiful woman before him was a seductress. Her auburn curls were wild on top of her head and matched the look in her brown eyes. Every move said tempting and enticing.

Chaka's stress was gone. Now he watched her intently wanting to flip her on her back. No words, just sheer will forced him to sit still, as she invaded his personal space. Closer than she dared to be, she licked the taste of salt from his lips. Mesmerized by the sweet scent of her favorite perfume, he surrendered.

Eve loved the way he smelled after a work out. More than that, she loved the control he allowed her over him when he was most vulnerable. Feeling daring, she pulled the wet waistband of his shorts and hissed at the sight of his hard dick. Salivating she felt the uncontrolled pulsing of her own sex as she lowered her mouth to his. Chaka's eyes rolled as he leaned against the wall. He enjoyed her licking, sucking and jerking him with her hands as he held her head loosely. The intensity from Eve's mouth was driving him crazy. He grabbed a hand full of her hair as she continued to nurse on his erection.

The low growl was the only sound she heard before he yanked her away from his lap. Turned on by his weakness she straddled him, commanding him to fuck her.

If all she wanted was to experience the pleasure then Chaka fit perfectly. However, she wanted to feel more than the passion she confused for love. Desperately, she needed to feel the tenderness and the intimacy that came with being in love. Quietly, she rode the wave until she felt her stomach muscles tighten. Damning the moment, she became angry that her body had betrayed her heart again. Slowly the desire retreated and she was forced to accept that she would never feel the closeness that other women talked about on television and she read about in books.

She was angry that he left her unfulfilled and empty after they made love. If all she wanted was a nut than Chaka had done that perfectly. She wished she could explain the feeling she read about but never experienced for herself.

Although, Chaka hated to admit it but the man he wanted to be was in conflict with the man he was. He straddled the line and became what he thought Petra needed and gave Eve what he thought she wanted. The street was the only place he felt important. Among his crew, he was the man. Standing next to Petra, he was ordinary. With Eve, it was all a game.

There was no way he could pursue a relationship and be a hustler until he had more to offer–so he strayed. Selfishly, he gave Petra the only gift he would never give to any other woman. In an awkward way, he explained his love.

"My love for you should be obvious. No other woman can declare that I have given her the best part of me – my children." Frustrated that he hadn't expressed the love he desperately needed her to feel he continued.

"Do you really think it was a mistake Petra that you became pregnant?" Before she could answer, he would continue.

"Having Chanice changed the direction of my life forever. Hearing her cry for the first time made me different. I wanted to cut off my arm if it meant it would make her happy. Not so she would be quiet but so she would never feel another ounce of pain. Maybe in the beginning I did things to jeopardize our love. Running away, instead of working things out but even then that was to ensure you met your goals. I loved you then and I love you more now. There was never a competition between you and another woman. You are the woman that I live for. Not being with you is a sacrifice, one I will continue to make to ensure that our children never want or need anything."

Feeling as if he had finally conveyed the essence of his love for her he stormed away.

She heard every word he spoke. She even knew they were true but she could not accept it without the commitment. In her heart, she always hoped he would make her his wife. She heard the words just as he spoke the day he left her for the last time.

A blaring horn shook her from the memory. Now forced to accept yet another fact; he was gone.

As Quinton reached the limo, he ushered the women inside before he quietly closed the door. Without explanation, he dashed across traffic. Towering over Petra, he held out his arms offering her his condolences. Shutting out his pain, knowing she needed someone to help her through the tragedy of losing her lover, her children's father, and her best friend. Chaka's death was overwhelming and she wanted one answer. The shattered woman stamped her feet and cried uncontrollably. 'Why,' was all she trusted herself to say? Repeatedly she cried out why! Quinton believed he understood Petra's need to know why. He held her tighter praying that his arms would be enough until he could find the answer to her question. As she stood there crying and shaking, she imaged the voice of her daughter yelling I want my daddy. The image of CJ her son staring at her afraid to ask why he couldn't go too. Unsure of how to go forward she cried until she had no more tears.

Her outburst rocked Q. His strength slide as he held her still tighter. The tears welled up and spilled from his eyes as he breathed deeply trying to gain some control over his grief. Unprepared for the break down he wished Anissa could help him. All day he had watched the difference in the two women Chaka had chosen. Where Eve was rude, crass and disrespectful; Petra was reserved, classy, and almost regal. Experiencing this side of her left him feeling inadequate and yet again he had failed. By the time she pushed away, he was ready to let go too. Appearing normal again, she explained the reason she couldn't bring the children.

"Chanice and CJ were not ready for this. Remembering him in a casket," she continued, "just didn't seem appropriate. The boy has not spoken one word since I told him about Chaka," she hesitated, "and Chanice just keeps saying she wants to see her daddy. I couldn't saddle them with this burden."

Both Anissa and Eve sat stunned at the affection Quinton offered the stranger. Anissa's heart sank, as she looked on horrified. Eve immediately recognized the woman from the church. The questions were screaming loud in her mind as she wished for the right answers. Why was Quinton offering this distraught woman such solidarity? Was she a friend of his or Chaka? Most importantly, why did she receive special treatment? The bitter taste in her mouth showed all over her face as she moved toward the door. Eve had finally, lost the facade she had fought all day to control.

Eve spoke first, in hysterics. "Who the fuck is that ugly bitch?"

Before Anissa could think of any answers, Eve ordered the driver to take them across to the parking lot.

The driver explained, "The path is blocked by last-minute observers."

Eve spoke through clenched teeth. "Don't play with me! Honk your horn and go around those pretentious bastards." The anger she felt had ballooned. She was seeing red and welcomed a confrontation as she slammed her back into the cushioned seat and crossed her arms as if she was a spoiled child having a fit.

The driver took his job serious and silently prayed the young man knew what he was doing. With respect for the situation, he spoke again. "Honking a horn is forbidden in a burial ground."

Eve glared at the driver through squinted eyes as she slid to the door.

Anissa reached for the handle just as Quinton opened the door. He practically pushed Eve back across the seat as he sat opposite her. Unconcerned with their questions he refused to answer. "Who is she," they both asked in unison? The scowl on his face should have been a warning but neither acknowledged the look. Tired of the litany of questions he easily silenced Anissa. The glasses he had been wearing sat on his lap as he met Anissa's glare head on. Although, he had not spoken one word she understood the meaning: shut the fuck up.

Eve, however was relentless. She spoke to him as if she had forgotten her manners.

"Quinton, I asked you a question and I expect a fucking answer," she demanded.

"Evil Lynn," he pronounced her name, "ask me no questions and I won't have to tell you a lie."

She turned her angry eyes on him, like daggers aimed at his face.

"Self-serving son of a bitch," she spat, just above a whisper.

Anissa's mouth flopped open as she watched the two people that meant the most to her insult one another.

"Evil, listen to me," he demanded. I am not going to tolerate you much longer, so I am suggesting you get off my nerves."

The words eased from Quinton's lips but the venom that they held was clearer than the words spoken. She could push if she dared but

Quinton was in no mood for her or her theatrics. The emotions from the funeral, along with the drama of having to continue on the path they had set weighed heavy on him. Eve wouldn't get the chance to add anymore pressure than he was already feeling. Staring at her, he wondered could she have set Chaka up to be killed.

6

According to Buck

Buck stayed behind to make peace with his fallen friend. Staring at the open hole, he waited, for the right words to form. Nothing he attempted seemed appropriate. Every thought he felt was unreal. Ashamed he allowed the comforts of rage to engulf him.

The sparkle in his eyes was now the look of a possessed man. The pleasant mask and contagious smile hid behind his cold heart and the menacing glare. The words fell from his mouth as he felt them.

Pacing back and forth, he cursed the wind that swirled around him.

"You protected Earl's bitch ass for too long and now look. Your arrogance made you believe that nigga did not have the heart to get at you. You ignored every one of his threats but look at you now. He's living and you…" Buck didn't have the courage to complete the thought let alone speak it.

"On everything I love I promise that niggas days are numbered. He better start praying so he can get into heaven cause he gonna die."

Alone his tears poured, guilt rode him as he begged Chaka for forgiveness. Buck believed he failed his Godchildren by allowing their father to die. In the cold he made more promises hoping that they could somehow change the direction he knew he was about to take. Friendship was the only thing constant in his life. Quinton, Dave, Danny and Chaka were his responsibility and he had failed them like they had failed him so many years ago.

Buck realized he'd got caught slipping the moment he felt the pain in his chest. The force of the blow almost leveled him on the dark pavement.

"Damn Danny," he yelled at the twin. Dave wasted no time taking up for his partner.

"Stop crying you big baby! That's our point," he laughed.

The twins waited for the retaliation. Quinton brought the ball down court knowing that he was going straight to the hole. There was no referee to call fouls or an audience to cheer them on. This was street ball. The bumping, pushing, and holding gave him all the incentive he needed to get around the twins. Before Danny could recover from his laughter, he was holding his lip.

"Y'all doing a nigga dirty! What you trying to be the baby body guard?" Buck smirked as he teased Danny.

"Stop whining and come wit it."

Dave step just beyond the backboard and shot the ball across the court to Danny. Danny turned in time to see Buck waiting like a Mack truck. Afraid of a head on collision he tossed the ball back to his twin. Face to face, Dave tossed the ball up in the arch toward the hoop. In midair, Buck swatted the ball to the ground. In disbelief, they watched as Buck clowned.

"Get that weak shit outta here. You play ball like a bitch."

Out of breath he yelled, game over. Buck walked away from the court three games later with a swollen lip and scuffed knees. Quinton had scraped the skin off both palms. Danny had torn the seat of his black slacks trying to keep up with Buck in his hard bottoms. Dave had run head first into the pole going for a lay-up. If the reason they were there wasn't so sad it might have been comical to watch them play.

Earl had known exactly where they would end up. Every time they were upset, they went through this ritual. This was as common as Quinton's compulsion to repeat everything twice. On the other hand, the twins were notorious for having a trunk full of liquor to douse any pain. Buck, however, was the wildcard even back in the days. He could easily sit in silence or punish them on the basketball court like the brut he was.

The bag rattled as Danny checked the amount of liquor left in the bottle. Memories flooded them as they each remembered why they were there in the first place. Chaka would always say that wasting liquor was like wasting good pussy- just a sin and a shame. Instead of the tradition of pouring out some liquor for the brother not there they raised their plastic cups and recited the litany as if it were their own words.

Earl's false bravado and his poor sense of choice made him waltz over to the men standing in the playground drinking. He was not a welcomed guest even if it was a public park. The reverie ended and angry men stood, each wanting an opportunity to kill the man they suspected was responsible for harming Chaka. Quinton pushed past Buck, sensing the danger. Spit collected in the corner of Bucks mouths and his eye went from sad to pure evil. The fact was Earl was living on borrowed time but they had to put some distance between the murders. The streets were watching and no one wanted to take an unnecessary chance with the court system. Earl raised his palms. As if surrendering to some unwaged war.

"I'm only here to offer my deepest sympathy."

Quinton eyes glazed over, his heart raced, and his palms burned to slapped the shit out of Earl. Knowing he needed to remain calm, he waited. Dave and Danny both closed the circle around the culprit responsible for the pain they felt. However, Buck found the words.

Buck's menacing glare, followed by the candid words, was everyone's thoughts.

"We heard you. We appreciate your heartfelt sympathy, now please leave."

The snarl that came after should have sent Earl running to his truck but he stood firm. This was Earl's moment and he planned to take it. With no choice, he let his mouth get his ass in a world of hurt. Quinton didn't have patience and Buck was just a fucking brut. The two together couldn't out-finesse him at this game. He sneered at Buck. Besides, everything he knew about the duo was hand wrapped and delivered to him by someone held in high regards. Someone inside the circle.

"Damn, nigga, you would think your big dumb ass would have learned: since your man is gone, anybody could be touched."

Earl knew they suspected he was the cause of Chaka's death. He also knew they would wait before they went gunning for him. However, he was planning to come after them first.

Quinton was elated as he hung his head. Buck punished Earl for being dumb enough to say what he thought. He didn't even get a chance to pretend to reach for anything let alone defend the rain of punches. The first blow shattered Earl's nose and the second cracked at least two ribs. The countless stomps to his body following his collapse left Earl unconscious. Buck put more effort into each blow as he relived the cries he heard at the church earlier that day. Dave and Danny only moved to stop Buck when they realized he was actually smiling with each blow that connected with some part of Earls already limp body.

"You one dumb motherfucker. I guess playing in traffic ain't dangerous enough for your simple ass." Buck was mad and delivered each blow with his words.

The other men standing nearby prayed Buck would kill Earl and the shit would end in peace. Street justice would have served its purpose.

Danny laughed hysterically. The moment made him want to kick Earl's ass too. Feeling a little vindicated, Dave got in a good head shot before they walked away. Buck was kicking Earl's ass and talking shit like it was an old fashion "get the belt" whipping.

When Earl finally came to, he looked around to discover he was alone. His ego had been stomped, snatched, and damaged almost beyond repair. As he struggled to rise off the ground, Earl realized Buck's weakness. Damn the investigation and fuck who knew what. There was no way would he have allowed his nemesis to live another day. Holding his ribs he stumbled to his car and smiled knowing that Quinton and Buck would be joining the beast that set this rivalry in motion. The sight of his blood as he coughed was the serum needed to make his words ring true. The heat he planned for them would have demented all over it. Someday soon, Buck would turn against Quinton giving him the chance to murder them both.

Bucks dreams were getting the better of him. Alone and away from his crew he allowed his grief to swell.

The first night locked up was the worst. The constant sound of metal slamming was mind altering. It stole his breath away, his stomach clenched, and his heart pounded. Fearing the unknown worked him over. The wide space was more than intimidating; men were huddled together talking and making jokes as if they were not serving time behind bars. One kid was hankering down in a corner looking scared to death. The putrid smell radiating from him saturated the room. To taunt him seemed cruel but occasionally someone would go by and throw something in the guy's direction and he would jump every time. Buck was determined to stay out of unnecessary trouble but he was hell bent on remaining true to the man he was. Walking in the facility opened his eyes to an underground world of chaos. Silently he prayed to live through the experience. Fear, resentment, and confusion transformed him into a hostile urchin. His face stayed screwed up in a scowl. His eyes moved constantly as he watched for trouble heading his way. Nothing in his life prepared him for the outcries of men in the night. Someone was always in some shit. The things going on behind the wall were oblivious to family and friends on the outside. The guards only responded it seemed when it was too late. One night Buck watched as two men set another guys socks on fire for amusement. By the time the guards acknowledged his screams, the fire had reached his legs.

The day had come for him to prove his heart was still in his chest. Walking into the bathroom three guys were whispering. The little nigga in the group decided that it was pick on Buck day. So he yelled in Bucks' direction.

"Where you from kid?"

Buck had heard the question but pretended to be busy taking care of his business. He didn't look around or respond. Scram was all of 5 feet and was yelling as if he was a big man.

"Yo, you kid where you stay?"

Buck knew what was about to happened. It didn't matter if he was from the other side of the moon. The lame ass duck nigga wanted to catch rec. The frown on his face never softened, neither did the base in his voice as he responded.

"Brooklyn," he paused "you know me or something?"

Ole boy seemed stunned that he received the response with such venom. It was clear the big burly black motherfucker had no idea who he was.

Buck wanted to laugh as he watched the fronting ass nigga rise up and walk towards him. Suddenly the familiar feeling that came when he was kid surfaced. The energy he needed to wage a good battle. Help him feel alive instead of ashamed at his predicament. Pounding on a niggas head might have been what he needed to get rid of all the stress that troubled him.

Discarding his wet socks and t-shirt, he went straight to him. No "what's up homie." No words were exchanged. The light reflected off the edge of the razor that flew out of homies mouth. Buck never felt the rip in his shoulder while he beat the boy's head against the ceramic basin. But he felt the pain in his kidneys from the guards as he lay on the floor. Blood was everywhere. The two cats that were with the troublemaker had left the area by the time Buck came too. The taste of blood made him hungry for more. He could feel an awakening that threatened to keep him in lock down forever. No way was he going to leave here alive if he needed to defend himself again. He would have another charge while incarcerated and the murder would stick.

One day while preparing for a visit an older man approached Buck.

"Son why you here?" He asked in his slow gravelly voice.

The joy that Buck felt surrendered to hostility. The question was simple but the answer was complicated. How could he explain that he was here by choice? That he took the responsibility for the actions of his entire crew because it seemed like the right thing to do. No one would understand that although his Grandma Bea's sad eyes and broken heart would probably haunt him. He had to stand up and be responsible. Even now as he worked the words around in his head, it did not seem so smart to have pleaded guilty. However, sixteen month's seemed better than everything else he was hearing.

Instead of waiting for an answer, the man left Buck to contemplate his response.

Jahson Holden needed to quiet the resentment that had found shelter in his heart. He contemplated all the things he had given up and decided that the punishment was far greater than the crime he had committed. His chance at a football scholarship washed down the drain the moment he heard the heavy iron doors slam. The girl that had made him smile was probably out enjoying time with another man smart enough not to be caught. In addition, worst than it all his friends were off enjoying freedom. Giving little or no thought to the sacrifice, he was making in the name of friendship.

Drifting off to sleep Buck dreamed about his first love. Angela had gone beyond the sex; she had managed to find a friend in her lover. The debate over who said what first always brought laughter to the young couple. Angela's version of their first meeting was comical.

"You were acting up on the court. Fucking up the game, letting niggas fly by you and your teammates, you were blowing the game. You posted up in the lane drooling from your mouth instead of playing defense. I thought Uncle Baldy was gonna give me a kiss cause you were so distracted. He claimed I was a better bet than the losing motherfuckers he had on his team." Buck laughed until tears came to his eyes. His boys were ready to beat his ass by half time because he kept trying to show off for her. Chaka's reputation and two grand were on the line and Bucks big ass was trying to close line motherfuckers instead of playing his game.

As real as the day he experienced it, he dreamed the first time he met the beauty.

She stood less than five feet from him, dressed like an outsider. Most of the chicks in Brooklyn dressed the same but she was claiming Harlem USA. The green and yellow Benetton sweater barely covered her ass. Her jeans sported a hole in the front right knee and a rip just below her left ass cheek. Standing there observing the game was this fully bloomed sixteen year old with one green and one yellow Chuck Taylor sneaker. A bag covered in the letter G slung over her shoulder and some designer frames sat on her face. Her hair pulled back in a ponytail that flipped about, as she got excited over another point scored. Although her Uncles team was playing, she was torn between family loyalty and lust.

Buck's team was whipping ass and the five-feet-five-inched diva was there, cheering on the opposing team. At half time, every nigga on the court that didn't fear Baldy was trying to holla at shorty. Buck was relentless in his attraction. He watched as she shot niggas down with a sweet smile and a no thank you. Meanwhile, he was prepared to holla at her Uncle if he could get him the hookup. "Who that?" Buck asked while running back to the bench.

"That's Baldy's little niece from uptown," Chaka answered. "You slow motherfucker get your head in the game and after we get this dough you can take a trip to mickie d's or sumthing."

Chaka had turned two shades of red chastising Buck. That was all Buck needed to hear. He zeroed in on the ebony beauty with dimples and made his way to her.

"Hey shorty, my name is Buck," he said dripping in sweat and panting in her face.

"Angela," she replied with a sweet smile, "but I know your momma didn't name you Buck."

"Nah, that's my name in the street – feel free to call me Jahson," he confessed.

"Nice to meet you, Jahson," she countered. Angela claimed him quickly by untying a green handkerchief that was on her bag. She offered him her rag and watched intently as he wiped the sweat from his face. In the matter of seconds, the relationship had begun and everyone that witnessed the small gesture talked about it for weeks.

The game was over and Baldy was cussing out his team for losing a game and his two grand. He threatened to have niggas up' til they each got him back the money he loss on their non-playing asses. He put Buck on blast, "my niece had those niggas cumin' in their pants and y'all motherfuckers still got your asses whipped." Disgusted he threatened Buck softly.

"I bet not catch you hanging around my dinner table you big bastard," he laughed.

Buck couldn't resist and yelled back. "What you cooking?"

Baldy turned around and winked at Buck. Secretly he under-

stood his nieces' infatuation with the burly bear. He reminded her of her favorite Uncle. She could not resist; curiosity had gotten the better of her. She needed to know why his nickname was Buck.

"I guess there is more than one reason. My weight might be the most obvious: big, strong buck." Angela giggled; that made sense to her. "But the other reasons would only make sense to me and my crew. I got the nickname for being a hell raiser, and it stuck the moment I started by playing football. I hold the record in my school for the most sacks on a quarterback. We don't call them sacks anymore; we renamed it 'bucking.'

"Okay, I can understand that. I prefer to call you by your name, Jahson," she smiled.

"I got a few questions of my own. Why haven't I seen you around here before?" The sadness in her eyes left him feeling insensitive; she answered the question as if she needed to prepare herself for the words as they left her mouth.

"Long story short, my mother and I just moved to Brooklyn with my uncle Baldy's family. Maybe another time when I know you better, I'll explain."

The game should have been the highlight of his day. But Angela managed to outshine the profitable victory. He didn't feel a need to be extra, he allowed the conversation to flow smoothly. It was easy to leave the thug in the closet as they walked around getting to know one another. Buck was an original Baker Boy 5; chicks were walking around calling out to him hoping for a little of his attention. Disappointment showed on most of their faces as they watched him bop down the block with the stuck-up bitch from the court. The young couple walked the streets oblivious to the smiles, frowns, talking and laughing. By the time the sun set Angela was beyond infatuated. Buck was charming and the thought kept Angela interested. She dated a number of clowns in her young life but none of them compared to him. She had been wondering how it would feel to just lean over and kiss him. Damn, she chastised herself for wanting to make an impression but it couldn't be one that would spoil her reputation. Her mother taught her men only took the good girls serious. When a girl gave away her goodness too easy, she got no respect. She wanted

Buck to come running when she called.

Standing in front of her door, she gave into temptation. Buck was standing trying to think of the perfect way to end the date when Angela leaned and kissed him. Buck could have pissed in his pants right then. At that moment, the door closed in his face. The prettiest girl on the block had kissed him while he was standing there looking dumb. By the time, he recovered from his blunder he was smiling like a lotto winner.

One memory flowed into the next as he remembered the day she offered to cook for him. Buck had gotten into the habit of hanging out at Baldy's house around dinnertime. However, that evening no one wanted to cook. Angela decided she could make something very quick. Slamming kitchen cabinets, she decided on spaghetti. Angela was good at a great number of things but cooking wasn't one of them. She counted off items as if she was a chef. Tomato sauce, noodles, onions, a green pepper, and ground meat were all the things she needed. Standing there, she convinced herself she could do this. Ms. June walked by the kitchen watching as her daughter tried to cook a meal. She sat next to Buck and offered her condolences as a warning. Buck laughed and prayed it wasn't as bad as her mother claimed.

Forty minutes later, Buck sat in disbelief at the mess on his plate. Angela was looking and waiting for comment. Sweat formed as he tried to think of a good way to get out of the situation. Buck knew the chances of hurting her feelings were great but he wasn't about to end up with food poisoning. Tact, wasn't his strongest quality so when he blurted out, Angela eyes grew large and angry.

"What the hell is this supposed to be?" he asked.

Ms. June laughed so loud, Buck felt badly for the beautiful non-cooking chef. But not bad enough to eat it.

"It's spaghetti," she answered nervously.

Buck smiled slowly to keep from laughing. He suggested they walk down to the pizza shop. Angela was embarrassed but she still expected him to try it before he discarded her hard work. Mad as hell, she yelled.

"You should have said that before I attempted to make this nasty shit." She couldn't resist the laughter that boiled over as Buck stared at her like she had two heads.

Ms. June attempted to quiet the cursing Angela was about to start.

"Girl, get your non-cooking ass down to the pizza shop and bring back a beef-patty. I don't blame that boy for having the good sense not to eat that mess."

"Angela," she yelled after she stood over the plate, *"did you even cook the noodles... why they so stiff lookin?"*

Angela thought about it for a minute before she realized the noodles were a little undercooked. In her defense, she cried.

"The box said cooks in 12 minutes and that's what I did."

Her mother was enjoying her daughter's failed attempts.

"Did you put water in the pot or did you just put it in the sauce undone?"

Angela stormed to the door to keep from answering the question.

The young couple was tougher than glue to separate. In their eagerness, they explored their emotions. Buck made no beef about Angela's reluctant to hangout with his friends and their girls. She was very adamant that his street life was separate from their time they spent with one another. When he and his crew did the things they did, she wanted to be nowhere near it. However, when he returned home she wanted a phone call or visit. For the first time in Buck's life, he was living with young love. It was exciting and scary. The thought of being with any one else was unnerving. She allowed him to be whoever he was.

Buck woke from his dream immediately, accepting that this would be the only way he would experience the happiest times of his life - in his dreams.

7

Back in the day

It was girl's night out for Anissa and Eve; but not just any club would do. Union square at 14th street was promoting a battle between boroughs for the best rappers in the tri-state. Eve was convinced that she had to be there the moment she found a flyer at work. However, she was hell bent on being there when she heard the hype on the radio. Gassed up and ready to party, Eve called Anissa with their party plans. Anissa sound reasoning was more than she could deal with.

"How are we supposed to get there?" Anissa asked.

Eve wasn't concerned with the details, all she knew was they would be there if she had begged, borrow and steal.

"Don't worry. We going and that's it. Make sure you ready when I get to your house tonight," she concluded.

Damn! What to wear? She asked herself as she hung up on Anissa before she asked another question.

Tonight's contest was a real excuse to be extra. Four well-known acts to come out of the surrounding areas were representing. The crowd would determine the borough that was the king of the rap game. Kane was representing BK in his cut up eyebrows and his high top fade. MC Shan was holding his corner with the boys from Queensbridge, and the Bronx was flooding the dance floor for the infamous KRS 1. The Wild card was the only female rapper in the room, MC Lite.

Sam I cram to understand you, had the partygoers in an uproar. The sound was every ones cue that MC Lite was there to represent.

The cold didn't derail Eve's plans. The moment she walked out the train station and saw the line, she was beyond excited. Scanning the crowd, she hoped to see someone they knew that would let them cut, but no such luck. Anissa was annoyed. Her legs, hands, and face were freezing.

"Look at that line, we gonna freeze to death before we get in," she complained.

The complaint didn't slow Eve down one bit; she was determined. Anissa soon realized Eve wasn't going to leave so she stood in line, mentally counting the people ahead of them. As the bouncers allowed another set of people to go, Anissa breathed easy. The line was moving faster now that they were almost at the door. Finally, they were next when Anissa began checking her attire to make sure she was dressed appropriately.

Her black leather bomber with fox-fur around the hood was stylish enough, but she was catching cold in her ass trying to be cute. The duo huddled together as the wind coming around the corner slapped them about. Too afraid to move and too cold to stand still, they thought of things to take their mind off the wind.

Security seemed to be the only ones enjoying the freezing weather. Eve wanted to get next to any one of the burly men holding down the door until she noticed the portable heaters keeping them warm. Suddenly she changed her mind as they stood around laughing at the huddled patrons.

Anissa was people watching to keep her mind off the hawk. She got interested the moment she observed a crew stomping by in forty-below boots and three-quarter goose downs.

"Damn," she thought each one was finer than the last. One guy walked up to a guard handed him something, and the red velvet rope was removed for him and his crew to enter.

Undeniable Anissa had hit the mark. Sporting her favorite pair of jeans ripped to shreds in the front, a colorful sweater with the four legged horse riding high on the left side and her fresh out–the- box Gucci sneakers to pull the assemble together. She was more than excited about getting into the club now. Six of the finest black men she had ever seen had given her their stamp of approval. Her confidence soared.

Eve was undone as one guy whispered to her to save a dance for him, seconds before he ducked inside. Until that moment, she had reservation about her outfit. But the not so subtle complement made it all worth while. Donned in a pleated mini skirt, thigh-high stockings, patent leather Mary Jane's, a black t-shirt, and a homemade-cropped denim jacket, she was on fire. However, her knees were cold, her face was frozen and her ass was out. Still she wouldn't leave the line. The outfit was a copycat of an outfit she saw in Elite magazine. Her face lit-up as she patiently waited to get inside.

The sounds of loud bass danced on the walls and vibrated the ground beneath their feet as they heard the crowd scream.

Anissa noticed the person walking toward them first. "Oh shit," she whispered and stared. Knowing that Eve would probably find something wrong with the dark chocolate brother dressed to impress in his Shearling coat and the matching hat, she kept her secret. The closer he got the more Anissa openly gawked. Something about him made her feel daring and sexy. She would have been embarrassed, if he didn't smile. Suddenly he was in front her. She was trapped by the energy—his energy. Quinton did not slow his stride as he neared the door. Not once did he divert his eyes from hers. It was almost as if she was willing him to her.

"What's up," he said to the bouncer, as he strolled by grabbing Anissa's hand in the interim. Eve gripped her other arm and rushed along with the two as if they were waiting for him to get them in all night. Barely, a head nod, and definitely no words were exchanged as they walked through the doors. Together the trio waltzed passed the security, jogged down the ramp and entered the club without as much as a hello. Just inches from the steps that led to the dance floor Quinton whispered, "I'll see you later for our dance."

As quickly as he claimed her, he stalked off in search of his friends. Eve towered over Anissa with her mouth wide open.

"Close your mouth woman before a man comes along and puts something in it," Anissa instructed her best friend.

The shocked look covered Eve's face as she declared, "Damn, that man was fine and generous! Girl, you best get at him before he finds him another chick to spread his generous spirit with."

Normally Anissa could ignore Eve's less than crass comments but it irked her nerve tonight. Just once she wished Eve would give thought to things she said instead of allowing anything to fly out of her mouth. However, she knew that wasn't going to happen anytime soon so she might as well move on.

The deejay swept them up in the beats as his mix-mastered the turntables. Still too cold, to jump on the dance floor, Anissa did a mean chair dance. Meanwhile, Eve stood just beyond the dance floor rocking from side to side. Caught in the look-see Eve disappeared into the jammed pack floor. Anissa got up when she heard her song. The sounds of Biz Markie's notorious beat box boomed from the speakers.

The deejay was taking no prisoners. Everyone caught the fever. Song after song the girls danced and enjoyed the festivities until they heard the high-pitched sound of the host declaring that the battle was going to begin.

The sweat poured off Anissa as she danced with a young man in front of their chairs. Glancing around the room, she pretended not to be looking for Mr. Fine. The truth was Eve had a point, ole boy was fine as hell and she wanted to get to know him better. Finally, she spied her benefactor standing across the room with a glass and chatting with a cluster of men. She toyed with idea that he seemed familiar but quickly dismissed it. She believed she would have remembered anybody that looked that good.

He had found her hiding space two seconds after coming to the dance floor. Quinton was confident in his game and had no qualms with approaching Anissa but decided that to let her get her dance until he was ready to dance with her. Occasionally, he would look over to see if she was having a good time. More than once, they caught the other looking their way but both quickly diverted glances before things got too obvious. Enough was enough. He raised his glass in a mock toast at the pretty pecan tan beauty. Tired of the cat and mouse, he didn't bother to wait for a response. He walked over to her with a glass of champagne. She wanted to scream but decided to appear nonchalant about the whole situation. Nothing she did stopped the voice in her head as she reasoned. Somewhere someone was smiling on her because guys like Quinton went for chicks like Eve with her caramel skin and long wavy hair. Plastering a sweet smile on her face, she worried what sweaty mess her face must look like. The thought disappeared when a chicken-head in a tight shirt and boobs for days started dancing with Quinton. Anissa felt like snatching a braid or two from her head until Quinton smiled politely and continued his stroll. The victory was hers she mentally sang, as she stood awestruck by his entire attitude. Her mouth was dry as a hot summer day. Besides, she realized he was too close to check her breath. Frustrated, she wished she could run to the bar or at least get a stick of gum from Eve. Anissa debated between losing the seats closest to the stage to get something to drink, or standing there with hot breath, waiting for Quinton. All intelligent thought went out the window when Slick Rick's unique storytelling banged off the walls. The bass was ricocheting off the walls and caught the couple up in the vibes. Anissa and Quinton shook, slid, and two-stepped from one song to the next. Neither seemed to mind that there was little room to do much more. In the center of the dance floor, a group was doing a dance routine as the crowd surrounded them. When Anissa began to fan herself, Quinton took her hand and led her over to the bar. The dilemma over whether to leave the seats ended and Anissa never gave it another thought.

"What are you drinking?" he asked.

She ordered a ginger ale. Playing the game was only part of the tricks Anissa had in-store for Mr. Fine. She pretended not to hear above the music forcing him to get closer to her ear. Next she squeezed in front of him behaving like the room was too crowded for her to stand any place else. Finally, he caught on when she began batting her eyes at him.

Shortly after exchanging pleasantries, Quinton offered his new friend and her company a ride home. Anissa's first response was to decline but after thinking about braving the cold home, getting a ride seemed like an act of chivalry. Batting her eyes and smiling wide, she accepted his offer.

"Thank you, but I must warn you we live in Brooklyn," she said above the loud thud of music.

"No big deal. I've seen your face before and I'm sure I can handle two little girls."

Anissa was startled at first by his confession but then decided she was being paranoid.

"Okay, I look familiar to you," she said with raised eyebrows.

"Yes," he answered without offering anything further.

"Where do you think you know me from?"

"Bushwick. I play ball in the park at the corner of your block every Sunday morning. I've seen you and your girl hanging out on your stoop many times." Quinton snatched her free hand and pulled her across the floor to met Chaka and Buck. Buck was the first to voice his excitement.

"Nissa! I didn't know you partied."

"Every now and again," she explained as she watched Chaka's face light up.

"Hey, shorty, I haven't seen you in a while," Chaka exclaimed. The pair exchanged hugs and Anissa spoke with gleeful eyes.

"I didn't think I would ever see you again! Give me my whistle."

Chaka laughed and explained to his boys that he and Anissa went to Peewee camp in the first grade. He borrowed her whistle on the last day and never returned it. They were laughing when Eve two-stepped her way over to the small gathering. That night, the group hung out well into the wee hours of the morning, chatting about life goals and lying about experiences. When Buck left to visit a female friend, Chaka offered Eve a ride home. She gladly accepted.

By the time Quinton arrived in Brooklyn, Anissa was out cold. She moaned when he tried to wake her and turned sideways when he tried to get her out of the vehicle. Although, she slept the entire ride home he wasn't too eager to end the chance meeting anyway. Taking her home with him seemed like a good plan, until he had to explain how she gotten there. Anissa woke up late in the afternoon, wondering why she was not in her bed. Panic set in until she got her bearings. Glaring at the broad, black back of the man lying next to her she prayed she had not gone home with a stranger. Anissa raised the blanket; relieved to see her bra and panties were intact. Quinton rolled over and barreled into her as she leaped from the bed. He smiled at his guest, as she stood practically naked in his room, wide-eyed and terrified.

"Good afternoon, Ms. Anissa," he spoke through the grogginess of his voice.

"Hey! How did I get here? How come you didn't take me home?"

Quinton sneered, "First of all, your ass is heavy and you sleep like the dead. Secondly, I didn't take advantage of you while you slept and laid your ass down before you caught a cold."

Anissa rolled her eyes at the demanding jerk that lay there, barking orders and looking good as hell.

"Do you ever ask anyone to do anything or do you just pull them along and bark orders?" She asked, looking around his room.

For a man, it was tasteful with a gold-plated wrought-iron bed frame and matching side tables with lamps, and the biggest television she had ever seen in a bedroom.

"Nah, normally I club a woman over the head and carry her where I want her to go. Sort of like what I did to you last night," he countered.

That afternoon, they slept in turns. Anissa watched the rise and fall of his thick, defined chest and long neck. She stared at the expressions he made as he dreamed. She pretended to care about what he dreamed about when he slept. The truth was she needed anything to take her mind off his fingers entering her in her most private place.

While Anissa drifted off to sleep, Quinton kneaded her breast while measuring the size in his large hands. He palmed her ass and finally flipped her over to climb on top of her, forcing her to open her eyes.

"Dammit, you Neanderthal! You could have waited until I woke up." Anissa pretended to be angry but couldn't wait to feel him inside her.

"Take those things off," Quinton demanded.

Anissa eased out of the bed, nervous, slowly removing her sexy panty-and-bra set. She stood there, less than perfect, in front of his lustful eyes. Somewhere in her subconscious, she found the false bravado. She issued a challenge.

"I am showing you mine now show me yours."

Quinton slid from under the covers and dropped his draws as if he were the most confident man alive. The sly grin that etched across his face made her laugh aloud. "Why are you standing here looking like you stole the cookie out the cookie jar?"

"This is why."

He pressed her to wall with his body. Softly he touched her until she surrendered. By dropping her guard, she experienced the ultimate pleasure. Any place his hand touched, his mouth followed. He seemed to be practicing or preparing for something. Just as Anissa expected the experience to be less than fulfilling, Quinton made her purr. He traced the length of her arm with his finger and brought the palm of her hand to his mouth. Using his tongue, he traced a small circle in her palm. The simple act seemed a bit bizarre at first, until he blew in the same spot and the wind caused her to tingle below her waist. Next, he sucked her middle finger slowly, allowing his tongue to lead the trail. There was nothing masterful about his skill but more like instinct. He wanted to make her remember his touch long after he released her.

While Quinton toyed with Anissa's body, he whispered for her to open her eyes. At that moment he touched her breast; she thought she would melt into the floor. He allowed his finger to trace along the dark inner circle of her nipple and his tongue followed. No words describe the pleasure she felt as he stroked her nipple with his mouth. Applying just enough pressure and alternation between sucks and teasing licks, she felt the dam break. The water flowed down her legs and pants escaped from her mouth. Her back arched all by itself and she pulled him to get closer. Her chest heaved as she gasped for air but Quinton had only helped her experience a small bit of pleasure. Taking both nipples into his mouth at the same time forced Anissa to whisper curses. She stroked his head as he found ways to make her moan.

He leaned away from her, just a bit, to look up into the face of the woman he would possess after today. Anissa closed her eyes and tried to relax from the tension Quinton had just created. Just when her breathing seemed to find a normal rhythm, he slid his hand between her thighs. The moistness that covered his long finger was all the encouragement he needed. As soon he pulled his fingers from her fold, he slid his tongue in its place. Her mouth flew open and she stared down at the body that kneeled beneath her. Quinton hoisted her from her wide-legged position and placed her in the center of the bed. No moments wasted as he climbed between her legs again and took pride in every moan that escaped her lips. He felt the pressure she applied to his head and knew that he had found another source to pleasing her. She was short of begging him to just fuck her when she felt the pit of her stomach do a somersault; the heat rose from some unknown place, the most racing feeling covered her entire being and forced through the pit of her core. She covered him in her juices.

Anissa had experienced sex before but this was her first orgasm and no way could she live without feeling like this again. She leaned up on her elbows and stared at the comical look on Quinton's face.

"What," was all she could trust herself to say.

"I'm a Neanderthal, but you must be a mermaid because you just tried to drown me."

Shamelessly, Anissa hunched her shoulders and smiled.

"Look at you. A half hour ago you stood in front of my bed, all shy, like it was the first time you had taken your clothes off in front of a man and now you lay here naked and unfeeling to my emotions."

Anissa laughed aloud, offering no answers and happy in her recent discovery. Quinton straddled her as she just stared at the slight curve of his hardened penis. Lying there, she heard the sounds of her favorite song called "Stars." Quinton and she had indeed come so far from the freezing cold to his bedroom and no one could convince her she belonged anywhere else.

The shrill of the phone broke Anissa's pleasant memory. She debated if she should answer but the annoyance would only persist. She raced across the room, and answered. Quinton's baritone voice broke through, "Hey babe."

"Hey."

"Are you alright?"

"Yes," she answered.

"Were you asleep?"

She was shocked at the tears that slid from her lids and angry that he had not come home the night before. She sighed.

"No, I wasn't asleep. I was just wondering when you were coming home."

Quinton's answer was void of any emotion.

"Maybe I'll see you tonight."

Anissa did not argue. She had learned that it was wasted energy. He would not respond to the vilest of her attacks and only punished her sexually when she was utterly disrespectful with her taunts. She did not wait for an explanation. She just hung up knowing that the one action made him angrier than any words she could form at that moment. It did not seem appropriate to tell him that Chaka was no longer there for him to impress.

She could not bring herself to say the words that lay dormant in her heart. So many nights she had wanted to ask what had Chaka done to warrant so much admiration. Buck even had the ability to get Quinton to leave a warm bed on a frosty night. Buck reserved his intrusions for the issues that they had to handle as a group. Chaka, she thought, used his friends. He wanted them at his disposal but they had to wait for his compliance. She had learned the art of reserved silence if she wanted Quinton to pacify her in any manner. Just as she cried openly, she heard the sounds of Eve moving about in the kitchen.

"Don't mess up the kitchen, greedy. I just cleaned it," Anissa yelled from the living room area.

Eve walked to her friend and stared at her face.

"Why are you crying?" she whispered.

"He didn't come home last night. I am just so tired of waiting for him to see my worth. I am more than a dumping ground for his semen. I deserve to be happy, don't I?"

Eve stared, wide–eyed, before she could answer. She had to be careful; Anissa was always the levelheaded one in the friendship. She was the main reason the two couples lived under one roof and shared the expenses down the middle. Far too many nights passed when either she or Anissa would take missing. As to stop all the unnecessary yelling and questions, she had formulated the argument that convinced Chaka and Quinton the women would only end up in the other's house anyway and privacy was a matter of her and Quinton residing on the second floor and Eve and Chaka claiming the third floor. The ground floor served as a dining and living room area with a full operating kitchen and bathroom.

"Go wash your face, Nissa," she demanded. "Quinton hasn't changed since the first day you met him and he ain't going to change if he sees you hysterical that he didn't come home last night."

Anissa understood Quinton had to deal with his issues. However, she didn't want to be sacrificed while he found a way to cope.

Twenty minutes later Eve was lying in her four-poster bed when she heard the front door slam. Seconds later, she rose from her lying position, ready to run into Chaka's arms. Grief erupted as she realized those were not his footsteps. As the foot landed on each step, it confirmed Chaka would never again come through the door. In the center of Eve being she had been searching for the closeness with Chaka, instead of enjoying the time they shared. Now he was gone and she was alone. The thought provoked all kind of insane questions.

Quinton peered around the door to find the bedroom empty and reasoned Anissa must be upstairs with Eve. He would not climb the steps and he refused to call her; she had to have heard him come home, he reasoned. Anissa could not bring herself to move; she wanted him to return home and now she wished he would just leave. The confusion that tore at her heart made her lean back into the chair. A few hours later Quinton went searching for Anissa. He found her asleep in the oversized chair, and his heart ached that she had been waiting for him and he had come too late. He kneeled at her feet before hoisting her into his arms. The small display of affection reminded him of their first night together. Lying next to her, he sniffed her hair, kissed her forehead, and silently promised to be a better man to her.

Anissa could not miss an opportunity that might not ever return. She leaned into him, kissing first the tip of his nose and finally his lips. She forced him to lie on his back as she straddled him. The moisture returned to her face as she peered into the sadness of his eyes. His hands touched her face and she pecked at the center of his hand as the tears dropped from her eyes.

"Don't cry. I'm sorry," he offered. He wanted to assure her everything would be fine. Although, he wasn't so sure that was true. Everyday brought another wave of emotions and questions but tonight he surrendered to the woman that held his heart. She could not talk. All she could do was cave to the need to feel his arms wrap around her back. She needed to touch all the places she had missed lately.

Anissa peeled away her nightgown and pulled the belt on his robe. She sat perched atop his erect penis as he held her hips. At a turtle's pace, she lifted and lowered herself onto him, refusing to look away. She had hoped to steal a piece of his heart just for herself, something he could not take back after the moment has passed. With precision and control, she lifted one hip and lowered the other. There were times he would make her beg him to just stop teasing her and give her all of him. However, tonight the tables had turned every so slightly. Quinton lost the battle of wills and closed his lids to allow the feeling to capture him.

"Open your eyes," Anissa whispered. He could only surrender to her request. He felt her muscles tighten and relax as she rode him into a fury. "Tell me you love me, Quinton," she begged just as she felt the familiar feelings that came when she was about to climax.

Quinton complied once, saying the words as if he would never get the chance again. As the last word left his mouth, he roared. Anissa's chest thundered against him. They clung to each other all night, afraid if one let go, the other would not be there in the morning. Respectfully, they separately cried together, realizing that life could very well change for them from this moment.

8

Missing You

Eve cried in the darkness, wishing that Chaka had just one more night. She talked to the stilled image of him on her dresser.

"Why can't you just come home one more time? I needed to hear you laugh at me for one misguided attempt at something or another. I need to feel your cold feet against me while I complain. Please," she begged the portrait. There was no one that could fill the void losing Chaka left behind. The miserable thought occurred too late. She really did love him. She had been running in a circle for the intimacy she already possessed. It was clearer through her tears, the pounding of her heart and the tantrum that rose in her soul.

The moment she heard the glass breaking, Anissa flew up the stairs, two at a time. She burst through the door to see Eve's body crumbled on the floor, hysterical. Quinton followed. The sight that held him captive just at the doorway made him quiver. It took all the will in him not to go to Eve's broken image. Softly, he spoke to Eve.

"Come on, baby girl, you can't lay here in this glass."

After she covered her face, he demanded, "Get up!"

She could verbally spar with wild animals and win but with Quinton, he provoked her to fight back.

"Get your simple ass off the floor before we have to go to the emergency room tonight!"

When Eve realized he was talking to her, she snarled.

"Fuck off, you black bastard! It should have been you lying dead on the ground instead of Chaka."

Quinton agreed. "You're absolutely right but in the meantime get your special ass off the floor until I clean up this mess."

She leaped at Quinton with the agility of a panther. Nano-seconds before she clawed his face, he snatched her hands.

"Now that's the unbarring evil witch I know and love."

The truth in her words intensified the guilt he carried. The hurt in his eyes was evident to Anissa but Eve didn't give a damn about his feelings. She wanted him to replace Chaka. Selfishly she wished Anissa was suffering the loss instead of her. Short of telling Anissa, she glared at them.

Anissa's anger was burning a hole in her chest.

"I don't understand how two people that love one man so much could be so mean to one another. You both need to accept that we are the one's left to deal with Chaka passing." With as much sympathy she could muster she spoke.

"Eve wishing it were Quinton isn't going to change shit."

She turned to Quinton with her eyes blazing.

"You hollering it should have been you, well where would I be? You didn't give that thought before you started changing places."

Turning around she left Quinton and Eve, hoping they understood the damage they were doing to one another.

Quinton pretended to have the answer.

"Evil will probably be the victor in that battle."

Eve had recovered and was demanding her respect.

"Stop calling me Evil, you bastard!"

He huffed, "I'll be calling you Evil until the day you bury me next to my best friend. Now get your evil, silly ass out of here until I clean up this mess."

The last words had shut Eve's mouth. She had not given any thought that Quinton could be suffering a loss. She was there as he cried openly, yet it still had not occurred to her that anyone might miss Chaka as much as she had. Slowly, her outburst subsided but she would let his fool hearted emotions change her mind.

The smell of his favorite cologne enveloped her the moment she opened the door. Determined she touched each thing as though it was him. She grabbed his favorite suede jacket, fingering the fabric, feeling the softness and trying to stay just beyond the memories that claimed her every time she dared to look in his space.

Eve had to believe there was life after Chaka. Accepting it however was another dilemma. She needed the love and protection he provided. Torn between her fears and being loyal to him she debated with her heart. When should she date? Was it even appropriate to clean out his closet so soon? What would folks think if they knew she wanted to move on with her life? Shamefully she wanted their approval but didn't have the courage to speak. When Chaka was around their opinions never mattered. He was her only responsibility and now she had no one.

She made a pile of coats, pants, shirts, and shoes for Goodwill to pick up the following day. In tears, she worked through the pain of losing him. Almost everything she touched she wanted to keep. Giving them away, she believed was like giving away the years they shared. Blindly, she tried to pack the boxes without seeing anything. At last thought, she decided to keep a bottle of his favorite fragrance and all the photo albums. There were two albums. Inside one she found a hospital bracelet of a girl child name Chanice Dubois. Her faith in their love was shattered. The date showed four year ago. Inside the album there also were recent pictures of the child. She had a smile identical to Chaka's and the pattern of her freckles was identical to his own.

The pounding in Eve's chest forced her to look away. There was no way in life she could put the book down and walk away. She had to confirm her suspicions. Eve was certain there was an explanation. There had to be. This child was too young to have been born before they met and to old for Eve not to have known she existed. There was a piece of hair in the compartment marked "the baby's hair," and a navel cord in the compartment meant for that. Eve thought she would go insane when she saw the picture of a smiling Chaka and a woman that seemed happy. The face of the woman was very familiar but she couldn't be distracted by it. She needed to piece this scenario together before she hyperventilated.

Her breathing quickened as she tried to find a legitimate reason for the display of photos. Tears formed but refused to flow as she held the album close to her chest. Anger began to coil in the pit of her stomach. The anger she had felt the morning of his funeral returned as she realized he had betrayed the ultimate trust. He had a child with another woman and kept it a secret. He had violated their relationship and now she wondered what other secrets he had taken to his grave. Before Eve allowed the rage to fully claim her, she lifted the second book. The very first page in Chaka's handwriting declared, "My first son. Chaka Xavier Dubois weighed in at nine pounds and eleven ounces. At birth he was 22 inches long and the color of paste." She held the book, hyperventilating over the realization that he had two children. "Holy shit," she whispered. "This motherfucker has two children."

She thought, *I'm sitting here unsure of how to act and he was playing me for a fool.*

Quinton came into the house as Eve began screaming. He raced up the stairs without thinking. She was kicking boxes and throwing clothes about as she cursed. Her hair was wild on top of her head and her eyes were red as beets. At that moment he knew she must have found something to prove Chaka had a family outside of her. Her words were more than a declaration of truth, "I can't believe all this time and you've had children hatching all over the place! I can only image how many times you waltzed in here from being with your children and lied."

Eve stopped ranting suddenly. She turned to see Quinton standing in the very spot that brought her to this revelation. She smirked at the smoldering image that bothered her more than Chaka being dead—it was that Quinton was alive.

She accused him, "You knew, didn't you?" She rushed on before he could explain. "You knew about his bastard children and never said a word."

Quinton did not bother to offer her any words of encouragement; he did not owe her any answers.

"I've hated you for more years than I cared to admit but now I have good reason to hate. You helped him betray me."

He stood still with his head hanging low allowing Eve her right to vent. She did not want or need a shoulder to cry on, she needed to place blame. Quinton had not expected to feel guilty when Eve finally found out the truth. The emotion claimed him as she blamed him for never mentioning the children after. Then it occurred to her maybe Anissa knew also and she had not said a word either.

"Does Anissa know too, Quinton?" She demanded an answer.

"No," he answered without much thought. "If Anissa knew you would have known before I could have gotten the words out of my mouth."

Eve crossed the floor to stand in Quinton face. She had gotten so close to him he could feel negative energy dancing all over her.

"I suppose I should thank you for keeping all of his dirty little secrets."

Quinton met her angry eyes and began to explain that he thought telling her would have brought him joy.

"Eve, this was never my secret to tell and as for telling you after, well, that was a decision I didn't think you could handle."

Suddenly she was able to put the missing pieces from the funeral and the pregnant woman in the photos.

"That was the woman at funeral. The one you and Buck kept holding on to and comforting. You sorry motherfuckers! Y'all showed the bitch more loyalty than me and I was his woman. Now I understand she was his baby mama," she spat.

He tried to reason with her. He would learn that was a big mistake. Eve was not rational and anything he said would just add another nail in his coffin.

"Stop talking! You kept his secret because you never believed I deserved Chaka's love." She shook her head at the truth. "Well, it seems he earned everything he got in our relationship. He lied to me and I did the same fucking thing to him."

The resentment of knowing he had been living a double life made Eve want to hurt him. However, he was gone. Even in death, he managed to make her feel like a fool.

Hours later, Anissa sat in the passenger seat opposite Quinton, mad as hell.

"Quinton, you have to try and understand how she must feel. From his grave he was able to destroy all the love they shared by keeping this secret. A secret she had to discover all by herself while trying to find a way to live without him. She can't even confront him." Quinton sat opposite Anissa wishing he hadn't expected her to side Eve. He was pissed that Anissa even pretended to understand Eve rational. She gave her opinion knowing that Quinton would be hurt but she was on Eve's side this time.

"Every chance Chaka got he berated Eve being the woman he created. Calling her money hungry but he started out giving her stacks to shop with in the beginning. Then calling her self-centered when he made her his show piece. You can say what you want but the way she is acting right now is about the way I would if the shit was reversed."

Anissa sensed there was so much more going on beside just the love/ hate relationship Eve and Quinton shared. The tension between the couple was strangling them. Q could not believe Anissa saw logic in Eve's drama. Eve had been less than loyal over the years. Although, his judgment and loyalty were measured by his long time friendship he still believed Eve's wrongs were utterly disrespectful. Chaka managed to keep his family hidden from almost everyone – there was not even a whisper in the air about them. However, every step Eve took revealed a new scandal involving her and Earl.

"You don't really know all the trouble she caused," he uttered.

It was too long coming and secrets did not stay hidden for always. Anissa's curiosity wore a hole in her mind as she debated over the facts. Quinton began to show his dislike for Eve shortly after they moved into the same home. "Why do you dislike her so much?"

She watched him shake his head and then she watched him open his mouth and close it again.

"Leave it alone, Nissa. Let it go," he demanded.

Anissa turned her entire body to him. The look on her face was fear mixed strangely with determination.

"I've asked and even pleaded with you to tell me the truth. Every other time you said leave it alone and I did out of respect. Not this time."

The cryptic statement was code for an ultimatum waiting in the background. There were few times when she outright demanded anything from Quinton but on the rare occasions she did so he could not deny her. He lowered his head in his hand. Slowly, he spoke. The deep breathes he took before speaking was a sign that the truth was heavy as the burden he carried on his shoulders.

"Chaka and I were having some problems. That is a long story going back to another time. By the time you and I started messing around nobody was safe from the drama in the streets. Hustlers were catching cases for trafficking like fly balls. Sentences were coming with letters instead of numbers. The boys and I were looking for a safe exit. I personally didn't know any man that threw his hat in the game and just walked away with everything in tact. Maybe you lose your values or quality of life but either way you suffer a loss. Call it being naïve but we thought we could be different. It was just a matter of planning. We were pups in the game by the time I met you. Our real respect came from the things we did as kids to keep money in our pockets."

Anissa had heard the stories involving the Baker Boys 5, but she knew Quinton needed to build slowly. It was his way of doing things. "We sold cakes by the slice, brownies, cookies and anything else that we could cook in Ms. Sadie's kitchen. Natural as rain we joined the drug game. It was simple as selling a little bit of weed. Our reputation as the Baker Boys 5 took on an entirely new meaning. Then it was a little bit of whatever. Finally, we had a lot of everything.

The dude that Eve used to fuck with before Chaka name was Earl. No one really knew Eve was dating the lame. Seriously, I don't think it would have mattered if Chaka had known. He seemed to want her trifling ass all-the-more after he found out.

You and I were spending so much time together; it was just a natural reaction that Chaka and Eve would see one another. No one ever expected there to be anything more than a little fucking to happen. Especially since we all knew Petra was due to have Chanice any day.

Anyway, they started seeing each other regularly but your girl neglected to tell Chaka she had a man at the time they hooked up. Buck found out some months later and tried to warn him but Cha wouldn't listen. When Chaka confronted her she lied and the real bullshit began. All behind some snitching and some pussy this shit got outta hand."

Slowly he stopped speaking as if to allow Anissa the chance to completely understand what he was saying. Quinton hands expressed every period and punctuation as he continued talking.

"One night Eve was sitting in Earl's car when Chaka rolled through the block. He did not say anything; he just tooted his horn, to let her know he had seen her. She made up some story to Earl about Chaka harassing her or some shit. In the middle of the club, Earl pulled a gun on Buck. He threatened to kill us if we kept fucking with his girl. Tempers flared and promises were made. That night there was no turning back or so we thought. Buck and I left the club heading home to gear up." To emphasize, his point Quinton took a deep breath.

"Before either of us could make good on any promises, Chaka came out of nowhere. He was just as amped as we were but I guess after waiting for Earl to come out Chaka lost his steam. He flipped shit telling us Earl wasn't a real threat. Like jackasses we listened to his bullshit. He convinced us to let the nigga live. Eve came out first and Chaka snatched her up by her collar whispered something in her ear. That ended that. She was sitting in the car waiting for Chaka to come. When Earl came out, Chaka stepped to him about his threats. Without raising his voice or so much as a threat, he squashed the bullshit. That still didn't make me or Buck feel any better. We wanted at that nigga.

Do not miss understand, Earl was the man among his men. However, Chaka was the bigger nigga back then. If it was about money, we were getting it. Other things came into play like creditability and even respect."

Anissa took a deep breath because she was not ready for the details Quinton laid at her feet. She knew about the beef between Chaka and Earl but she thought it was simple rivalry. She never knew Eve was part of the game.

"We were all making money in the street but Earl's name was spoiled years ago. He set us up to save his ass when we first got in the game and started hustling. Earl could have showed out but he was a lot smarter back then. The key was making money. No one wanted to loose his freedom over a bitch. Eve might have been Earl's girl before but getting in the car changed that and the rest is the drama that follows."

Anissa was stunned speechless. Before she could completely understand Quinton's confession, he continued.

"It didn't end there. That was really just the beginning. Chaka beat Eve's ass that night and dared her to go get Earl's simple ass. For a while, Chaka and Eve had broken up and since she could not get next to Earl any longer, she just kept after Chaka until he started up with her again.

It didn't matter to Eve the trouble she created. Every few months it would be something and most of it centered on her interaction with Earl.

By Christmas that year, Earl had reestablished his crew and was really grinding hard in the mean streets. He had a tight little group of boys running with him so he thought he could be disrespectful. Eve went to a party hosted by Earl. She was there for about an hour when Earl threw a drink in her face and told her to go call her man. He claimed it was about time they settled some issues."

You ever hear the saying add liquor act foolish. That's the perfect description of Earl's scrawny ass. Anissa saw where this was going and even remembered part of the story after and the drama that took place afterwards.

"Eve didn't have the heart to tell Chaka what happened but one of Buck's lady friends witnessed the situation and called Buck to explain before it was swept out of control. Buck did not call anybody, he just showed up at the party and raised hell. Most of the cats at the party were men that we grew up with or men with whom at one time or another we crossed paths. They did not have anything to do with the drama and were not about to get in the middle of another man's problems. Earl's crew whipped Buck's natural black ass that night. Not before Buck told him he would see each man personally. Buck pleaded with Earl to grow some balls and kill him, or he would see him again. 'Every time I see you,' he said, 'I'm going to beat the natural bitch out of you. You either going to stop hustling or get you some real killers in your camp.'"

Quinton relived the fact that Buck could have died that night and the truth was Q still wondered why they had not done him in.

"Chaka isolated Earl and forced him out of the area completely by supplying hustlers with the best work at the sweetest prices. The plan was simple: undercut anything Earl might have dreamed of doing. Niggas came at us looking for help when Earl did them dirty. Chaka being the man that he was helped more than he turned away.

It took a minute but by the summer Earl realized he was not getting any love in the streets so he took his act somewhere else.

"But of course, he had to smear a little shit in Chaka's face about good ole Eve. She forgot to tell anyone she fucked Earl before the Christmas party and she went there to tell him she was pregnant. She reasoned it was not Chaka's child, so it had to be his. That was the reason he threw the drink at her trick ass. He also gave Chaka the receipt for the abortion that Eve had a few days after the drink incident. After all the drama that silly evil bitch caused, Chaka still carried her. She was his woman. I tried to convince Chaka he was making a huge mistake and that Eve's games were going to get one of us killed."

Anissa watched Quinton's face turn to pure bitterness as he told her almost everything. Suddenly, she regretted ever asking him to tell her the truth; now she had to examine the things Quinton had shared with her. She had to try and not harbor ill feelings for Eve for playing so many games and although Quinton had not said it, she now knew he believed Earl had caused Chaka's death. She shifted slightly in the seat, stared at the brick walls of their home and hoped they could somehow get past this moment. Anissa just began talking as if Quinton might be listening to her rambling.

"I know you have valid reasons for being angry with her, but Chaka forgave Eve."

Quinton barked, "Anissa, don't finish that comment, please, because you and I are still alive and Chaka is buried in a box not far from where we're sitting right now."

The stress of the moment forced Quinton to reveal things that gave him trouble sleeping.

"All day he was with Petra and kids. He told me he was in for the night. About an hour later, he called to find out where Eve's trifling ass had gone. Right then everybody's life changed. Instead of telling her ass to walk, he went to meet her on Furman. He asked me to meet him there because her car was broke down or some shit."

Anissa tried to control her breathing because she knew Quinton would kill Eve easily if he had proof she caused Chaka's death. She wanted to stop Quinton but she let him continue.

Quinton caught up in his version of what happened, he had not even noticed Anissa's bizarre behavior.

"I didn't see Chaka's car right away, so I pulled into the station on Furman and then I thought maybe he meant Aberdeen. I doubled back, and there was no Chaka. Eve's car wasn't there either. I pulled on the sidewalk opposite the stations and waited a few minutes. I called Chaka's phone but there was no answer. I drove to the curb on the dead end of Furman and that is when I spotted Chaka's car. There were two people standing with him. I did not recognize either of them, so I got ready to do battle. I stared in my best friend's eyes as he was shot in the chest at point-blank range."

Anissa's mouth flew open; her hand palmed her forehead as she rocked back and forth. Quinton had seen Chaka's murder.

The words tumbled from his mouth as he spit. He had to explain. "That one shot was all they got off before I started bucking, but it was no use. They got away. It was almost as if they were from the 'hood because the niggas knew exactly how to get up the low wall without getting into the direct line of fire. They both positioned themselves in the little alcove that separated the church from the bingo hall. Worst yet Anissa, neither nigga fired another shot – I was practically in the middle of the street. They climbed up the low concrete wall and disappeared in the park. On the ground, Chaka," he stammered, "There was blood everywhere. Since that night I haven't slept easy, knowing I could have saved Chaka, had I reacted quicker."

Anissa's mind raced as she sat helpless watching her man take blame for Chaka's death. She grabbed Quinton as he banged his head against the headrest and cried. He wanted to tell Anissa for more seconds then imaginable he stood frozen watching his friend die. However, his shame kept him from saying another word.

9

On my own

The process of grieving had created a great deal of tension. Living with the idea he had a family all this time and calling Eve a cheat made her madder than the betrayal. Her confusion ended and she blamed everyone for keeping Chaka's life a secret. She even convinced herself that Anissa was mistreating her for some unknown reason. The time had come to put an end to the drama and just move on. Storming back and forth, she whispered her resentment. Foolishly, she believed in the friendships.

Financially, she was prepared to get her own home but it nearly destroyed her to sit opposite Petra and know Chaka had taken out a policy for her. He had taken care of her separate from his two children. He carried that bitch when she was his wife! Not just some mistress. The bulk of the property, distributed evenly between his children. The remaining businesses split in thirds with Eve. In the aftermath of his death, he had tied Eve to the unrelenting toad Quinton and that simpleton Buck for the rest of her life. Although they now were her partners, so to speak, she was determined to get from underneath their controlling hand. Planning would be difficult without her safety net but she would be free. The proverbial prison would not hold her down. Mentally, she was already out of the home, the friendship and the business relationship she shared with them all. The confines of these walls were too much to accept. Today, she was liberating herself and the mourning would end the moment she exited these doors.

Anissa walked into the house just as Eve slammed her footlocker full of clothes shut.

"Eve, you home?" she hollered from the foyer. Eve did not answer. She wanted to be in the wind by the time Anissa came home. Instead, she raced down the steps with a backpack.

"Yeah, but I'm heading out just now," she answered just as she slinked past her former friend.

"Every time I want to talk to you, you're never home or you're leaving," Anissa whined.

Eve's lack of response was bone chilling: she opened the door and slammed it without a word. Quinton was eavesdropping just behind the basement doors and he would have cursed Eve out but had decided it was time Anissa and Eve dealt with their own battles.

Several months had passed since he confided in Anissa regarding the real reason he loathed Eve's very being. Since that time he had noticed a change in Anissa behavior. Almost as if she knew something and had chosen not to share. He opened the basement door as Anissa moved past it.

"Hey, babe you just getting home?"

Anissa did not trust herself not to break down and tell him what just happened, so she retraced her steps and headed to their bedroom. Suddenly Anissa felt different she felt insecure when it came to Eve and her motives for being so mean. However, standing near Quinton and the "I told you so," look on his face made her tired of the entire ordeal.

"Yes, but I'm tired. I'm going to lie down for a while."

Hours later, Quinton was in the kitchen cooking pasta and sauce when Eve sauntered by. She waltzed straight to the kitchen, opened the fridge, grabbed an apple and slammed the door. He would not respond to her antics. She had been trying to start a fight for some time and he never replied to any of her rude behavior. She was an attention hog and he was not about to be caught up in that drama. They stepped around each other and no words left their lips. Eve rinsed her apple; he stirred his sauce and she glared from the corners of her eyes at him. In her thirst for drama, she slammed her hand on the marble countertop and declared, "I'm moving out."

Quinton's answer was patent rude boy, "I'll try to miss you, Evil."

Eve was just as predictable as time. The announcement was not out of due respect, but some sort of warning. His natural reaction to her behavior was always the extreme; he called Buck.

"Get over here now. Eve is about to pull some shit."

Buck had long ago tired of Eve's rude manners and told her as much only once. He had held her with the same regard he would a long-lost cousin. They did not exist and neither did she.

"Give me ten minutes," he sighed.

Anissa woke to Eve dragging things across the floor and slamming doors. Rarely did she go upstairs uninvited. Especially since Eve seemed to be distancing herself. Anissa walked into a mess of boxes and clothes scattered everywhere.

"What's up girl? You spring cleaning," she joked.

Eve stared at Anissa and decided her exit should at least be cordial since they had been through so much together.

"No, I'm moving out. It's about time we all got our own space and lived our own lives."

The painful look on Anissa's face made Eve ashamed at the nasty attitude and the neglect of their friendship. The initial hurt disappeared and her anger was fresh. Although Eve was taller than her former friend was, the venom that flowed from Anissa mouth made her feel rather small.

"You're just moving in the middle of the night? You planned this — knowing your conniving ass you were not going to say a word. It's just like you to up and leave without so much as a goodbye or nice knowing you."

Eve was stunned, but recovered well.

"Shit! Nice knowing you," she hollered. "I can't say it has been a pleasure. Between you and the beast, I've had more than I can stand. At least now I know how you really feel about my conniving ass."

Eve's attitude did not impress Anissa.

"Your shouting hasn't moved me. Eve, you have always been prone to drama, so I guess expecting anything else is my fault. You are stomping around here when it's not our fault that you are feeling miserable. The truth is you create every bit of drama that comes your way."

Anissa was so pissed off she could not hold her tongue any longer. "Good riddance, you self-serving drama addict that wouldn't appreciate a good friend if she bit you in the ass!"

Quinton did not bother to referee the incident; he knew Eve was bark with very little bite. As for Anissa, she was angry but the sight of him might force her to beat Eve to death. For years, his woman had campaigned for Eve. Now she had to accept that her plea for peace was in vain.

Buck came through the door in the middle of Eve's tirade. He didn't bother looking for Quinton. He knew where he was after smelling the sausage cooking. Buck raced up the stair until he was in the thick of the drama.

"Okay, Anissa. You have had your say. Now get the fuck out of my face before I whip your fat ass," Eve threatened.

Anissa's chuckle startled both Buck and Eve. Buck was an instigator; he wanted to see Anissa beat the hell out of Eve. Knowing that what ever caused this battle was Eve's fault one hundred percent. He stepped out of the way.

"You would rather slap Buck's big ass than to tangle with me right now. Goodbye, bitch," she snarled.

Eve's cell phone jingled, saving her from having to put up or shut up.

Buck laughed aloud when Anissa marched down the steps. He could not leave without adding his two cents.

"All these years, Eve, I thought you had some heart – you were just perpetrating." As he doubled back down the steps, Eve yelled.

"Whatever, you big burly bastard! Try and answer the door."

Quinton spoke plainly and got down to business. "Who the hell are you?"

That was easy for Pop. He was nobody right now but soon enough, he planned to make the hood familiar with his presence.

"Forgive my manners, partner. My name is Pop." He extended his hand like a true businessman.

Buck caught the fever that claimed Quinton.

"Nah, nigga. Where I know you from," he barked.

"I hustle with some dudes on the dark side," he answered a little intimidated.

The dark side is an invincible line from Moffat and Knickerbocker, all the way down to Linden Street.

"How you know Eve?" Anissa asked, blocking Bucks path.

"I met her about eight months ago at a party in the Village," he lied.

Stunned the trio yelled, "Eight months ago."

Eve sauntered to the rear of the house, claimed Pop's arm and slammed the keys on the kitchen counter. They left the house without further fanfare. Anissa was beyond angry and would have gladly whipped Eve's ass if Quinton would let her. Buck left the drama at the door seconds after he began eating.

The energy changed once Eve had moved. Instead of relief, Anissa worried more. Quinton had become more distant, coming home with just enough time to sleep. Claiming he was out all times of day and night making a better life for them. In front of her eyes, he had turned into the clone Chaka had left behind. Ranting and raving was the couple's only communications. Quinton's insults were vicious but Anissa was lethal. Once during one their matches he yelled, "You need to get a life."

In the beginning, she would cry and hide from the hurtful words. Anissa found her voice, "Motherfucker I had a life! One that included a loving relationship. But I guess my lover is still trying to impress a nigga that's dead and buried."

Quinton would have responded but he knew the sting was long overdue.

Meanwhile Quinton and Buck were heading two rising empires. Every precaution had to be established, especially now that they would be a target for anyone with the heart to challenge the crew. The first step included them hiring a staff that could maintain the legal businesses and properties. Freeing them the chance at working on their secret businesses. The Dirty Dozen and their shifting responsibility were first on the calendar.

10

Serving time as a youth

Jahson Holding sat opposite the two people he had trusted most with his life. Clothed in an orange jumpsuit and his head hung, fighting back tears as he prayed the words were not true. The words were boulders placed on his heart. Through clenched teeth, he asked how she had died.

"She was killed in a car crash last night on the Conduit. Some nigga she was riding with was racing and he lost control of his car."

Quinton could not help feeling that delivering the horrible news was like standing in quicksand. Next to Quinton in the bright orange chair, was Chaka, lost in his own misery at being helpless to the man that had saved him more times than he could count. Although Buck was the only one serving sixteen months for possession of marijuana with intent to sell, Chaka, Q and Earl were just as guilty. In retrospect, Buck had the most to lose by going to prison but he did what was natural when it came to his partners: he protected them. He had been protecting Chaka since second grade so this was just another step in the course of their friendship.

Chaka chose his words carefully, "I can only imagine how you feel."

Before Chaka could complete his thought, Buck exploded.

"Nigga, you can't imagine my pain. The thoughts of Angela are the only reason I'm surviving this bid." His volume of his voice rose but the depth of his words could have sunk the titanic.

"The day the judge sentenced me, I asked for one thing. Please protect her until I come home. Both you motherfuckers failed. You sitting here imagining my pain and this nigga sitting here looking at me like he gonna break down and cry. Fuck that shit you talking."

Buck leaped from his seat bitter, resentful, and angrier than he could ever remember. In jail, there was no room for weakness. Despite his attempts at holding his tears at bay, he was breaking down. Just inside his cell, he collapsed and allowed the tears to flow like a raging river. He banged his head on the concrete wall and bit his tongue to keep from screaming. Blood gushed from the sides of his mouth as he held his mouth open, but refused to let the sound escape.

He opened his eyes and saw the letter just inches from his face. It was in Angela's neat cursive. Leaning forward he grabbed the envelope, hoping to make the words of her death less true. He was searching for a clue that she would not be alive by the time he received her words of encouragement. In some bizarre way the letter had taken him to her. He pictured her as she wrote the words that he would remember for the rest of his life.

Boldly she described missing his gentle loving touch and needing the opportunity to try all the things they only imagined. She begged him to forgive all the things she had done in his absence. She explained that nothing could erase the purest and most innocent love she experienced with him. She had ended the letter promising to see him in her dreams.

The last line of the letter brought the hulking physique of a powerful man to his knees. Love was such a small word, he rationalized later, but it had the ability to destroy everything in its path. The only woman to love him was unprotected. Now she was gone. Shame, rage and now a lost love had taken over his miserable existence. Buck cried as he begged God to send her back to him.

The morning sun was no better then the night's moon. Buck opened his eyes and felt the ache in his chest. The best part of Buck laid buried deep as the regret and bitterness rose in its place. Snarling about the days seemed longer. It was if he welcomed a challenged. His mean mug was permanent. He was rude and unforgiving to the slightest infraction. Shortly after Angela's funeral, he received a letter from the state granting him release.

It should have been a happy moment but instead he began reevaluating the direction of his life. He resented his crew. They had failed, while he had given up a chance at a good life. He wanted to prove all the people that predicted he was headed for prison wrong. Instead, he helped the prediction to come true. He had broken his grand Bea's heart and left her sad. Angela cried every time they spoke on the phone. Any chance at a football scholarship was over yet, Quinton, Chaka, and even Earl's snitching ass was free enjoy life. He reasoned the news of his release was another sentence. Things had changed too drastically, and he didn't want to deal with his so call friends at all.

Some nights were harder to sleep than others were. Buck had done his pushups – sit-ups and numerous curls but he still could not relax. Silently he laid there and the images of Angela took over.

There in his bedroom, standing in front of his bed was the perfect being. He could smell the essence of anticipation as she nervously unbuttoned her scarlet silk shirt. Tossing it casually to the floor, she turned her back to him, causing him to worry. For a moment, he wondered if she was still going to make love to him.

"Turn around Angela. Show me how bad you want to do this," he whispered.

She twirled around and dropped her bra at his feet, showing off seductive eyes and shining the brightest headlights he had ever witnessed. There she was, standing in front of him naked from the waist up –just smiling.

"You behaving like you're a pro, so let's see how well you shake that ass and get out of those tight-ass jeans with your boots still on."

Angela stopped cheesing and realized she had a problem. She had practiced this strip tease all week. Dancing with and without music, she tried different looks in the mirror that made her feel sexy. There was not going to be anything smooth and sexy about her next feat. Triumphantly she unsnapped the button on her leather jeans and shimmied until her pants were just past her butt. She rotated her hips from left to right and slowly pushed them to her thighs. Buck lost his mind as he stared at her triangle. He leaped from the bed and tackled her. Heaving her high in the air, he slammed her on the bed

*and snatched the jeans and boot off. Unashamed of his obvious lust
he dropped to his knees at the foot of the tiny bed and buried his face
in her black velvet. Angela had heard girls talk about oral sex but
her first experience was confusing. Unable to hide her pleasure, she
moaned loud enough to encourage his efforts. She cursed when she
felt the small fire building in the pit of her stomach. Her chest heaved
and she slammed her head from side to side.*

"Oh God," she begged, "Please don't stop."

Buck's eyes flew open just as Angela pleaded in ecstasy. His jaw
went slack and his fist clenched; he tried desperately to see his beloved.
The dream was over and he was back in the tiny confines of his tiny cell.

His eyes fluttered closed as he tried to see the vivid image of Angela
squirming about at his touch. He wanted to capture that feeling once
more. In his desperation, he had not realized that he had cried out. Buck
was losing control of all his faculties, just for this one last touch.

An understanding elderly man passing Buck's cell whispered, "Just
hold on a little longer son – just a little longer and it will all be easier."

The old man's words of comfort carried Buck until he could go home.
His only friend in jail offered him another word of advice before he was
free.

"Son, don't allow this mistake to dictate your life, get past it. There is
a world out there waiting for you to conquer – do it for me."

Moments after his release, Buck decided to make peace with Angela.
The pain and guilt of having left her alone weighed heavy on his spirit.
However, her dying while he served time left him crazy.

Chaka sat in the beat-up Monte Carlo Cutlass, waiting for his bro-
ken-hearted friend. Finally, there he was standing at the electronic gates.
From the distance, nothing about Buck seemed to have changed, except
he had bulked up and his glare was more menacing. Standing next to him,
he realized Buck had changed. Their greeting was cold; it lacked any of
the qualities Chaka thought defined their friendship. There was no excitement in his eyes or even a hint of happiness that he was a free man. If

there was every a time in Chaka's life he wished he could change a bad decision, this was one. He did not know what to say to change the mood so he said nothing.

Chaka's quietness evolved around the fact that he had not protected Angela. In his selfishness, he had not even bothered to speak with her outside of the pleasantries of seeing his friend's girlfriend.

Privately he admitted he was a little jealous of Buck's strength. Buck never stops trying. There was no situation too big for him. When they were younger, the pudgy kid with crazy fighting skills would not allow anyone to pick on him without a fight. It wasn't the same for Chaka. He had been the target of more than one bully. Meeting and befriending Buck changed that forever. Chaka however, never shook the fact that it was Buck that saved him from getting jacked almost everyday of his elementary school years. Instead of being grateful he resented it when they were older. He hated that Buck could go anywhere and most men either moved out his way or greeted him simply because of his size. Meanwhile Chaka always had to earn his respect.

Friends were not supposed to have resentment towards one another. Chaka was happy he never had to explain why he harbored the feelings. Men did not discuss the things that made them weak, or the animosity they harbored from their youth. However, seeing Buck made him ashamed of things he done to hurt his friend.

At the cemetery, Buck searched the grounds until he found the stone dedicated for Angela Plumbton. Without fanfare or singing choir, he knelt and kissed the bronze-colored plaque. There was not a tear left to shed or an apology left to ask for. He sat quietly until he could allow the words to form. He poured out his heart and promised to love Angela for all his days. The minutes that passed were like seconds as he thanked her for loving him and being his best friend.

The air that escaped from his lungs burned as he vowed to make the guilty pay for the pain they had inflicted on his beloved. Just as quietly as he walked to the grave, he found himself wandering back to the car. Chaka's meaningless chatter forced Buck to accept that no matter how angry he was, he needed to control his emotions. He could not allow anything to interfere with his plans.

Arriving at Grand Bea's door had brought finality. Chaka climbed from the car and handed Buck a set of keys.

"These are for the car. The others on the ring are for you when you are ready," he announced, as if it were some big surprise.

Buck hunched his shoulders in response and turned to leave his friend standing on the sidewalk.

Buck's homecoming was uneventful. There wasn't a group of people waiting for him or even a home cooked meal. He was alone with his thoughts and resentment. After a few days, he took a chance and left the house. Not two blocks from home, he ran into Chaka's mother.

Ms. Sadie put an end to Buck's self-inflicted exile. She summoned him to her home to have a talk. The moment he stood in her kitchen, she turned and smiled. There he was the teddy bear trying not to look as sad as he felt. Understanding his loss she wanted him to feel and know she would always be here for him. Opening her arms, she wrapped him in a mother's hug and rocked him until she was ready to let him go. The reception made Buck feel loved. For the first time since being home, he was sorry for staying away from the house where he played as a child. He had to admit in his anger, he hadn't given thought to the other people that did love him and wanted to know he was okay.

The petite woman placed a platter full of his favorite foods before him and watched him eat. She couldn't have been happier to see he still loved to eat as much as she loved to feed him. Giggling she reminded him of all the times she had to cook extra because he pretended to be taking food to his grandmother. The truth was Buck would eat the food long before he got home. Slowly she got serious and shared her feelings about life after loss.

"Buck it's not easy to accept losing someone we love, either in death or if they just move on to someone else. However, it's better to know that special connection than to wonder about it all your life."

Ms. Sadie wanted to encourage Buck beyond his grief so she continued until she was sure he understood her point.

"I'm proud you haven't allowed the setback to cripple you and for that, I could not have chosen a better friend for Chaka. My son is a better man for having you in his life. I remember not being able to get any of you to leave as children. Do not allow your disappointment in them to stop you all from growing. I know they let you down but you are as incomplete without them as they are without you."

The words made sense. Ms. Sadie had completed the task. She hugged her surrogate son and begged him to try to forgive his brothers. He'd listened to everything she said, he even tried to forgive them but the pain wouldn't subside.

Days later Buck leaned back in the barber's chair relaxing, wondering if he had the courage to forgive Chaka and Quinton. Laughter and complaints buzzed through the shop but it was the peaceful feeling that helped him make up his mind. Being home and able to do something as simple as go to the local barber and talk bullshit, seemed like a privilege after all he been through. He watched little kids running back and forth waiting for their turn to get in the chair. He watched as mothers dropped their son's off and talked to their favorite barber. It all brought back memories of him, Quinton and Chaka as young men.

Ms. Sadie was all smiles the moment she saw Buck enter the room. Although she had asked him to forgive them, she didn't think he would show for Chaka's party. Standing in her elegant cocktail dress, she couldn't wait to show the rest of the boys her surprise for them. The healing could truly begin as long as they were in the same place at the same time Ms. Sadie reasoned. Chaka rose as he watched his friend stroll toward him in his black leather pants, matching leather shirt and fedora pulled slightly over his right eye. The two men embraced as though they had not seen each other in years. But more than anything, they knew this was not about time; this gathering was about forgiveness. Despite everything, Chaka wanted to appear unmoved by the gesture of seeing his burly brother in the walkway. His eyes glistened as he bowed his head to hide his joy.

Quinton observed the camaraderie. This was a welcoming, Quinton thought, that was long overdue. Finally, he could relax and enjoy the night. The night went by as each man danced with every woman brave enough to shimmy nearby. A cameraman captured the true essence of the trio's friendship while they sat side-by-side, laughing, and clowning around. Buck left that night feeling as if he had eased a small burden. Quinton left elated that his right arm was now intact. Chaka left smiling because he knew just how much his brothers meant to him.

Ms. Sadie posed for a picture with the young men and she kissed each as if it would be their last chance together. She proposed a toast to Chaka, wishing him a merry birthday and happy life in peace with his closest friends. Each man understood the meaning and bowed his head, paying their respect for the wisdom bestowed. Buck marveled at the number of women that found him attractive. In his state of bereavement, he had not bothered to appear available or even interested. He stumbled about, restoring his Monte Carlo and staying away from anything that would remind him of his loss. Now he understood the other part of staying away was that he had missed the tender touch of a good woman. Sasha came out of nowhere it seemed just as he was about to pull off. He had seen her since he'd come home but he kept meaning to call her. It always slipped his mind.

"Hey bad boy," she teased.

Amazed at seeing her he leaped from the car pulling her into a huge hug. She laughed when he let her go because she had missed their friendship too.

"Damn, Sash you looking good," he said as he twirled her around.

Sasha blushed, thinking the same exact thing about Buck, but she didn't dare say it. All her teenage life she had a crush on him and he never knew. She kept the secret from every one including him.

"Thank you. When did you get home and why haven't you been to see me," she asked in all one breathe?

Ashamed of the answers he lowered his head but kept his smile in place.

"I've been home a little while, but I wanted to get my head right before I started visiting my peoples you know," he admitted.

"That doesn't excuse you," she answered with her hands on her hips.

Before long, Buck was sitting next to Sasha in her apartment listening to music and reminiscing about their days of playing scully in the middle of the street.

Quinton leaped an inch off the floor the first time Buck pulled up alongside him in the Monte Carlo. The French coffee exterior gleamed. The ivory-colored interior with coffee piping complemented the smile of the driver.

"Damn, big boy," said Quinton, "you have made this baby pretty as hell."

Buck nodded. He had done well in restoring Mable. The excitement etched across Quinton's face eased Bucks reservation about his color choices.

"What you name her?"

"This is Miss Mable. She got an old soul with a hot-ass body and pretty as any of tomorrow's next best thing," Buck clowned.

"Nigga, you did alright restoring this pretty bitch. I'm ready to go get me a Caddy and see what you can do with that."

Buck leaped from the driver's seat, allowing Quinton a chance to really see the detail he had put into his ride. Quinton sat down and got familiar; he turned the ignition and listened as she purred. He slammed the door, reclined and adjusted the mirrors. If Buck didn't get in he would be left right there because Quinton was ready to ride.

Quinton yelled, "You better get in or I'm gonna leave you standing right here." Buck laughed as he sat in the passenger seat in amazement at Quinton's theatrics.

"Let's go to Atlantic City. Give me the chance to open her up and see what she can do."

Buck smiled in agreement and they glided into traffic. The car sat suspended in mid-air and the tires stroked the pavement with the touch of a well-skilled lover. Buck nodded his head to the words as the flowed through the alpine speakers. Quinton smiled and laughed as he accelerated on the parkway. He weaved in one lane and dashed into the next with the agility of a panther. Yelling above the music, Quinton spoke, "This must be what it feels like to ride on a cloud."

Buck laughed. "Just remember this is my ride. You got to get your own."

The flow changed as they found themselves on the Jersey Turnpike. Quinton stopped at a rest stop to fill up the tank; in his excitement it hadn't occurred to him to invite Chaka along for the ride but shit, he would tell him about it when they got back home. Buck shook his head at his friend as he watched Quinton push Miss Mable to full throttle on the open highway. Her smooth response impressed Quinton even more as he sailed past sign after sign. The tollbooth clerk uttered her approval as she claimed the fee before they headed down the road.

Buck leaned over his friend and began flirting.

"Hey, shorty, can I see you again?"

He asked with a sincere smile. Her giggle and wink answered that question. Buck pressed a laminated card in her hand and asked that she give him a call.

Twenty minutes had gone by before Quinton got the nerve to ask his friend about a time not so long ago. He hadn't apologized for not holding up his end of the bargain when Buck got locked up and he wanted him to know he knew it. He also understood Buck's distance and he didn't want anything to come between them especially, not something that he could be forgiven for. Unlike Chaka, Quinton valued Buck's opinion and he valued his friendship more.

"I can't tell you how sorry I am for not protecting Angela better, man. I truly hope you can forgive me."

Although the somber mood held the car and its occupants, it did not change the fact that Quinton had broached the subject by offering his condolences after so much time had passed.

"I know how much you loved her and it's really good to see you flirting and getting on with your life. I also have to believe that anything I say now is little said and little done but you must know, Buck, I would have done anything to take away the pain you felt that day."

The words rang true enough to Buck but he was still angry that time had come and gone for him and Angela. Gritting his teeth, he finally spoke his first words of forgiveness.

"I have to believe that you wouldn't have wished something so miserable on me. But most importantly, I have to accept that Angie is gone."

Quinton was awe-stricken by Buck's response but there was nothing more to say. The next few minutes of the ride they played, "Remember when."

Buck started. "Remember the time Chaka got his big-ass head stuck in the bars at P.S. 73?" They laughed.

"Remember the night old lady Ruth's dog chased you for two blocks?"

Quinton followed. "I still got the bite mark on my ass from the vicious beast."

"Nothing beats the night we got caught trying to smoke some tea leaves in Chaka's basement."

Neither could stop and before they realized it, the neon signs were welcoming them. Four hours later, Buck was driving back to New York with a serene feeling in his chest. In his bitterness and exile he had forgotten the realness that he learned being friends. Snoring beside him was one of the men he felt he could bare his soul to and never regret that he had exposed so much. He rationalized that during the party, he had taken a first step but now he was ready to move forward.

The following days found Buck, Chaka, and Quinton forging a greater bond. They were preparing for a future that had no glass ceilings. The same tenacity it took to hustle cookies in school, applied to amassing property in the hood. But the challenge had always been how they would amass fortune in the street. During Buck's prison stay, he met a few brothers that had been balling in the world. Some were eager to tell the tales of life on the outside. The elderly man that whispered, 'Hold on son,' impressed Buck the most.

The man explained that he had seen so many different miseries in life that jail seemed like a step up from the hell he had been living. He was 66 years old awaiting sentencing. He had killed two men for stealing a cheap bottle of wine from his liquor store. The leather-faced man smiled easy and joked as if life did not really mean anything to him. Buck listened as the man shared a life filled with waiting for a better day. He had done all the things people claimed he was suppose to do to be a man. He worked hard, married a beautiful woman, had a couple of children and still he didn't see the better day coming. He out lived his wife and both children grew up and went on their own to make futures for their families. All he had left was his business. Still no better day seemed to come. Tired of living, he was sitting in the store one cold night when two guys came in to buy liquor. But at some point they decided to rob the place too. He told Buck with a straight face.

"If they had taken the liquor without paying I don't think I would have been so angry but one guy told me today was my luck day he was gonna let me live. Well, something clicked in me and I told that son of a bitch that it was my lucky day but it wasn't so lucky for him and I shot him."

Stunned, Buck couldn't believe he had heard the man right. In his slow time, Buck tried to make sense of the words. Patiently, the man waited for Buck to ask why he had done that instead, of handing over the money. Buck finally found his voice and he didn't disappoint either.

"I was tired of waiting for the better day. I was tired of doing all the right things for all the wrong reason and never seeing the rainbow that everybody talked about but nobody I know ever saw. By the time they brought me to court I knew my life was about as good as it was ever going to be so I might as well enjoy the rest of it."

None of it made sense to Buck right away and even later when he heard of the man "hanging up" it still troubled him but he tried to get the sordid message from the man's story. Buck decided that it all meant stop waiting for the "good life" and just live the one you have.

The trio stumbled in the beginning over the right paths and the right women, even the right way to get through red tape that threatened them at every turn. However, with every block, they took on the prism of knock it down or hurdle it. Either way, they had to keep moving. It seemed since Buck's homecoming he had thought about his old buddy more and more. Especially when he wanted to fall back and wait for the better days.

11

Accepting Evil

Chaka had taken Eve from the only place she'd ever lived; her momma's house. He gave her money and other material things while he ran the streets and did his dirt. Gone were the days of spending time with her or caring about her day. If he paid her any attention, it was to criticize or chastise her about something she hadn't done right. But Eve lived with it believing it was all worth the drama if she could live like a queen. Immediately, after sharing his bed he began playing another game Eve wasn't prepared for. If she showed any resistance he wouldn't come home. He'd stay away for days at a time until he knew she was damn near stir crazy.

Just like an animal, put them in hostile territory, they either adjust or die. Eve learned to cope. She learned the game and began provoking him when she wanted to run the streets. He set up rules that she'd purposely break, provoking Chaka to head out.

They found the drama queen lying on the floor of the bathroom in her wet clothes, crying. She did not believe she had peed and not one of them cared enough to help her. Chaka demanded her to get her funky ass off the floor and wash.

Eve's whining grated on everyone's nerves. Chaka was being down right disrespectful. She accused him of a fatal disease: a drunken man speaking a sober mind.

"Shit, Chaka, tell us all how you really feel about Eve and her selfish behavior."

Stunned into silence, Chaka staggered back to the living room and reclaimed his seat on the floor. Quinton moved in slow motion as he retraced his steps to his overstuffed armchair. Anissa helped Eve undress and she sat on the toilet as her best friend bawled at the insults Chaka left in his wake. The tension was a reflection of the drama.

The following morning Eve rolled from the bed, hung over, in search of anything to wear. She had decided that Chaka's character assassination would end that day. Even if it meant she had to leave him. As she stumbled through the room, she noticed he was gone. At some point during the wee hours of the night, he had left the house. She timidly walked down the stairs, afraid to look down. First, the sweat poured off her body as the bile threatened to leap from her throat. Next, she felt a dry heave and forgot about the fear of falling; she rushed down the steps. Eve would have been embarrassed at being hung over if she wasn't more concerned with making past the kitchen. Just as she reached the ivory porcelain, she hurled.

Anissa and Quinton stared at each other and snickered softly as they listened to Eve pray, "Lord, I promise to never drink again."

Eve stood in the doorway of the kitchen, mad that the smell of breakfast sausage left her stomach rumbling. For the remainder of that day the trio sat in different stages of drunk. Chaka's disappearance had proven that the time had come to either shit or get off the pot. Although, getting off seemed like the right thing to say, she was not ready to give up the things he provided. By nightfall, Eve had a plan, and leaving wasn't an option. Being with Chaka had gotten her many of the things she did not want to live without. Proof was her home, with furnishing supplied by every expensive company she could find. Clothes that cluttered two walk-in closets, shoes, and all the accessories any woman could ever want. He could call her any name in the book but she planned to hold her corner until someone better came along. For a few insults, she promised to continue to rape his pockets and save her love for another.

Eve reasoned that Chaka deserved every pain he felt. Far from being a dumb woman, she knew he was out there cheating but none of it really mattered. Many times, he would leave home in the middle of the night, claiming to have to deal with some business. Chaka's defense for Eve complaints were simply reversed bullshit. He claimed the only reason he ran the streets so hard was to keep her in the fashion of spending his fucking money. If that did not quiet her nagging, he would yell insults to hurt her feelings. Chaka hadn't realized his theatrics or insults didn't work anymore. He was too busy doing his own thing to notice. In the sanctity of their bedroom, she hatched a plan.

Earl was not the man she dreamed about at night but at least for the time they spent together, he managed to cater to her whims. Eve accepted since Chaka didn't give a damn she would go about living it up like a single woman. However, she learned the meaning of discretion. She couldn't afford to let Chaka or anyone else get wind of her doing dirt too. Earl seemed like a good enough candidate, especially, since they were fucking before she met Chaka.

Anissa had tried to convince Eve that making a way outside of her man friend was the best route. That was all nonsense in her mind. Eve had thrown her head back and declared that ordinary hoes have to carve out a future but if there were a man in the streets making money, she would find her a benefactor.

Chaka was the only lover she had that could whisper from across a room and she would cream. The more he berated her, the more Eve searched for all the qualities she deemed she needed in one man. Meanwhile, she screamed, "I love you," at the top of her lungs every time Chaka appeared. Eve's resentment festered into a great big mess. She hated that she couldn't stand Chaka but she didn't have the courage to leave. She wanted to smear shit all over his face when she had found someone more deserving of her love and affection but no man seemed suitable. It didn't take long for the affair with Earl to get out of hand. Since Earl didn't have to take care of her, he was very attentive. He was affectionate and accommodated any request that left her lips. If she wanted to spend three-days on the beach he provided the relaxation. When she wanted to see a play, he made it possible. They just had to see it outside the city limits. If she just wanted to lie up he was right there to hold her hand.

The night of Earl's Christmas party, she admitted to herself all her game playing landed her in the middle of a deadly triangle. Pregnant and unsure of the father, Earl seemed like the right choice. The years of fucking Chaka without protection had not even caused a scare. She just assumed he could not make children. Earl had tricked Eve. She felt, in his eagerness to shower her with attention that he was willing to accept any responsibility that came with his mistress. However, Earl explained that his real motive for fucking with her was to have bragging rights over the lame man she had chosen over him.

The party was in full swing and Earl marched into the room, playing the part of a real don, dressed in all black with a bimbo at his side. However, Eve wasn't the least bit impressed. Her arrogance would allow her to believe any woman Earl fucked with was fit to handle her luggage let alone claim her throne. Standing near the bar waiting patiently for him to notice she was there. She didn't give a damn about being seen. Eve was on a mission. It didn't take Earl two minutes to know she was there. Two of his henchmen had whispered Eve was standing at the bar wearing the hell out of a little black dress.

Earl begged off from the ring of women vying for his attention and bopped over to her. Eve winked as he caught her eyes and stared her down. The compliments were flying out of his mouth as she kissed his cheek. The open display was a mystery to Earl. Eve had always proclaimed that discretion was necessary when it came to their relationship. They stood oblivious to onlookers and clung to one another without any concerns — this was Earl's house and no one would violate the trust by running back to Chaka.

"We have to talk," Eve spoke with the right amount of seduction and mystery. Earl's smile broadened; he misunderstood the word "talk" and thought she said "fuck," judging from his reaction. Almost instantly, his dick hardened. Eve slid her hands to the front of his black linen pants and stroked the average-sized member. Too eager to allow this opportunity to pass, he snatched her hand and lead her to a massive room with mirrors on the ceiling and pristine floors.

After the door slammed, he tossed Eve against it, pulling up her dress with one hand, and unzipping his pants with the other hand. Earl was not her very best lay but at least he knew how to get her juices flowing. He bent his neck and was stunned Eve only wore a garter belt. The art of seduction was a waste on men like Earl. He could not fathom the real meaning of Eve's brazen attitude and sexy dress. He wanted to fuck and got right to business.

He lifted her leg and then repositioned her.

Earl commanded her to turn around. Eve eagerly obliged his request and pushed her ass out giving him better access. He bent her at the waist as she pressed her hands against the door for support. He slammed his hardened penis into her and waited for the chorus of "ooh shits" to fly from her mouth. He flipped the fabric away from her bare ass and pounded harder. Slapping her cheeks he listened for the curses of encouragement.

"Pull my hair," she demanded, "slap my ass, and pull my hair." Never losing the rhythm, he smacked the flesh and yanked at her hair. The slippery warm place he was pleasuring squirted juices as if he had just turned on a faucet.

"Dang, baby, this pussy is too good," he offered between pants, pounding, and pulling. Feeling the full effects of Earl's strokes, Eve stroked her clit just as they began the height of their climax. He clenched his jaw tight and mumbled some inaudible curses, releasing semen straight into her cave. If she were not already pregnant, this would have definitely been a night of conception. Eve followed, screaming a litany of curse words. They stood motionless until they could feel the passion subsiding.

The arrangement worked out precisely as Eve had planned. Now that she had taken care of Earl's first priority, she needed to tell him her real reason for coming. The early affection left along with their climax as Eve began her litany as to why she had graced his function.

Earl's jaw fell open. The laughter began slow, controlled, and changed into a cynical howl. However, the harsh words left Eve cold.

"Bitch please! You come in here talking about being pregnant. Fuck that shit. Tell your man he about to be a daddy."

He opened the door as if to dismiss the conversation and Eve rushed behind him on his heels. The bimbo appeared at his right arm and handed Earl a drink. The chick did not feel threatened or even moved by the act of Eve being full center with Earl.

"Look, let's just discuss this shit in private," Eve demanded.

Before Eve could form another word, Earl threw the drink directly in her face, leaving her humiliated. As an afterthought, he spoke with cold eyes and bittersweet manners. "Come see me when you handle your little problem."

Dumbfounded, a few people openly gawked while others just did not care. With a broken spirit, Eve left the party. She got home and thanked God that Anissa was asleep and Chaka was not home.

In the shower, Eve scrubbed her body as though she would never be clean again. Exhausted, she went to bed only to dream about the mess she had created. In her dream, Chaka was choking her senseless and Earl lay inches from her body, breathless. Common sense had prevailed; she knew if she even attempted to tell Chaka about Earl's disrespect then he would have 101 questions and the result might be her getting an ass kicking. She promised through the tears that this secret would ride with her to her grave, along with all the others.

Eve opened her eyes and feared that her worst nightmare was about to come true. Chaka's face was beet red and his eyes matched.

"Tell me your dumb ass didn't go to that party last night," he pleaded.

Eve could not trust anything that came from her mouth so she just breathed deeply, preparing for the drama.

"I know you're the most self-centered bitch in the world but to go to Earl's party and think for one minute it was going to be a secret was the second dumbest thing you've ever done."

The puzzled look on her face confirmed that she needed to know her first dumb move.

Chaka ignored her pained expression. He paced back and forth until the idea came to him.

"You want that nigga, right? So guess what, I am gonna send you to him. Get up," he shouted, pulling her by her hair. She complied out of sheer nervousness. He tossed her a pair of jeans and a sweatshirt. She hurried into the items, thinking he would kill her right now if he knew for sure how far things had gone between her and Earl last night. Chaka held her at the base of her neck, pushing her about until they worked themselves to the front door. In the heat of the moment he would not bothered to give her a winter coat or shoes. He pushed her through the door and calmly told her to go see Earl. He could at least buy her a coat and shoes.

Eve stood horrified by Chaka's cruelty. They had been down this road before but not once did it occur to her she could find herself without a place to call home. The wind whipped through the meager cloth and she really began to understand the severity of her situation.

"I'm standing her barefoot and pregnant, in the cold, with no place to go," she whispered as if hearing the words would make them less true.

She turned to knock on the door but Chaka stood there on the other side of glass pane with his nine pointed at her face. She lowered her head not in shame, but in arrogant anger. Nope, she was not about to be shamed by one of Chaka's theatrics. She twisted the knob and found herself locked out. The smirk that filled his eyes was evil as all day.

The idea came like a light bulb: Anissa had to have heard the commotion, but she never came to Eve's rescue. The angry smile struck a cord in Chaka. He had learned that Eve was medieval if pushed to far. She banged on the door and begged him for a pair of shoes and at least a jacket, so she could get off his property. Chaka tossed the ratty sneakers on the carport, along with a spring jacket. Grateful she would not die of pneumonia, Eve gathered the things and left.

First, she walked toward the projects and finally she retraced her steps and entered the house through the basement. Chaka was on the third floor and had not a clue Eve could have the balls to come back after he tossed her on the sidewalk. On her way upstairs, she stopped in the kitchen and grabbed a butcher knife. Slowly she crept to her bedroom and watched Chaka as he lay with his back to the doorway. She stepped lightly to the edge of the bed. Just as she found the courage to pounce, Chaka leaped from the bed in a battle stance. Her natural reaction was one of anger and contempt. His actions forced her to a place she did not dream existed in her. The target was Eve's face. He slapped her and watched in horror.

As the tears stained Eve's face, her head went slamming into the wall. She found her bearings and raised the knife above her head. The force behind the blow she intended would have killed him if she hit her mark. The deranged look in her eyes and the sinister grin were enough to prove she intended to kill her benefactor today. The battle had insured one of two things: either Chaka would kill Eve or she would kill him.

Anissa and Quinton came in as the screaming erupted from Eve's mouth. Neither Quinton nor Anissa raced to the direction of the mayhem. They had both become accustomed to the danger zones and waged wars on the third floor. Carrying grocery bags to the kitchen took precedence over stopping the battle. Quinton was the first to speak in defense of saving Eve's life while she still had one, while Anissa busied herself putting away boxes and frozen foods.

Chaka's raised voice alerted the two levels below that maybe this time it was more serious than usual.

"Bitch you want to cut me," he asked, as if the thought of her cutting him was the most outrageous thing in the world. Eve did not verbally respond. She swung the knife in an arc and nicked his shoulder. The punch sent Eve sailing across the room. Banging in to the walk-in closet, she slumped at Chaka's feet. He grabbed her shirt and lifted her to her feet. As he dragged her to the door, he planted his foot in her ass and kicked her past the threshold into the hall.

Quinton reached the landing first, Anissa was huffing and puffing as she followed as quickly as her feet would carry her. Chaka stopped them both in their path.

"There is no need for a family conference. This bitch has finally worn out her welcome here."

The defiant look on both Eve and Chaka's faces left them bewildered. In a short time, something had gone terribly wrong and the sight of Chaka's blood caught Anissa's attention. She raced about to gather materials to clean his wound and bandage him up.

Eve made threats and promised to get even with Chaka for tossing her outside without shoes and for hitting her.

"You'll get yours motherfucker! I promise one day you're going to get yours," she yelled in hysterics.

Chaka laughed in her face. "That lame bastard Earl? He's too weak to come up against me. If it will make you feel better tell him to come see me."

The sobbing stopped at the mere mention of Earl's name. He was no longer an option after he had insulted her beyond repair.

"Earl ain't the only motherfucker that can't stand your bitch ass! I'm sure of that," she whispered as she wobbled down the steps.

"Well, stupid, when you find the motherfucker dumb enough to go up against me, tell'em come see me."

Eve's face stung as the wind blew around her. Anissa completed the task of repairing her man's best friend as quickly as possible. She raced down the steps to discover Eve had disappeared. The anguish that covered every inch of Anissa was enough to give her a mild heart attack. She prayed that wherever Eve went that she would be okay.

Quinton came downstairs hours later with a pained look on his face. His back was straight and he was not willing to discuss anything that happened earlier in the day.

Eve took her chances and called Earl. He listened to her troubles and decided that he could somehow benefit from her banishment. He took her to a hotel and got her a suite for a couple of days. He promised to help her pay for the abortion and to keep everything as discreet as possible.

For New Year's Eve, Chaka, Buck, and Quinton were hosting a Hustler's Convention. Exiled from the festivities was the only man that Chaka refused to forgive. The energy was high and harmonious with the festivities that surrounded the occasion. Half the people moving around the club were either working for or reaping the rewards of the Dozen's success.

With great sacrifice to life and relationships, the vision had materialized better than they dreamed it. Fifteen men comprised the Dirty Dozen and that night they stood proud of their successes.

Their status was explosive. Anyone not down was certainly trying to find a way to get down with them. Full-length minks swept city streets as all fifteen men exited luxury vehicles that could fill a small car lot. They ranged from milk white to midnight black. Men thin as a rail to beefy and brawny. Flat-out fine and straight-up ugly as hell, but not one man was representing less than a million-dollar attitude. Buck was extra with his flair, donning a mink baseball cap and matching jacket.

He joked, "You clowns ain't ready. Y'all still playing hustler while Daddy making all the money and representing success like a king out this bitch."

Women openly drooled at the spectacle of men. Each man stood about as though he was more important than the next, smiling, and winking at the long line of patrons.

"Damn, homey, these women ain't playing tonight. I think somebody trying to catch a sponsor," Dave said as he high-fived a few comrades.

All the millionaires sauntered about the club meeting and greeting, gangsta leaning and scoping out the competition.

The conversations bouncing off the walls reflected the changing of a new year. Old friends chatted while new ones celebrated.

Quinton loved watching the success of men. It was the reason so many ran to the game. Every man wanted more than he had--there were rules to this thing. The goal was to earn a million dollars. These men had done that more times than they could count and he felt honored to be among them. The pressure to be better is constant but the moment you arrive the feeling is euphoric. When a man donned ice from ear to pinky ring, he was making enough to eat well. Flossing lightly with platinum and gators, he was stuntin' a little better than average. The big dogs were showing -out in sables and minks, dancing on crocodiles, flashing Rolexes and were riding high-handed in luxury vehicles.

The women were taking it to the next level of fascinatingly fabulous. There were a cluster of women donned in designer duds and fashionable shoes. Strutting back and forth, batting eyelashes so long they could have been wings. Hairstyles were just as outrageous as the makeup. The glitter that draped off their necks, wrist, ears, and fingers was enough to open a fine jewelry store. As the hour got closer to midnight, the crew entered the swanky disco, claiming their place in the VIP section. A platform was erected in honor of The 12.

Eve and Anissa's ivory limousine rolled to a stop just outside the door of the club. The driver opened the door and waited as the duo sauntered by the security, looking like leading superstars. Short of a runway, these women were representing the major money and big things their counterparts had established. Anissa's ebony sable dragged the ground despite her three-and–a-half-inch Jimmy Choo sling backs. She was regal in her forties-style dress. It draped across her shoulders and gathered at the front; the length of her dress was full length, touching the tops of her shoes but the back hung just at her tailbone. The silver ensemble complemented the bob-styled finger waves that framed her face, right down to the single-tier diamond earrings and huge carat perched on her left hand. However, nothing outshined her smile, it brightened the dark room. She had brought a real royal sense of class to the world of gutter fabulous.

The second after Quinton and Chaka left the house, Anissa opened the door for Eve. The men of their life had lost their minds. Anissa and Eve were friends until they said differently. Chaka was going to have to accept that fact. The chance to stand in a room full of wannabe divas and pretentious folk was Eve's legacy. Anissa was there for morale support and they all knew it.

Eve's coat remained closed until finally handing it over to the club manager. The female mink was sparkling jet black under the overhead lights. Any words used to describe the sexy caramel sister with serious style were inadequate. Heads turned in her direction as she walked towards the bar. Despite the fact that she and Chaka still had not spoken since the incident, Eve was determined to shine like the Don's Diva. Standing at the bar, she searched familiar faces and nodded greetings to all the right hustlers.

Most of the women were stunned that Eve was really so beautiful. Because of the rumors, they just assumed her ugly ways were the proof of an ugly woman.

The high-backed gown dipped low in the front, barely covering her perky breasts. The slit in the center of the dress revealed one thigh every time she took a step. Eve worked the room, greeting people as though she was the host--smiling and offering compliments. She moved about just enough to call it dancing but not enough to reveal too much already-exposed flesh.

By the time, they made it to the VIP area restricted for the Dozen, and their female companions, corks popped, and every one was heading straight for a merry New Year. The young woman seated at Chaka's elbow was none to happy to see Eve floating about, hugging and kissing members of the crew. If looks could kill, Eve would have dropped dead from the many daggers aimed at her back, front, and side. Purposely she avoided greeting Chaka and his little friend.

As the countdown began, Quinton positioned himself behind Anissa and whispered in her ear, "Damn sexy, you got a man?" Anissa liked the game and lifted her left hand to answer his question. By the time they were at five, Chaka had moved about a foot away from the beautiful woman and was heading toward Eve. Four — Eve retrieved a flute filled with champagne. Three — Chaka was steps from being directly in her path. Two — the couple stood face to face. One — Eve touched Chaka's face. "Happy New Year" bounced off the floor and walls and tumbled out of the speakers as couples and strangers celebrated the dawning of a new year.

The traditional New Year's Eve song played softly in the background while the Dirty Dozen offered 15 toasts, paying homage to fallen soldiers and prosperous futures.

Just as quickly as they had ended days before, they were back to being the number one couple.

12

Getting Even

Eve had betrayed Earl and she would pay for her neglect of his feelings. Not to mention, every lowlife knew that he was shunned by his archrival. Desperate times were calling for desperate moves. Earl managed to quietly leave in the night like a thief to set about his plan. He headed south to align himself with some get-money soldiers that were making a name for themselves. Ian was having a little trouble staying focused and Earl needed a new start. Helping his cousin seemed like a win-win situation. He would help set up shop and show him the best way to turn profit on even the worst product. In return he figured to make a little money and establish his own crew. Surviving had been Earl's greatest achievement and today he would start learning to live.

As the business grew, an unspoken debt was rising. With newfound dollars in Ian's family, egos and confidences soared. He began to buy into his own hype, setting his own plans into motion. The timid curiosity he felt about Earl had snowballed. The time had come to ask questions.

"Why you really down here in the dirty when you could be home in the Rotten Apple, making money," he asked.

Earl's answers were always barely truthful.

"I was having a hard time finding real soldiers willing to put in work."

Ian understood that answer because he had taken his share of losses until he got the right crew together. Ian's eagerness to repay his cousin had everything to do with pure greed. Something else was in the works but Earl was not about to share just yet. The drivel tossed about the room between the cousins was as simple as watching two con men making the other his mark. Earl witnessed Ian's crews come from meager street urchins to real money chasers. He fantasized that if he just had a few good men, he could really show Ian how New York cats put themselves on display. Across the marble table, Ian imagined that if he offered to help Earl set up better at home, he could eventually snatch the business from beneath his feet and make Earl into an earner for him instead of a boss for himself. Grimy and grit were staring each other in the face but they had no clue they were just dirt.

Days turned into weeks and weeks into months when Ian finally approached the subject of helping Earl on his feet. The topic came on the hills of Ian seeing his first million dollars, free and clear.

"Cousin, listen. We have everything on sound footing. It's time you went back home and paved the way for us to expand."

His words were clever enough. Earl became an actor in the matter of minutes. Faking surprise at the generous offer, Earl shook his head slightly.

"I didn't come down here for you to help me in NY. I came to get my head right before I went back and re-established for myself."

Ian, in his own arrogance, could not see the trees for looking. Earl was playing him but greed was in Ian's way. He smiled pleasantly and spoke as if carefully choosing every word.

"There are plenty hungry cats down here looking to get a hand up in the world. You need soldiers that do not give a damn about the reputations of cats running the streets in your 'hood. Strangers somewhat to the area, I got that here — you could pick any six men and clear town and country on their eagerness to make money."

Earl covered his face with both hands to hide the smirk; he had caught his mouse. When he uncovered his face, he looked pained and spoke through labored breathing.

"If we do this, we have to come to some sort of agreement."

Ian grinned as if he had just hit the lottery.

"Okay, whatever you deem fair is payment enough."

Earl was willing to reward his cousin a king's ransom for his efforts – knowing he only intended to break the terms as soon as he was strong enough. Ian accepted without fuss, thinking it would be easy enough to snatch the entire pie from Earl when he was earning the right numbers. Ian counted on his soldiers staying loyal to him. Meanwhile, Earl counted on Ian's greed to cause a straight up mutiny. The terms negotiated and the deal was sealed as they puffed on fat, neatly rolled ganja. No shaking hands and toasts — just puff, puff, and pass between the men — proved that business made strange bedfellows. As quietly as Earl had left town he returned with a new swagger and his killing squad.

Earl was delusional when it came to his real potential. However, he had learned while sitting about in the south that patience was important. Even more important was the act of surprise. Patiently he watched the self-proclaimed Dirty Dozen operate. Quietly he learned the habits of the main core of the crewmembers. Earl had deemed Buck the weak link in the core and decided that even if he killed Buck; they could still operate without the muscle despite their loss. Every man was willing to hold his own when it came to his money. Quinton was smart enough to handle the business but he lacked the finesse it took to keep men loyal without humiliation and fear. Eventually, Earl believed with Quinton at the helm of the empire, he would ruin it by his own tyranny. That meant Chaka had to be dealt with properly; there could not be any proof that he was the real murderer.

Experienced enough to know that as long as no one could prove his involvement, he would have a fighting chance at the Dozen's entire operation. Money could quiet any suspicion and killing a nigga was the answer to blackmail. Earl had been circling the wagons for months, he thought about everything from the prime moments to the reaction of their women.

Opportunity was a key factor; his first order of business was to learn the habits of the targets. Eve, he imagined, would be his sweetest victory. The chance to see her broken after Chaka was dead and buried would be the best revenge he could have for her betrayal.

Learning Chaka housed another family only a short distance from Eve's watchful eye stunned Earl. His undying dedication to Eve was tarnished but he would use that information for a better day.

Although his children's mother was pretty, she was definitely not as beautiful as the sultry, sexy Eve. One quality intrigued Earl — she seemed to walk as though she were oblivious to Eve's existence. She was normal; she went grocery shopping dressed as a parent of two children bound for success, and met her man at the door with a respectable hug and kiss before sending him out into the world. She did not seem any extra or caught up in the gutter-fabulous lifestyle Chaka could so readily offer. Even her home was just ordinary and understated, in comparison to the gigantic brownstone Chaka shared with Eve. True to a hustler's creed, he had kept her away from the game. She lived just far enough away to be invisible but close enough to touch. If all else failed, Earl would make Chaka pay with the loss of this comfortable place he had hidden behind Eve's back.

Further investigation revealed that seeing his children every day was his only habitual act. The nigga even shredded his bad boy persona when he went there.

The dimensions to Chaka made Earl laugh as he realized he had been coming at this the wrong way for years. The real estate business operated like any well-respected company. A small staff assigned and handled the daily regiments. While, Chaka rarely stopped by he was hands on from the phone. The staff's payroll, were computed and distributed by an outside company.

The eagerness to get on with the get on had Earl on pins and needles. Even pulling a petty larceny robbery to set things in motion seemed better than sitting around waiting. The window of opportunity to catch Chaka was too small to commit the heinous act he had planned. Frustrated, he realized there was a required sense of commitment. Sticking to his original plan was the best route. Time was only a factor to Ian's investment and he could finagle for a while.

Earl had become bored with Chaka and his regiments but he needed an opportunity to shake up the Dozen's foundation. Trailing Buck was a good idea until it became clear Buck couldn't be caught slipping. He had no bad habits that were worth mentioning. From the looks of things, he wasn't a good choice either until he spotted him parked in front of Baldy's home. Baldy left the house without as much as a backward glance. Seconds later Buck walked up to the steps and entered without knocking. Earl sat from afar because, he was not sure, if Buck had a key or if the door was open. However, he was certain he was inside, no doubt boning Baldy's current girlfriend.

Earl devised an alternate plan. He could use Baldy to set the Dozen's camp in a tailspin. Two hours later Buck exited the house and drove away. Earl stayed to see how long before Baldy arrived – and as he suspected, Baldy came home within the hour.

Ecstatic at the revelation Earl bopped his head. Now he needed a way to get a little birdie to whisper that Buck was mowing Baldy's' lawn. As Earl and his henchmen debated on the best way to expose Buck's indiscretions, they were also preparing for the next point of attack.

Quinton was proving to be the easiest of the trio. He was a day walker and at night he went home, to the club, or visit one or two of the women he had stashed about the place. Earl surmised if he moved too quickly, Chaka and Buck would band together and flood money into the hands of prying-eyed neighbors to find Quinton's killer. But it was the only move that made sense and he was the easiest target. This was proving to be a project that Earl might not be ready to handle alone. Earl's crew was keeping a low profile but they were also itching to meet some of the natives. So far they were away from their friends and family and getting a woman was difficult if you didn't have any bread so Earl had to fix things quick.

It became clear almost immediately, which member of his six man crew was a ladies man. Pop seem to know his worth too. Maybe it was his cat-like eyes, black skin, and pretty spinning waves. The country rooster made the city chickens cluck loud every time they passed by his yard. Unbeknownst to Earl, Pop was sexing one of Buck's lady friends regularly. The late night creeping paid off even bigger than anyone could imagine.

Sasha told Buck about the incident at Earl's Christmas party. Then she hoped it would help Buck make a choice and be with her as more than one of his many flings. However, it didn't pan out the way she expected and her hopes dwindled into nothing.

After months of hanging on, she began hanging out in the streets and becoming less available to Buck when he got around to calling. She'd met a country boy she claimed to Petra on the phone one night. "He is too cute girl but I don't know though he may not be the one but he is doing me justice in bedroom," she joked. Petra laughed at Sasha. It had always been the same with her. Meet a man, have a good time, kick him to the curb to wait on Buck. She had been doing it so long Petra had named it 'waiting for Buck, the saga.'

In her search for real-love, Sasha was betraying trusts. Undeserving whispering had placed her in the middle of a battle that she could not handle. It was the usual bring-a–bone, carry-a-bone syndrome. The fact that she may have spoken out against the wrong man never occurred to her as she began telling all of Earl's dirty little secrets to Pop.

Pop was listening and doing his own mathematics; the time would come he was certain this information would land a golden rainbow at his feet. Pops plan worked well. Share a little information, pay her a little attention to get her to telling things she did not know she knew. Cater to her freaky nature and wait for her to tell everything else. Everyone seemed to be plotting on someone else's weakness.

13

Everyone harbors some ill will

Quinton had been living in Chaka's shadow for so long he grew tired and angry. However, he learned to suppress the emotions because it gave Quinton anonymity. Everyone believed the image created around Chaka. It was too easy for Quinton or even Buck to allow Chaka to take center stage. But none of them rode his coat tails. They earned everything together. In the sixth grade, Chaka was the only freshman getting respect from older kids because he knew how to jostle. Nevertheless, Quinton's genius showed him the direction to take his operation from nickels and dimes to dollars. They were only peddling cookies, and cakes but they were doing the things no other sixth grader dared to try. In a matter of the minutes it took to get to the next class, they were all fifteen or twenty dollars richer. Every morning Chaka supplied the teachers with a coffee cake, and by the afternoon, they were back for any other goodies they could buy. Chaka argued for about a week before he realized the profits had almost double off the teachers alone. The math was simple giving away a cake only made the teachers allies in the game. The business was so lucrative they were able to supply Danny and Dave with goodies. They sold to their friends in Catholic school. The first year was more exciting than a graduating senior's prom.

Together they were the most popular clique in junior high and by the time they were in high school, they had made a name for themselves. Chaka went to South Shore with the twins. Buck went to Jefferson and Q had to trek the furthest to King High School in Manhattan. In the ninth grade, they were able to buy all their school gear. Nothing but designer labels were gracing their closets. The footwear was unreal for ninth graders. The most important thing was it was all legal money. When their wants became more extravagant, pushing desserts were a secondary means of getting money. They began looking for other means to get their hustle on and advance them to the next level. The summer of the crew's sophomore year, they were selling weed, along with brownies. Buck had convinced them getting away with it would be easy because they had been selling candy for so long, no one would pay them any attention. They would just assume status quo. The game was the next step but none of them had any connections except the local guy that sold bud. Chaka kept talking about the Rootsman but no one knew him well enough to approach him. Shit, they usually sent someone in the weed spot to buy for them. The discovery that Earl's father was the man they purchased weed from was a small part of a big revelation. His pops was the only Jamaican in the hood peddling pure, homegrown, potent ganja at the time. We called him the Rootsman for his superior product and he charged us double what he charged his regular clientele. He claimed it was because he was trying to discourage the young boys. The truth was he wanted them to fail and open the gate for his son. Back then, Earl was timid, wore glasses, and did not really care about friends or money. He went to school, and rarely came outside, so no one knew much about him.

The Rootsman's plan would have worked if he truly understood that the boys were not just pretenders. They were hustlers, with heart, a loyal set of customers, and respect for the game at large. However, their lives changed. They made Earl apart of their circle. That was the only thing to do to keep their secret. Chaka's mother was a hawk and if she saw the boys hanging over there too much she might suspect the reason. Among their peers, they were the only sophomores that partied with seniors. They were teenagers making grown-men money.

Ms. Sadie had always served as their accountant in the early days but when the bank got too big, she started asking hard questions no one had the courage to answer. However, they were clever enough to try to hide the extreme currency. The selling drugs had tripled their profits in less then a week, as word got out the cash flow was sick.

One Saturday morning, Buck, Chaka, and Q sat around the kitchen, eating breakfast and talking about the party that was taking place that night. The yellow walls and ivory and yellow linoleum seem brighter than usual. Ms. Sadie stomping down the steps was the first sign something was wrong. The flapping of her slippers and the curse words were the next signs. When she slapped Buck in the back of the head, Chaka and Q had the good sense to leap from the table and get out of harm's way. It did not stop her from chasing Chaka into the dining room, where she cornered him and pounded on his forehead with her open palm. By the time she dispensed Quinton's punishment, it was clear she knew they were no longer the Baker Boys 5 but were full–scale, tree-peddling hustlers. Although Q towered over her, she made her point.

Instead of offering a slap or swift pounding, she grabbed his ear and pulled Q to the basement door. Chaka followed the mayhem with wide eyes and Buck sat still, hoping this was all a bad dream. Friday, Chaka got an insane idea from the Rootsman; to line the boiler room walls with aluminum foil so he could begin preserving some reefer plants as an experiment Ms. Sadie was so mad it was scary for the boys. As reached the last step in the basement Quinton began praying. Not moved by his fear Ms. Sadie let them have it.

"You, Quinton, are the oldest in this group," she hollered. "I expect you to have more sense than my irresponsible son and the football star. But no, you just as dumb as they are, allowing them to leave this shit down here like I wouldn't find out sooner or later."

They didn't dare try and explain, especially seeing there were not any words in the English language that could possibly help them now. She snatched sheet after sheet of the light tin and tossed it at them. The plants and dirt flew across the room after she toppled tables with both hands. She turned medieval when Chaka began trying to salvage the disaster on the floor.

She shrieked, "Motherfucker, if the police had come in here, my pretty ass would be locked up and your selfish ass would probably be on the way to being somebody's bitch."

She was a comedienne standing there describing the dilemma that they would have faced, but not one of them cracked a smile, let alone laugh. After restoring the basement, she called Q's mother at work and told her. Next, she called Buck's grandmother and nearly gave him a heart attack as she vowed to beat some sense into his head. Buck became a runaway that weekend. He did not return until it was almost time to go to school Monday morning. He claimed to have been sleeping on the roof of his building but they suspected that one of his groupie senior girlfriends probably let him spend a few nights in her room. Despite their parents' best efforts they could not walk away from the calling.

Ms. Sadie was not about to be defeated by the outlaw behavior. She tried to steer them in the right direction, all while trying to protect them from the biggest pitfalls in their path. With all the money they had saved, they had enough money to open a bakery. However, they weren't interested. They wanted to quit selling pastries and get their other hustle on full time. Chaka moms nearly hit the roof the day they claimed they were done with the small bakery thing.

"You simple bastards will continue to cover your asses and sell whatever you were selling before y'all decided to become pot connoisseurs," she hollered.

In disbelief, their smiles fell and their mouths hung open. She rushed on before anyone got the notion to question her demand.

"I was a numbers runner for twenty years and never went to jail once. I was above reproach even when the cops suspected that maybe I was doing more than frying fish on Friday nights and hosting cards games on Saturday. They could not touch me because covering my ass was the first priority. So you criminals will continue, like I said, to cover any ideas that might get your asses caught up." Ms. Sadie didn't care how they felt about her demand. It was clear she was their advisor and if any shit went wrong, one or all the crew would suffer her punishment.

They listened and the success was evident as they counted out the money each day. Still Ms. Sadie's support neglected to prepare them for some of the other problems. Envy was coming at them hard; the older hustlers were plotting while the boys in their peer group were scheming too. The nickname for their crew was the Baker Boys 5 and each member experienced the pressure of someone looking to capitalize at their expense. Buck was adamant about the next course of action - eliminating any more drama.

"Any product lost or money stolen is a personal attack on our reputation and we couldn't have our reputations tarnished." His eyes were fire engine red and his nostril flared as he pounded his fist into his open palm. "I don't know what y'all planning but my money ain't nothing to play with. The next nigga dumb enough to look like he want to tangle gonna have to fight for his life," Buck yelled.

The nervous laughed surrounding Chaka's basement was proof that they had not completely thought about the ramifications should anyone test their strength. Buck, it seemed, had not only thought about it but had taken the lead to prepare them for battle. He produced a black semiautomatic weapon and held it up for examination. Chaka's eyes sparkled as he held the cold steel, while the twins smiled and nodded. Q stood just a few inches from Buck and wondered where he had gotten the gun. Q thought it was the prettiest black thing he had ever seen up close. It looked nothing like his mom's old .38 with a band aid on the handle.

Buck passed the gun around. Q fell in love with the feeling in the palm of his hand. Chaka was hyped as he asked all kinds of questions.

"Where you get that gat? How much did it cost? Is that shit new? Where can I get my own?"

Buck answered each question like a professional gun dealer. He told them about the number of bullets the clip held, how much it weighed and the handle had a special kind of material that did not leave prints. They were all amazed at the level of information he shared, seeing they just wanted to point and shoot. That afternoon they had taken the next step without even thinking it may not have been worth the hassle. What seemed worst was that no one cared about the warnings that came with the decisions they were making.

False confidence was making them foolish. The following Friday, the Baker Boys 5 were attending a sweet sixteen birthday party in Queens. Together they walked into the community center, greeting familiar faces and making new friends with some of the girls.

The deejay was playing all the hits and the area reserved for the dance floor got crowded quick. It was so hot in the place some people stood in front of the building, dancing. It was easy to tell they were visiting, and did not know anyone except the birthday girl. As the night was ending, everybody gathered around talking when some neighborhood cats walked past. Tanya was the girl celebrating her birthday. She was thanking every one personally for coming out when one of the guy approached Chaka. "Yo, kid, you know me?"

Before Chaka could respond, Tanya interrupted. She stood directly in front of Chaka and yelled, "No, he doesn't know you, but I do. So stop trying to start trouble." The clown moved on and his crew left, but the Baker Boys, knew they would be back. As they said their goodbye and headed for the nearest train station Buck spied the group first. .

About two blocks from the Jamaica Avenue station the clowns stepped to them. Survival took over as they stood hoping they could make it home in one piece. Fists were swinging and no words were exchanged. Before they knew what was happening it was like sixty niggas out there, trying to take their heads off. Buck drew his heat and fired a shot. The popping sound deafened Q for the remainder of the night. It didn't matter because after the shot rang out, the boys' crew took off for the station.

The train was pulling in when Buck leaped the turnstile. Chaka was behind the twins and Q brought up the rear. They had not bothered to see if anybody had followed them, they were just happy none of them was injured too badly. That experience changed how they looked at life – there were no more good and bad guys. Now it was the Baker Boys 5 against them. The gun had served its purpose: better to have it than need it and wind up dead. That was our first real lesson in self-preservation. The fact that they lived proved they passed that test. They also accepted there would be many more.

After Buck came home from jail, he was understandably angry. The fact that the crew seemed to move without him had to feel like a betrayal. He even seemed bitter that Angela had died in the car accident and punished his friends for not being more responsible for her well being. At first, Quinton was angry that Buck stayed away. They hadn't caused the accident but after a while and a lot of consideration, Q missed his friend more than he held on to his anger. Quinton accepted if all things had been the same, he might have blamed Buck and Chaka also. It didn't matter , Quinton decided to respect Buck's isolation and wait for his return.

Chaka however, pretended he wasn't affected. He even went as far to say forget Buck. He would return when his pockets were hurting. All Chaka's insensitive remarks were just a testament to his self-centered manners. Quinton chose to ignore Chaka until he was forced to remind him Buck had been bidding for them. They owed him their freedom and maybe their lives. None of them except Quinton thought about the things Buck may have gone through to survive. Chaka knew he wasn't exempt from the drama because he happened to be lucky enough not to be holding the bag at the time. That fact usually brought him down off his perch but nothing changed the reality that Chaka was sometimes less than a good friend. Quinton was grateful for Ms. Sadie. He knew she was instrumental in getting Buck to forgive them.

Guilt rode Quinton as he thought about life after Chaka. His relationship with Anissa was suffering and he didn't have time to fix it. He worried about Buck more because he seemed to still be running around chasing an illusion.

The Dirty Dozen were showing resistance in the beginning. They didn't believe that Buck and Quinton had the business savvy of Chaka and began expressing their ideas about dismantling the crew. Buck was clearly not even entertaining the idea. He stood his ground knowing Dave, Danny and Quinton would lay down the life of any nigga in the room dumb enough to test him. That wasn't his concern. Bucks real concern was that one or more of these fake ass busters could have killed his partner. Judging from the way they were behaving the killer may have been in the mist. Sparks flew when money came up short for the legit businesses but Quinton was a tyrant when the illegal kitty started taking loses. It was a matter of getting to each man and securing the plan was still intact. The buzzards were hovering but the Baker Boys 5 weren't taking one short lightly.

The Annual barbeque was the meeting place. Niggas were walking on grass in dress socks, knee shorts and gators like they didn't own sneakers and play clothes. Buck reminded each man the real reason they were able to stunt so wonderfully and it had nothing to do with their own premonitions.

"This thing got started because collectively we put our heads together and made it work. You can pretend this is your thing and Chaka was repaid but you motherfuckers are committed to the bigger picture," Buck continued. Danny and Dave, stood vigil next to a picnic table listening and watching the reaction of each man hoping for a negative response.

"No one wants a nigga here if he really wants to leave. That's not what this was about but everyman here still owes for the initial venture that started this shit. You niggas ready to settle your debt now and walk," Buck asked. Buck had to reign in his emotions before he spoke again knowing the answer to his question but it was all about representing the facts. True to his status he was a brut but he had more sense than they had all given him credit for. "The rules haven't changed just some of the faces. Each man that wants to leave owes an exit fee. The fee is the same for every man whether he earned it or not so I want to know is there any man here ready to pay," Buck continued. Danny almost laughed out loud as he watched a few of his comrade's faces drop. Dave didn't waste time holding his laughter. He didn't give a damn. Quinton was impressed as Buck waited and watched for any one of them that was tired of living the good life. Most of the niggas sitting on the benches were walking invest-ments. They had credit cards, beautiful homes, fancy cars and a number of businesses but they all had hella spending habits. Only six men sitting in the circle of fourteen could say that they could pay the exit fee right now. Four were the original members of the Dirty Dozen. The other two dudes were from Jersey and Philadelphia. They were close enough to reap the knowledge Chaka had been trying to plant. They learned the lessons had claimed their loyalties despite all the rumors of a takeover. Buck now knew he had six men in his camp for sure. No one books or accounts were a secret. They were a conglomerate in every sense of the word. They paid taxes and such on their legal businesses, hired lawyers, and gave to charity. He waited a little longer until a few others became restless with the silence. Buck finally had their attentions.

"Any man wanting to leave is more than welcome to do so just make sure you can settle your debt. There will be no hard feelings. Enjoy the barbecue," he said as casual as he could muster.

In the park the deal was sealed. Buck, Quinton, Danny and Dave all cleared up any miss understandings. Business was as usual. They had to keep on top of the game, search for Chaka's killers and keep the extension of their success in line. However, one more bit of drama had begun to unfold. Earl was back from hell with his bullshit. He had a crew of nigga's hustling and making a name for themselves. Soon enough they knew that situation could not be ignored. The ruler that was used to measure others was no longer in effect. Chaka was dead and it was becoming clearer Eve might have helped Earl kill him so the time had come to move against them both. The potential to get side tracked was evident, especially now with all the responsibility being handed over to Buck and Quinton. Danny and Dave had moved to the Carolina's and were carving out their fortune there.

Anissa had become angry with Quinton's long days and longer nights in the streets. She accused him of being more loyal to Chaka's grave than he would ever be to her.

Quinton tried to understand her anger but didn't know how explain his side of things. His lack of communication was a breeding ground for more drama. He was offended that Anissa didn't support him after he had always encouraged her to pursue whatever she needed to do. The argument built between the couple and Anissa got the last word.

"You're more loyal to your boys than me. But at night when you're too tired to take off your shoes, I do it for you. When you need me to listen to your plans and fears, I'm right here for you. Motherfucker who's gonna be here for me when they run you in the ground," she demanded.

Quinton was tired of her tirades and he learned to just sit quietly and let her vent. It was easier than responding. However, Anissa had the ultimate question.

"What are you going to do if you never find out why Chaka was killed, let alone find out who killed him," she asked. The question slid from her lips with more compassion then she wanted them to. Her plan was to make a point and get Quinton to see it was time to move on with their life.

Quinton didn't try to answer the question. He stormed from the house leaving her there alone to wonder if he would return. The thought never occurred that he might never find the answers to the questions that drove him day and night. Quinton had to find Buck. He had to help him make sense of it all. Driving, Q admitted to himself that Anissa was right. What would happen if he never learned the truth?

14

Acceptance and moving forward

Buck heard his alarm go off twice before he made his way to the window. Just as he pulled his pants on, he heard the annoying shrill again. He was mad as hell when he realized it was Quinton setting off the alarm. That could only mean a couple things: Anissa had chased his ass from home again or he was stressing over some shit that could wait until morning.

"Nigga, you could have used the phone, instead of coming out setting off alarms," Buck yelled.

He smiled, "Nigga, stop talking shit and let's go for a ride."

Buck hung his head knowing that it didn't matter to Quinton what he was doing before he got there. The plans were different now. He could never send Quinton away. It was his responsibility to take care of his brother.

"You mind if I go get a shirt," they laughed together.

"Yeah, just make sure a shirt is all you get while you in there."

Buck smirked at him and walked back into the house to find Sasha waiting by the door. She was redder than a chili pepper but she would not say a word about him leaving her after she'd had just gotten there. She tossed his shirt at him and threw some socks across the room. Before Buck could say goodbye, she was slamming the bedroom door. Seconds later, he was slamming the front door.

"You know you can fuck up a good thing when your ass is stressing," Buck complained.

Quinton groaned at his friend and laughed. "You six feet tall, the size of a double-wide trailer and you complain like a bitch."

Buck could not help but chuckle.

"That's alright because I hit like a semi-tractor trailer motherfucker," he yelled as he pounded his fist.

Quinton was clowning, so Buck knew he was trying to take the edge off whatever was bothering him. He would not let Buck have the last word, so he had to say something clever.

"Yeah and after that you sit down and cry like a baby for knocking a nigga out."

Buck only nodded to cease any further banter because whatever had him in the streets at this hour was serious. After driving for about a half hour and bobbing their heads to music, Q finally spoke.

"Anissa asked me what I would do if I didn't find out who killed Chaka. I did not know how to answer, so I left the house. It never occurred to me that I might not ever know the truth."

Quinton sighed and lowered his head a bit as Buck sat listening to him.

Buck leaned back and realized he hadn't thought about that as a fact either. Now he was searching his mind to find an answer for his friend.

It was like coming face to face with the boundaries they never accepted. Every time any one of them felt boxed in, they redirected their strengths and pushed uphill. Buck swallowed hard, hoping the lump would disappear, wondering when life got easier or if anyone ever really found happiness. The farce they had been living was closing in around them and just like that, they were sitting in front of our old junior high school. Bucks grandmother had been dead for years but he heard her speaking as if it were her sitting on the cold concrete steps, instead of Quinton. *You cannot start accepting failures now because you fought so hard to achieve your goals. This is no different, Jahson; press on.*

As easily as Buck heard the words, he repeated them, thanking his grand for always being there even when he could not see it. Quinton accepted the answer as if it was his last meal. Buck felt good for the first time in a long time. Thing about his grandmother or sitting there on the stone didn't bother him it reminded him of a time when he was happy.

Quinton was feeling a bit sensitive himself tonight. He started speaking like a man unsure about his future.

"There are two men in my life that I would have killed and died for: one is dead and Jah, you are the other."

Buck understood exactly what Quinton meant. However, the recent turmoil in their lives had Buck wondering if he was placing his all in an illusion. Chaka's death still had them in mourning. The culprit that caused his death was still walking around living and probably plotting his next move. The thought enraged Buck and he had to do something with that energy or he would probably wake up in jail tomorrow. He convinced Quinton it was time to take a ride.

Atlantic City's bright lights were as good a place as any to take off the edge. The ringing of machines, bright overhead lights and free drinks flowed like a river. They bounced from one casino to the next. Quinton had hit in Lucky Seven machines and picked the roulette table dry in two casinos. The house tried everything from changing dealers to dice; it did not matter. With the meager earnings, they got a two-bedroom suite and went to the club. Before the night's end, they were celebrating life instead of mourning. Quinton wanted to be devoted to his cause but understood the importance of letting up just enough to see past the drama.

Buck was a natural flirt so him meeting a cute dealer and trying to hit was his usual. She explained that it was against company policy to associate with the clientele. Thank goodness he wasn't a hound, so it was easy for him accept her answer and moved on. Quinton and Buck were sitting in a little cheese steak restaurant about twenty minutes from the casino when in walks the cutie. She looked even better without her uniform. Her hair was resting on her shoulders instead of pulled back in a ponytail. It took her all of two seconds to notice them. She walked over to our table and sat next to Q, smiling.

"Mister, you should be careful of the company you keep; he looks like a tease," she said and winked.

Being shy was never Bucks way. He knew if she was sitting there then she was interested in him too.

"It was Latisha, right," Buck asked as if he didn't already know the answer.

She nodded, looking shocked that he had actually remembered. Quinton excused himself and headed to the restroom while they got to know one another. By the time Q came back to the table, they had exchanged numbers. She invited them to a party later that night. Quinton was hyped about Buck accepting the invite. The chance had arrived to chase some women, drink, and party. That always had been a good way to relax.

The following morning buck heard him talking to Anissa on the phone, explaining that he needed to relax and he would see her in a couple days. Judging from the noise on the other end, she was less than happy about his taking off without saying goodbye. He pretended to be asleep until the conversation ended, only for Quinton to yell, "Get the hell up! We got shit to do today."

That meant shopping and these two men were as bad as two shop-a-holics.

Hanging around Eve and Anissa had given them a serious addiction to clothes. Anissa claimed that you could tell a lot about a man from his wardrobe. Years ago, they had taught them about the essentials for a well-dressed man. Eve was the first to shock them by declaring that jewelry was the smallest part of the ensemble. It was important, she schooled, but it could make the outfit. Anissa thought that coordination was the most important part. Eve felt it was the shoes; a man in a pair of cheap shoes was like a Cadillac with no gas: it ain't going nowhere. Armed with their lessons from long ago, they hit every store they could find that catered to their tastes. They had enough outfits for two weeks, let alone one party.

Latisha had called to remind them that the party was invite only and they had to pick her and her girlfriend up to make sure they got our invites. At twelve thirty, the ladies climbed into the rear of the white stretch limo Quinton decided to rent so they could really enjoy the night. Bucks date brought her friend Brenda. She reminded both Quinton and Buck of Ms. Sadie, the way she talked. She spoke plainly yet she was not crude. Her manner was easygoing. From the minute she got into the car, she hugged them both as part of her greeting. Buck got the feeling that was just her way. She made everyone feel good about their choice of outfits and promised them they were definitely going to enjoy the party. Brenda explained that she was playing host tonight for the company she worked with. They had signed a deal with a local artist and this was part of welcoming him to the family.

Everyone was impressed with the layout of the place. It was actually a strip club converted for the night's festivities. Buck didn't know how it happened but during the course of the night Latisha went missing and he ended up hanging out with Brenda. Quinton had collected a fan club. He was the only man in a booth with about six women and countless bottles of champagne. They were taking turns dancing with him, judging from the permanent smile, he loved all the attention. When Latisha finally resurfaced, it was too late. Buck wanted to stay with Brenda. Besides Latisha was a mess, her curls were limp, her lipstick was gone and she was drunk as hell. Brenda felt responsible and excused herself to help her friend to the limo.

Brenda was the only one to come back to the table. She confessed that Latisha went home early. The reason Brenda gave was lame but it was all right by Buck. He was not missing anything. The party was in full swing. The stage was crowded along with the bar floor. Music pounded from invisible speakers and everyone was having a great time. The deejay lowered the music as Brenda welcomed the rapper to the stage, handed him a bonus signing check, and turned the mike over to the guest of honor. A serious beat poured over the room and the rapper did his thing, spitting line after line. He had every one rocking in the place with his catchy chorus and his serious facial gestures. By the time the song was over, he had them hypnotized with his antics.

Brenda smiled like a proud parent when she came back to the booth. The women at the table complimented her on a job well done and expressed that she should be proud of the rising star on stage; he had a definite stage presence. When the night ended, Quinton had company and Brenda was still at Bucks side.

Brenda slid from beneath the covers and raced across the room straight for the bathroom. She came back with her hair less disheveled, smelling like toothpaste and Bucks T-shirt hung off her like a tent.

The first words out of her mouth were, "I'm starving."

Buck had been trained to be a man by every woman he had ever dated and complying with Brenda's big hint was as easy as picking up the phone. He tapped softly on Quinton's bedroom door to see if he was awake. Just as Buck headed toward the menus in the sitting area, Quinton opened the door with crust still clumped in his eyes. He looked behind him and stepped into the sitting area.

"Yo, kid what you getting ready to do," he asked.

Buck raised the menu and he smiled.

"I can always count on your ass to want to eat. Order enough for everybody," he said, heading back into his room.

Brenda called Buck into the room to see if he had found the menus. Buck smiled at hearing her say his name. No one had called him Jahson in a long time, except for Quinton when he was confused or upset. He still had not figured out why he had told her his real name. It just rolled off his tongue during the introductions and now hearing it was almost like he was human again. He took the menu into the bedroom and climbed back in bed. Brenda snatched the menu from across his lap and read the items on the breakfast list. He tried reminding her it was lunchtime but she kept right on reading.

"I want an open turkey sandwich with cheese, extra cranberry sauce and a pitcher of iced tea," Buck announced. By the time she put the phone down, they were laughing that she had ordered so much food.

She appeared comfortable in her own skin as she walked back to the bathroom and turned on the shower. He told her she could have another one of his T-shirts after her shower. She stuck her head out the doorway.

"Jahson, you planning to lie around dirty all day, or are you coming?"

Buck was too excited and certainly too much of a man to tell her no. He almost tripped over his feet trying to get in there with her. The only sound he heard besides the shower running was the sound of the door locking behind him. Standing inside the enclosed glass was the prettiest set of tits he had ever seen. Her breast weren't as perky as he originally thought but they were all one even color, including her nipples. He was transfixed. He had never seen anything like it and he had dated more women then he ever intended to admit. Staring at the water bouncing off her shoulders and rolling down her back he was hard as hell. It was mesmerizing to watch this woman do the most natural things they did. He wondered if the thought made him a voyeur. Sitting on the marble stool inside the shower and watching Brenda cover her body in soap and then rinse clean was mind altering. During the act, they touched each other with their eyes. Buck had experienced many levels of sex but he had to admit this was the first time he had experienced this.

"Wash my back, please," she requested.

Buck could do anything else but comply. He wasn't ashamed of his girth or shy about his manhood. The first chance he got she was going to feel the pressure from both he reasoned. He lathered her entire body from shoulder to butt. He traced letters in her back and dared her to try to decipher the message. By the time they left the bathroom they had written some vulgar messages on each other and promised to act out a few of those message after they had eaten. Brenda wasn't shy either. She was a real woman. She enjoyed a good meal, good laughter and great sex. Buck promised to provide all three by the time they said goodbye.

Their food was waiting for them by the time they came out of the bathroom. The four of them, Quinton, his date, Buck and Brenda sat in silence except for the smacking sounds and occasional burps.

"I think Buck's finally found a girl that like to eat just as much as he does," Quinton said. Brenda couldn't reply. She had a mouth full of food and didn't plan on wasting one second unnecessarily.

Their belly's were full and niggaitis had set in and Buck didn't wait for anyone. He went right back to bed. The chiming of the phone woke him a couple hours later. Before Buck could answer, it stopped. Brenda was comfortably sound asleep and barely shifted when she heard the noise. Buck knew he might as well go to the bathroom since he was awake. Stumbling back into the bedroom he found Brenda lying in his spot. She had stretched her body to its full length and drifted off to sleep. He was not about to try and wake her, Buck pushed her across the bed and reclaimed his place. Thankful she had kept it warm.

Brenda woke up, and laughed at Buck. "I was just trying to keep it warm that's all," she teased. Brenda raced across the floor heading to the bathroom. As she reentered the bedroom, she wonder loud enough for Buck to hear her.

"Is there such a thing as a black panda bear," she asked.

Buck shook his head and marveled at the idea every one described him the same way. He was a teddy bear, grizzly bear and even a cuddly bear but Brenda wanted him to be a black panda bear.

"You're a silly woman," was his answer to her question.

To prove him right she rained kisses all over his face until he started laughing. They couldn't have been more comfortable with one another if they had known each other a life time. Playfully, they wrestled until Brenda sat on top of Buck and declared she was the winner.

Brenda allowed her dreads to flow freely as she leaned in and kissed Buck passionately. Buck responded by holding her in a tight embrace. The feeling of her body was as perfect as their chance meeting. Silently they alternated between touching and kissing.

Brenda slid from his embrace to lie beside him and stroke his dick. Feeling mischievous she asked, "Why does Quinton keep calling you Buck?"

The sly grin that plastered over his face caught Brenda off guard. He flipped her from her back on her stomach. Without a protest or asking, he assaulted her with his member. Lifted on all fours, Brenda prepared herself to receive him inch by inch. She wasn't prepared her for the gentle touch. He touched her at first with gentle strokes. She encouraged him further by arching her back. With every deep breath, she jerked to meet his pleasure.

Buck used his body language to answer Brenda's question. Buck locked his fingers in her locks, gripped them and used them for leverage. Brenda turned her head slightly to get his attention. He raised his eyebrows and smiled. She couldn't understand the pleasure he was tossing at her. Just as Brenda panted, Buck hoisted her legs sending her upper body crashing into the bed. He squared his knees slightly and dipped into the pounding. Two thrusts later and Brenda was climaxing all over the place.

Her muffled plea was, "Don't stop, please don't stop." Suddenly she was saying things like right there and damn.

Buck was on fire. He wanted her to continue talking that shit to him. After allowing Brenda's orgasm to subside, Buck chased his own desire. The headboard pounded against the wall as he continued to stab at her. As an after thought, he flipped her onto her back again. With her legs still hoisted, he pounded and the sweat poured like a real workout.

Brenda felt the moisture before she opened her eyes to see the rain falling from his face. Down the path of his neck and back, that was definite evidence that he was laying down the gauntlet, so to speak. She used her pelvic muscles to stroke him while he crushed. Tightening and releasing, she had him timed completely. Bam! He bucked, she double clinched and then released, allowing him the chance to understand that she has a trick or two to offer in the mating dance. It was a challenge that could only last as long as he didn't erupt.

"Not yet, not yet." Holding onto the headboard for support, he allowed her legs to slide to the floor. Brenda smiled wickedly as she felt euphoric. When his heartbeat returned to normal, he collapsed in her arms. He coiled one of her locks around his finger, playing with the coarse feel just to take his mind off the act they had just performed. The lovers drifted into a quiet sleep for all of twenty minutes.

Buck and Brenda recognized the primitive sounds and laughed, knowing they had probably inspired all of the noise because of the fireworks set off on their side of the wall. Not to feel like they were peeping toms, they headed into the bathroom to shower. Half an hour later, Buck could still hear slight sounds and decided it was time to leave the room before he and Brenda ended up back in bed. Together the couple exited the room and headed for the casino, when Brenda questioned, "Are you hungry?" Buck laughed and nodded like a little kid.

In the restaurant, Brenda ate with her head practically in her plate, afraid to let her eyes linger on the face opposite her. Buck was concerned that maybe he had offended her in some way.

"B," he called softly. She smiled. "Yo, what's up?"

"I just realized I was still wearing my clothes from last night. I look like I spent the night out and haven't been home yet," she answered.

Buck analyzed what she was really saying without using the words. "That's an easy fix," he consoled her with his voice. "It's a matter of finishing our meal and picking up something for you to wear."

The days had gone by so quickly and now it was time to return home. Quinton was the first to speak once they got back on the road.

"Thanks, kid, for taking me out to have a good time. With everything that's been going on at home, I never get the chance to just relax and have a good time anymore." The excitement lasted until they were heading home.

Buck was concentrating on driving in the heavy rains, so he offered little verbal response. The bow of his head expressed every word he could have spoken. As they got closer to home, the dreadful feelings began to return. Together they entered Quinton's home through the garage and found the house empty. Buck headed straight to the phone to let Brenda know they had returned without drama. Quinton walked about the house wondering where Anissa had gone.

Most Sunday evenings she was perched in front of the television in the bedroom, watching some sappy movie. He tossed his bags in the bottom of the closet and did not give it another thought. Anissa stumbled into the house at around eight o'clock with an arm full of shopping bags. Buck rushed to meet her at the door.

"Always the gentleman, huh, Buck," she said with a smile.

In his deepest southern drawl Buck answered, "I aim to please, ma'am."

The giggling caught Quinton's attention. He came out of the kitchen with a sandwich in one hand and juice in the other. Anissa leaned her body into him. As angry as she had been just two days ago, it had now subsided. Quinton leaned down and kissed her. The small gesture made Buck smile. In his mind, it was a representation of what life-lasting love should be if there were such things.

"I see you been out spending money again."

Anissa flashed them a smile. "Yeah, just enough to make you wish you had been home for the last three days."

Quinton groaned, Buck laughed, and Anissa raced up the steps. She leaned over the banister and yelled, "Buck, Sasha called this morning. She said if you don't move your car by the time she has to go to work tomorrow, she's gonna have it towed."

"Oh shit, I forgot I left my car in her parking lot," Buck said, laughing.

Quinton yelled up at Anissa, "Don't take off your clothes. I want you to take a ride with me."

Buck climbed from the back seat to see Sasha standing in the doorway, wagging her fingers at him. Buck hunched his shoulder to offer an apology and Sasha hoisted her middle finger. He looked back at his friends, only to see them laughing at his dilemma. He hung his head real low and slowly walked to an angry Sasha. The rage was still in her eyes as he leaned her back and kissed her hard on the mouth. He opened his jacket and pulled out a teddy bear with the words scrolled across the stomach, *My man went to Atlantic City, and all he brought me back was this stinking teddy bear.* She accepted the gift, pushed him away from the door, and slammed it in his face. Anissa burst out laughing. Buck had done all he could to make peace. His only choice was to let her forgive him. The purring of his engine made him feel at home. After Quinton and Anissa had gone, Buck pulled into traffic and headed home.

15

Taking Chances

Monday morning arrived to find Buck and Quinton in the real estate office, looking over paperwork. It was a rare occasion when the two were there together. The doors swung open and in walked Eve with a briefcase and a smile. Quinton was the first to leap from his seat and Buck just sat dumbfounded.

"What the fuck you doing here," Quinton bellowed.

Eve flashed a two-hundred-dollar smile and sauntered to an empty chair.

"I'm here to make a proposal," she said, even tempered. She sat opposite the mahogany desk, folding her hands in her lap. She waited for Quinton to take a seat.

"I've found a property that needs rehabbing; it's in a great place."

She opened the briefcase and presented some information for them to look at. She continued after they glanced at the papers.

"The estimated cost is far more than I can stand on my own, but I thought maybe we could split the cost and make some money once everything is complete."

Quinton would have laughed had he not been in total shock. So he just sat. Buck, however, did not waste a second before lighting into her with contempt.

"Eve, you must have fell down and bumped your fucking head. You walk in here, talking about going into a joint venture for a piece of property. First, if we do any business, it would still be a part of this company's portfolio. Secondly, we could probably pay you a finder's fee to you for bringing the property to our attention." He continued, "Lastly, and most important in my book, I don't want to do business with a snake. You are about as trustworthy as a bank robber in a vault full of money. Now having said that, thank you for stopping by. It's a pleasure to see you leave." He dismissed her.

Eve sat stunned for a full sixty seconds. No words ever left Quinton's mouth. He could not fathom what she had been thinking when she walked into the office as if she was a welcomed guest. Slowly she got up from her position and turned medieval.

"So be it. You don't have to do business with me but I promise, soon enough you'll wish you had accepted my offer."

She stalked out of the office, slamming the door in her wake.

Storming to her car, Eve cursed underneath her breath. She was not watching where she was walking when she slammed into someone.

"Watch where the fuck you going, asshole," she growled before looking up.

If Eve had not been so absorbed in her own drama, she might have had the good sense to be a bit leery of Earl's presence. Instead, she opened her arms, welcoming him as if he were a long-lost friend. "Oh my God, it's so great to see you," she yelled. "What have you been up to lately?"

Earl pretended to be as excited to see her as she had to been to see him. Had he not been angry with her for her betraying his trust so long ago, he might have been more sincere in offering her the same warm reception. Together they stood chatting about old times and long-forgotten promises. Earl suddenly had the most brilliant idea, "Come, let me take you to lunch," he offered. Quickly Eve glanced at her watch and seemed mildly interested in accepting his offer, until he whispered, "It's been too long since we've really talked."

Smoothly he draped his arm across her should and led her in the direction of his Mercedes. She examined the ice blue big body with bugged eye headlights and nodded her approval. Earl was taken back by her blatant disregard for his feelings so long ago. He tried to suppress the anger that seemed to rise while desperately struggling to be a gentleman. Catering to her whims had been his life's mission until he realized that Eve always had an agenda and her top priority was Eve. Ushering her to the passenger's door, he waited until she was comfortable.

Sliding into the driver's seat he asked, "Pretty lady, where to for lunch?"

By the time the waiter had taken their orders, Eve was in her flirting mode. She positioned her seat as close as she could without actually sitting in Earl's lap, batting her eyes, touching his arm or hand at every opportunity and finally giggling at all his corny jokes. She even seemed to be hanging on his every word. Slowly she was disarming him of his guarded manner. Like old times, they were slipping from one topic to the next without a hitch. Lunch had been more than two friends catching up on lost times; it was a mating call of some sort.

As weird as it seemed, Earl was enjoying the flirtation with Eve and her carefree manner. She excused herself, heading toward the restroom. Her strut was mean and exaggerated, anticipating that Earl was paying close attention. Behind the closed doors, she checked her appearance, reapplied her lipstick, fingered her hair, and plastered a smile on her face.

Earl settled the check; he decided this was as good a time as any to position himself next to Eve. Now that Chaka was dead, he knew she was probably looking for someone to fill the void. Earl imagined that with the right amount of pressure she would run to him, the way she always had when Chaka dismissed or disrespected her. As Eve sauntered to the table, Earl rose from his seat to meet her halfway. Claiming her hand, he led her out of the restaurant across to the parking lot.

Eve wanted to touch Earl but she wanted it to be subtle. She had batted her eyes, wiggled her ass, now all she needed to was to add the crowning piece. Pretending there were crumbs in his goatee she stroked his face. The gesture, small as it was, aroused something in Earl. He pulled Eve into his arms with his large hands planting in the small of her back. Eve leaned into his embrace, standing just inches shorter. As the car pulled into view, she turned and offered him the sweetest kiss. The game had definitely begun but Earl had measured his steps carefully. He intended to drive her directly to her car tonight. Tomorrow might hold a new experience. He secured Eve in her car and handed her a card with his name and telephone number on it. Eve searched her bag and discovered she did not have any cards, so she wrote her number in his palm.

All during her drive home Eve kept wondering why Earl had not tried to take her home. The moment she got home dispelled any ideas she had that he was no longer interested. The message on the machine was from the melodic voice of Earl, inviting her to dinner tomorrow night. He promised to cook and be a gentleman, so long as she graced his doorway. He offered to pick her up, if she preferred. Eve was giddy with anticipation and had to control her breathing as she waited for him to answer her call. "Yes," she uttered seconds after he answered the phone. After ending the brief conversation, she wondered if Earl would be investing in her project. Then the thought occurred that he might not be financially capable of investing the amount of money she would need. Further contemplation of the situation left her thinking if he could very well afford the likes of his Benz, then there was no way he could not put up a little of the capitol.

Eve's one-track mind would probably get her in trouble with Earl if she did not handle things properly. She decided that she would not tell him about the tenement until she had a full picture of his financial footing. Once she had confirmed he could really afford to invest, she would woo him out of his hard-earned revenue. She would return it handsomely she thought, once she was able to turn a profit. Eve recognized the address he had given her. He lived at the same address so many years ago. She hoped that this was not a sign that he was just fronting in his big-bodied Benz. Eve climbed the steps to her bedroom and searched her closet for an appropriate outfit. The choice had to say so much – from "I'm sexy, and I know it" to "but I'm still a lady." She had not decided on the right clothes by the time she laid out on her bed.

The old apartment Earl shared with his father had been completely revamped. Instead of the six apartments from back in the day, there were now four. On the upper floors, they were duplex apartments. Earl welcomed his visitor into the lounging floor, taking her coat and greeting her with a glass of wine. The aroma wafting through the place tickled Eve's nose and her stomach growled. Just past the threshold, Eve looked around at the abstract paintings along the walls. Stepping into the kitchen, she was stunned by the island with the running water, all the stainless steel appliances, and the country nook. She leaned against the counter, watching Earl sauté vegetables and add last minute touches to the meal.

"Look around, woman, don't be shy," he said while continuing with his task.

Eve stepped up on the raised platform, impressed by the careful décor. The large sofa was black leather flanked by a white armchair and chaise. A red portrait graced the walls, adding drama to the room, but the real attraction was the sparkling parquet floors. Outside the bay window, she could see the moon shining bright and stars twinkling. The soft music purred through the speakers, setting the right amount of excitement to the night. By the time dinner was ready Eve had been through the entire first floor, marveling at the amount of work he done to make it look so perfect.

"Pretty lady, dinner is ready," Earl called to her from the living room. In the center of the floor, he had laid out a blanket, lit two candles, and placed the meals out as if they were at a picnic. Eve could not contain her excitement. She leaned into him and kissed him passionately.

"Thank you for making everything so perfect. I can tell you took your time to make tonight special."

Earl did not say anything. He seemed to be blushing. He raised the fork to Eve's mouth and watched as she chewed. Earl was turned on the moment he watched her pink tongue dart out of her mouth to catch the invisible juices that might have dripped on her lips. She definitely knew how to turn him on.

16

Changing Places

Anissa stormed back and forth, wringing her hands, waiting for Quinton to come out of the bedroom. She needed to discuss her current situation with him before he found out on his own. The phone chimed, interrupting her anxiety attack.

She answered and whispered, "Not yet. I'll call you back."

Quinton floated by her, heading to the kitchen. "Good morning, beautiful," he said with his head deep in the fridge. Anissa stood in the doorway, near tears, as the words flew out of her mouth.

"Quinton, I'm pregnant."

He did not respond right away, so she just assumed he had not heard a word she spoke. Before Anissa could repeat them, Quinton slammed the door to the fridge and began laughing. The sound was of a deranged laughter, not one of happiness. The first tear slid from her lids and the dam broke. There was no need in pretending she was going to be strong about this situation. She held herself together by wrapping her arms around her middle. He stopped laughing the moment he looked in her face.

"Why are you crying?" he asked.

Anissa did not answer. She just raced from the kitchen to the steps. Before she got on the first stair, Quinton stopped her.

"You're serious, Nissa? You're pregnant?" She did not trust the words to come out her mouth, so she nodded.

They were indeed becoming the family next door in their new life. It never crossed Quinton's mind as to whether he would become a father. He had been so content with Anissa that he did not think about a family.

"Stop crying," he said, embracing her. He rocked her in his arms until he felt her body relax.

Anissa pushed away from Quinton. She plopped down on the steps with her head in the palm of her hand. The initial reaction she had gotten from her man left her broken. She did not believe she had the courage to listen to him tell her to have an abortion or worse, to leave.

The silence was frustrating Quinton but he had to wait for her to speak. He sat beneath her open knees, placing his head in her lap, he spoke softly, "Nissa, please stop crying and tell me what's wrong." The heaving of her chest had long ago subsided but the tears kept skirting down her lids. In the confusion, they both were becoming angry. Anissa opened her mouth to speak only to shut it without saying a word.

Quinton's heart pounded as his frustration turned to anger.

He yelled, "Anissa, stop fucking crying and tell me what the hell is wrong!"

She looked at him as if he had injured her. Quinton leaped from his position, slamming his hand on the banister.

He bellowed, "I guess having a baby with me seems like the worst thing in the world to you." Just as he was leaving the house, he said softly, "Do what you want to do."

Anissa glanced up from her misery, only to see that Quinton had left the house with the door wide open. She could not allow herself to trust that he had said those words. She had been defeated by his last declaration and she would do just what she thought was necessary to keep the relationship the way it was. In her desperation, she had not noticed the look of hurt on his face when she would not speak to him.

Quinton came home and avoided Anissa as much as humanly possible. He would not come in the house until he was certain she was asleep. She could not sleep until she knew he was home. Early in her relationship with Quinton, she learned that she did not have the patience to wait on a man to provide for her. He encouraged her to attend school, if that was really her ambition. When she came home and decided that being a nurse was her calling, he supported her in every way possible. Because of that, Anissa had gotten a job at a local hospital in New Jersey. The staff loved her easygoing manner, quick smile, and work ethics.

One night Anissa declared, "I want to be a surgical nurse." The Christmas following her declaration Quinton went out and purchased a stethoscope. She remembered all the times he had been supportive of whatever steps she chose to take, such as helping her prepare for exams by forcing her to buckle down when she got too lax in her studies. She often wondered where that man had gone.

Anissa had begun reading extra into Quinton's words. "Do what you want to do," he said. She accepted that to mean he didn't want to be a father. She didn't want to be any man's baby mama. The weigh of his parting words made her angry. He should have been happy about the fact that this was the next step in their relationship. Determined to be strong she made a decision.

Quinton had known that Anissa loved him but he did not understand why she was choosing to terminate the pregnancy. He reasoned it would be better for him not to know when she decided to go. However, his love for her made him ask the hard questions.

"Have you made an appointment?"

"Yes," she answered while staring at his broad back.

"So you're really going through with it?"

Anissa thought it sounded as if he were accusing her of something and her anger flared. "I'm doing exactly what you told me to do."

Quinton was standing at the closet when he turned his full attention to her. She was riled up and wanted to fight. He had decided that he would not make it easy for her to do the vilest thing he could imagine. He did not respond right away. He climbed into bed next to her and turned off the lights, surrounding them in darkness. His words struck like lightning as he called her selfish.

"Don't pretend you're doing what I asked you to do. I just gave you permission to do exactly what you wanted to do." His voiced was strained, but the thing that struck Anissa was the finality. She did not respond. She relaxed in the pitch-black space wondering why he was pretending to care about her having this baby.

During the night, the couple alternated sleep. First Anissa as Quinton stared up at nothingness, then Anissa, as she stared at the rise and fall of his chest. Finally, they had both drifted off. Anissa woke first to find she was locked in his arms. She tried to pry from his embrace without waking him but he was already awake.

"Where are you going," he questioned.

"To the bathroom to throw up, if you don't mind," Anissa answered with the right amount indifference.

He was not moved by her attitude today. Either they would come to this decision together or she would carry his child full term.

"You sure you don't want to get up every morning and run to the bathroom for the next nine months," he joked.

Anissa rolled her eyes and hoisted her middle finger. Quinton's serious demeanor only changed when he was confused and Anissa knew this. In a matter of minutes, he was joking, trying to get her to hurl some insult at him. She could not oblige.

"Nissa, let's just talk about this before you do something that might ruin our relationship."

She did not trust herself to speak without wanting to stab him, so she stood and listened.

Quinton pleaded with her to complete their family.

"If this has anything to do with marriage, then fuck it, let's get married. If it's about money, I can secure a future for our child whether I'm here or gone. If this is about something else, maybe you do not think I'll be a good father, let's talk about that too. But I can't just allow you to walk out of here and kill my baby.

Anissa had heard all she needed to hear but the turmoil inside her would not permit her to be happy. Her arms flailed as her voice hit octaves she had not known existed in her being.

"I've been around this damn house worrying myself silly, wondering why you wanted me to have an abortion." She stormed back and forth. "Now you are talking 'why I want to kill your baby' Why can't you just say what you mean the first time? Instead, you have to create all this damn drama."

Quinton laughed at her hysterics. She had to laugh herself, but not before, she collapsed in his arms. Finally, they had come to an agreement.

Meanwhile, Armageddon was preparing to wreck havoc on all their lives. Eve had planned a memorial service for the first anniversary of Chaka's death. She orchestrated a last ride to symbolize that he might have been gone, but he would never be forgotten. At the cemetery, she had placed all kinds of white orchids and roses along his gravesite. In honor of his memory, she had rented a dining hall where everyone would go afterward to celebrate his life after his death. Eve had called Buck and asked him to help her with this, knowing he would not turn her down if had anything to do with Chaka. She had extended invitations to everyone, including Petra and the children. Petra chose to come alone.

Although Buck had reservations about Eve's real motives, he could not decline. Maybe, after all this time, Eve had really loved Chaka, he reasoned, and missed him as much as they all had. Quinton, however, was neither so forgiving nor trusting. He knew that Eve could be charming and calculating when she wanted something. Now, it was just a matter of waiting to find out what she wanted.

The service had gone well. People from all over attended, offering funny stories about their times with Chaka. Once again, people turned out to offer their condolences and marvel the memory of their friend. Although the gesture was heartfelt, Earl had changed it into an opportunity for him. During the years, all the members of the Dirty Dozen Camp had been somewhat of a well-kept secret. But Eve had unraveled the mystery for anyone in attendance. The crew operated like a well-run organization from the start. Chaka had been the head while his men formed all other parts of the body, sometimes alternating positions to suit the task. To honor their brother, the crew moved about in unity, sparking blunts or pouring out liquor in his memory, introducing loved ones or just clinging to the loss of their comrade.

Eve's excuse for betraying the Dirty Dozen was that they had shunned her and she promised they would pay. She intended to see them crippled, or die trying. Earl convinced Eve that she did not have to be tied to them if she truly wanted to be free.

"The smart thing to do will be to ask them to buy you out; give you a lump sum and walk away," he advised. Eve analyzed the situation. She calculated she probably wouldn't get the full amount she deserved if she took a buyout. But her reasoning was that money in her purse was far better than money promised. She also made a pact with the devil when Earl promised to help her, if she helped him. His most convincing argument for her was simply if the Dirty Dozen were on the run from the Feds, or had somehow fallen from the perch. She might not get the chance to get any of the money off the investment Chaka made before he'd died. Pure greed motivated Eve to help Earl even more. As a result, she stood just inside the hall, welcoming each guest and thanking him or her for coming when they left.

In an old, beat–up, black paneled van Earl sat with Pop, clicking pictures of all those in attendance. Pop marveled at the number of heavy hitters that rolled through the place in their Sunday best, outshining the sun, and flossing to no end. He could not help but wonder aloud, "I wonder how many millions we could walk away with if we just rolled up in that bitch and robbed them motherfuckers?"

Earl laughed at his protégé and began mildly chastising him for even giving thought to such petty larceny.

"There's no needed to rob niggas' pants pockets when you could walk away with the entire bank. That's why we out here snapping pictures, because when the sun sets on those frontin' ass Big Willies, we gonna have their entire operation for our own."

Pop felt chafed from the scolding he had just received. Six rolls of film later, they had captured the entire event: the Dirty Dozen, their cars, and the woman of the hour.

After every guest had gone away with their memory, Eve cowered in the dark corners of her condominium, wondering how she could have betrayed the love Chaka had given to her, for Earl's conniving plan. But it was too late; Earl would be at her home any minute with proof that she had been a key component. If the truth ever came out, she would not be fit to leave and was too evil to die. The reality of what she had done was grating on her.

Just as Eve thought she might not be able to live with the plan, she heard the buzzing sound that indicated Earl was indeed at the door. With the photos in hand, Earl strolled through the door straight to the kitchen. Eve's less than jovial mood didn't concern him; he was ecstatic. Pretending had long ago been Eve's claim to fame and today was no different.

She took a seat opposite her evil lover, waiting to sort out the puzzle of pictures. The first image was Quinton and Anissa standing next to a cranberry-colored Jaguar. The image caught Anissa at an angle, making her belly appear slightly rounder than Eve remembered. Then there was a photo of Quinton alone. All the pictures of the fourteen remaining members were similar. Eve could not help feeling like a traitor of the worst kind as she pointed out the faces and gave each name. She began to hate Earl for actually using her loving memory of Chaka to slaughter his friends. However, she felt powerless to move against Earl, as she had been a co-conspirator in this plot.

The master conniver in Earl had not cared how Eve would feel when he finished using her, but he did wonder how she would manage when he moved against her. As quickly as the thought had formed, he dismissed it from growing wings and clouding up his judgment.

Eve decided that although she was up to her elbows with guilt, she could not turn back now. It took great measure, but she cautioned Earl.

"Earl, you weren't the first man to try and stand against the Dirty Dozen. Certainly if you fail, I will be sending your body back to Jamaica for your father to bury. Don't misunderstand, I am committed to our plan, but be careful — one wrong move…" The sob that escaped from her throat stopped her from continuing.

Earl had the good sense to recognize the sincerity in her words and he hugged Eve tightly.

"Baby girl, you never thought I had the means to be The Man. That is the reason you ended up with Chaka in the first place. Don't worry, I'mma show better than I can tell you," he said with a sense of finality.

The pair parted Eve to the confines of her home and Earl to fine tune his plan. Eve had a plan in case Earl failed. She reasoned, with exception of Quinton and Buck, that the others would pledge allegiances to whoever could turn them profit. She figured that if Earl failed, she would help him capitalize on his mistake and then he would be indebted to her.

Across town, Pop was lying in Sasha's bed, waiting for her to come back to clean up the mess they had made. She waltzed into the room, naked as the day she was born, with a hot towel in her hand. For lack of a better way of putting it, Sasha was sprung over Pop and his masterful tongue. Never before had she felt the throes of an orgasm by the stroke of a man's tongue. The only condition would be he had to promise to do the trick with his tongue.

Sasha was a victim to Pop's insanely jealous nature over the idea of Buck and her ever having been a couple. She thought it was cute until Pop blacked her eye after finding a pair of underwear that Buck had left so many months ago. Through all Pop's fits, he had never once taken her outside the confines of her home. She was his dirty little secret and she had no problem with it, so long as he continued to love her.

Sasha had not a clue she was on borrowed time. Long enough to get any information on Buck and his whereabouts. So far, she had been useful in telling Pop a few places she believed he housed his drugs and some pocket change, but he hadn't hit the mother lode yet. Slowly he questioned her until she told him things even she was not sure were completely true. The little trust Buck had given to Sasha, she was willing to betray for a little lust.

Sasha had gone to the service to pay her respects, only to see Buck standing with a dark-skinned girl sporting a head full of locks. She could not help thinking she was not at all his type, yet they seemed to be clinging together during the entire time Sasha was there. Once she hoped she could talk to Buck but the dread head never left his side. The thought that Buck had gone out and created a relationship with someone other than her was enraging. Sasha had been his soft pillow on many nights over the years and he hadn't shown her so much affection. The envy sent her home to wonder why had she wasted so much time on him. Before she could make a fool of herself, her secret lover arrived to take away any hurt that may have surfaced.

Earl sat in the bowels of the basement, starry-eyed over the photos that told the tale of fourteen rich men in eleven states. He breathed in a healthy toke of his blunt and grinned. Earl stood and began talking aloud, repeating to himself how he would take away everything. The original remaining members of the Bakers Boys 5 were the brains, heart, and soul of the Dirty Dozen. Eliminating them would not be easy, but he knew their weaknesses. He planned to extort Quinton; no way would he allow his pregnant girlfriend to remain in the hands of a kidnapper. Quinton would see the cost as minuscule compared to the life of his family. Buck would rot in prison for the rest of his miserable life. The charge, Earl hadn't decided yet. The twins, he reasoned, would be a robbery gone badly and they would pay with their lives.

The shrill of the phone interrupted Earl in his plotting stages, but he could not afford to miss this call. Ian was on the line, greeting his cousin and hoping to hear good news. Earl reassured Ian that everything was handled according to the original agreements. He also felt contempt that Ian had the audacity to call with his foolish worries. Before Ian could fully work on Earl's nerves, he cut the conversation short, saying he had a few last-minute things to deal with. Earl illogically believed he would kill Ian as soon as he got the first chance. The haze was lifting as he envisioned himself the king of everything.

17

Testing the strength

Several weeks had passed and the groundwork had begun. Two of Earl's soldiers, on loan from Ian, had gone to North Carolina where the twins lived, to scope out the operation they had established. The first thing that became evident was that the twins had capital everywhere, it seemed. The big investment was the split-level strip club that opened every day of the week except Sunday. There was also a strip mall and several real estate offices, not to mention the illegal money they were making on the side.

Dave had become lax in his routine. He had been living well for so long, he forgot that envy's arm could be as long as NYC to North Carolina or as short as next door. Saturday night's profits had been counted and ready for depositing but Dave decided that he would handle it on Monday morning. Turning out the lights, he stumbled down the steps and headed for his car in the parking lot. The bouncers were still lingering around so Dave felt a bit at ease. However, he still had the feeling that someone was watching him. The hairs on the back of his neck rose as he stood near his car, searching the darkness for an intruder. He shook off the eerie feeling, hoping to dispel the thought that maybe he really was under scrutiny. Like a true general, Dave released the safety on his firearm and tucked it between his legs as he drove home. The dreadful feeling still had not left him by the time he secured his home and climbed the steps to his bedroom. His young, beautiful wife had been asleep for hours and did not move an inch when he climbed into bed. After lying silently for five minutes, he began to snore.

Outside the twin's home, there were two males in a pewter Saturn, contemplating their next move. The lanky driver decided it was just as well that they go back to the motel and wait until the wee hours on Monday morning to pick up the trail. In their investigation, they had discovered that Dave was a family man on Sundays. He went to church, came home, and played with his children. The duo joked that he probably fucked his wife only on Sunday nights, after the kids were asleep.

Dave climbed into his Range Rover with the deposits by his side and the gun between his legs. The ride was as ordinary as any Monday morning, but he would be on point. In true mannerly fashion, Dave held the door for two women and a kid to enter the bank before him. Despite the early hour, the bank was crowded, leaving him no choice but to stand in line. Suddenly, the eerie notions returned. Carefully, Dave turned to get a clear picture of his surroundings. Like a bright light, it hit him all at once. The young'un at the desk filling out a bank form had been in that same spot entirely too long. Slowly he glanced at the kid in his peripheral vision and began to observe. The lanky boy was dressed in NY fashion, no doubts about that, but his clothes were ill fitting. From the designer shirt that barely covered his long arms, to the too-big jeans that sagged, caught Dave's eye. New York thugs didn't tie their Timberland and old boy had his tied tight around his ankles. Even the jewels he wore suggested he was a hustler. So why was the young'un standing in the bank? As quickly as Dave assessed the situation, he decided he would have to eliminate this imposition without alerting his stalker. Finally, Dave was at the teller's window and the opportunity presented itself.

The young'un held his head down just long enough for Dave to leave out the side door. He doubled back to his car and position himself to see the young'un come out of the bank, confused. The look of frustration confirmed the feelings Dave had been experiencing. As a final effort, the stalker climbed into his Saturn with New York tags and sped off. Dave watched his rearview mirror every few seconds for his company. But the moment he pulled into the strip mall to open the sneaker store, he spied the familiar car. The fact that the young'un knew his next stop angered Dave and he realized if he did not control himself, he might reveal that he was aware that someone was trailing him. Dave climbed from the Rover, greeting his waiting staff with smiles and his usual pleasant manner. The aroma of freshly brewed coffee caught his attention. Dave found humor in the situation. Did his shadow take sugar or honey with his tea? The day was as normal as any other and since the young'un knew his usual moves, Dave went about his day.

The night, however, was another matter entirely. The strip club was hosting an invite-only party for the most exclusive patrons on this side of the Mason-Dixon Line. The usual patrons scheduled to attend, along with a few up-and-coming ballers. Danny had been at the club all day, overseeing that everything was complete. From the sound system to the dancers' costumes, Danny had even donned a pair of gloves and waxed the mahogany bar until it shined. Dave ambled through the double doors close to ten o'clock, irate as he could ever remember being. He stormed up the steps heading to the hidden offices, searching for Danny. Behind the massive desk staring at numerous closed-circuit cameras, sat a mirrored image of him.

Danny raised his eyebrows as he felt the negative energy ooze from his twin's pores. Dave couldn't catch his breath fast enough to explain that he had been right all this time; someone had been following him and he had proof. Danny began analyzing the situation. It was not for the money. The young'un had ample opportunity to snatch the money bag. Drugs could be what he was after but if it was true that the young'un was following Dave for a minute, he had to know that Dave never moved near those circles in North Carolina. Next, the bell sounded about the New York plates. Together the brothers yelled, "Earl!"

The answer was clearer than the bright shining moon and the twinkling stars. Earl had finally grown a dick. Danny picked up the walkie-talkie and told the burly bouncer at the door that they would be making an allowance for a special guest. He would let him know when the gentleman arrived. There were at least one hundred men in the club watching the show by midnight. Just like they had expected, the young'un arrived without an invite, but Danny's voice alerted the bouncer that he was indeed the special guest.

Dave was now at the top of his game as he yelled, "That nigga trying the represent the NY, but his bop ain't even right."

Danny laughed. "Only you would declare that the Rotten Apple has its own walk."

Neither man took his eyes off the screen as they trailed his every move. His first stop was the men's room. Next, the circular bar just off the deejay's booth and finally, he claimed a table that gave him access to the comings and goings of the patrons. The anger that filled the office was barely contained as the twins decided they would have the chance to deal with the stalker soon.

Two men were standing in the center of the room, having a very loud argument, when the twins determined the time had arrived. Danny went left down the spiral stairs and Dave went right. While the young'un was caught in the drama, the twins closed in on him from both sides. The young'un eyes bulged as he felt the steel pressed into his back. The bouncers were now dispersing the fallout while everyone watched. The crowd hadn't notice that the twins were even on the floor let alone they were stalking the young'un.

Danny led the young'un down the stairs to the invisible basement. The fear motivated the young'un to move quickly before the door slammed and sealed his fate. His heart lodged in his throat as he remembered the box cutter under his sleeve. The trio was a few steps from the bottom when he reached out with the sharp razor and tore into Dave's neck. The gush of blood frightened the young'un more than it affected Dave. Dave's retaliation was swift with a series of punches to the back of the young'un head, sending him sailing down the remaining steps.

Danny found the common ground to reason with Dave: "Let one of the girls take you to the hospital and I promise to stay here with ole boy and work out whatever I find out. I'll even save some for you."

Dave smiled at his twin, knowing he meant every word. The young'uns sprawled-out body enraged Dave. He secretly wished he could wake him up so he could kick the bone right out of his ass.

The moans alerted Danny that the stalker was finally coming to life. "The pain," he spoke, "lets you know you're still among the living. However, I would like to tell you some things. Either you are the dumbest nigga alive for walking up in my house, or you are the realest nigga Earl ever had in his camp. One thing is certain: you're about to be the realest dead nigga Earl once knew."

The fear betrayed the killer instinct the young'un had prior to hearing those words of death. Danny liked the emotion and decided to exploit it. "Save yourself, kid. Tell me what Earl is planning." Although the young'un was eager to live, he did not speak. Danny switched gears. He needed to get him to talk and fast; there were lives at stake. "What's your name, young'un?"

The boy whispered struggling to say his name. "Mac — Jaime McMillan," he answered, defeated.

The deep gasp clued Danny in that Mac just might black out again soon. He fired another question. "You dress like you from the N.Y., but where you from, kid?"

"I'm from Virginia." His voice quivered as he tried to breath and talk.

Danny was having problems completing the picture. He began to analyze the situation aloud. "Virginia? We don't run with them boys," he reasoned softly.

Mac thought he had a bargaining chip and decided he would cash it in for his life. "I run with a hustler name Ian. He and Earl are first cousins. I can help you out if you let me live."

Danny pretended to be contemplating the offer. He accepted by a nod of his head. Mac's breathing was ragged but if he was going to live, he would write the words to save him. Before he could speak, Mac passed out. In frustration, Danny rushed to his office to make a quick phone call.

The tension on the line wasn't missed by Quinton or Buck as they heard the dreaded words: "we have a red-eye situation."

Quinton was the only one to speak, "We're on our way."

Danny was shocked to see Dave back so soon talking with their prisoner.

"In your absence, our friend told me some things," Dave told his twin. "It seems Earl has this diabolical plan to kill you and me. He wants to take over our world. So, our young'un has been following us with another young'un for about three weeks now. He said that you agreed to let him live for some big secret."

Danny only nodded, so that Mac could get his words out without straining. "Earl is on his way here. He's driving with that chick Eve," Mac confessed. "She helped him set everybody up. He and Pop were at the memorial services taking flicks of the Dirty Dozen and they came up with the plan to kill you and your brother."

Danny's fury began to show. "Y'all was gonna kill the entire Dirty Dozen? Who you s'pose to be, the Mafia?"

The fear returned to Mac's eyes as he explained only the remaining members of the Bakers boys 5 were going to suffer. The sinister smirk on Dave's face said everything his mouth hadn't yet (you gonna die tonight).

Dave spoke, "I may die tomorrow but not before, I kill you tonight."

The twins established they had a small window of time to get this shit right. If they miscalculated even one-step, there would be unnecessary casualties. The Saturn had to be moved from the club's parking lot. That was easy, seeing that the only blind spot in the lot was the west side of the lot. As luck would have it, Mac had parked there. They helped him through the back panel and out a hidden door.

"Soldier, you alright to drive," Danny asked.

Feebly, Mac answered, "I can try."

The pain in his ribs, the throbbing of his head and his will to live was keeping him awake at the wheel.

"Follow that truck in front of you." A few feet away, Mac recognized the construction site. He began to sob like a little girl. When Dave climbed into the back seat, he accepted his fate.

He whined, "You lied to me, man! You said if I told you everything, you'd let me go."

The brothers looked at one another and hunched their shoulders. Dave wrapped an extension cord around the young'un neck until he was stilled. The brothers operated in perfect silence. Dave went to get the gasoline from his truck and Danny tore rags to ignite a fuse. The orange flames were shining in their rearview mirror as they left the car to burn.

It was not hard finding Mac's partner in crime. After a little research and some stalking of their own, ole boy was right where they expected, waiting for his comrade to return. Porky sat in the room, chain-smoking cigarettes, wondering where Mac could be. Twice he had tried to reach Earl, but to no avail. Ian was not an option unless he was face to face, so Porky waited and worried. The news reporter stood outside a construction site, where a body had been found burned inside a sedan. The police believe the victim had been strangled and then burned. The police were appealing to the public. *"If you have any information on the identity of the young male or information on this crime, please contact the sheriff's office."*

Porky was nervous as hell. This was not rocket science. He reasoned they had murdered his friend. He was not going to wait around for his turn. Porky left the room, heading for the front desk, when he noticed the imposing familiar figure. From this distance, he entertained the idea that it could have been Buck. Porky could have run a marathon on fear alone. The only sane thought Porky had was run. He turned and took two steps before he recognized Quinton. Trapped was the only other sane thought that came to mind.

Porky could not fathom dying without putting up a fight. As a result, he readied himself for battle. "I ain't here for that – let's go inside and talk." Quinton tried to appear friendly.

"Nah," was the only word Porky trusted himself to say. Before he could assess the situation any further, he felt the fierce pain in his back, then his legs went numb and finally he was lying face down on the ground. Buck was angry but he tried to save his venom for the intruder in their lives. The twins laughed, thinking it was just like Buck to render a nigga unconscious before he could say a word. Together they took the young'un back to the room, leaving him lying on the floor just inside the door.

Finally, Porky shuffled backwards. The image of death and being burned alive clouded his judgment. "What the fuck you want?" he asked with false bravery. Nothing was ever said to him. They had what they needed and Porky knew it by the smiling faces. "Just kill me, motherfucker," he spat.

Dave raised the gun shot the hulking image in the leg. "You can die slow or quick, based on what you have to say," Quinton offered.

Porky smirked. "You ain't giving me shit. Death is death, so do what you do, bitch!"

Dave eagerly obliged their victim. "We ain't here to break a soldier, just to get some information. See you in hell," he saluted before firing the weapon at Porky's head. Together the brothers walked out as if they had not just committed murder. It did not matter what happened from this moment on, so long as Earl understood once and forever that life would be a serious of ducks, dodges, and bullets flying.

18

The last straw

Earl had convinced Eve that they needed a well-deserved vacation. Some time to talk about their future together. Eve was not the least bit fooled by the gesture. She knew this was about the twins. All her life she had lived in a bubble on a need to know bases. Finally, she had to know the truth. She had decided she would ride with him to get whatever information she could about Chaka's death. Suddenly it seemed important to know the truth. The morning skies were dreary looking as Earl loaded Eve's travel bags in the trunk of the luxury sports utility vehicle.

The silk scarf, wide sunglasses and ear plugs gave Eve an appropriate look for traveling. She was pretending to be a jetsetter this morning, despite the hateful moods that covered her being. Eve had been awake half the night, rehearsing the words to say to get Earl to confess to killing Chaka. She needed to know why he had decided at that precise moment that Chaka had to die.

Two hours into the drive, Earl asked her to get him water from the cooler beside her feet.

In her foul mood, Eve had not noticed it was there, packed to the brim with everything a road trip needed. Snacks were in the bag, perched on the back seat along with a host of music.

Playfully, Eve punched Earl when she saw a battered Volkswagen

Beetle. "Punch buggy," she yelled. He could not help but laugh, "You're still one silly-ass woman." The couple had been on I-95 south for a while and Eve decided it was safe to begin a dialogue. Shifting in her seat she asked him, "What attracted you to me?"

"Who the hell told you I was attracted to you," he teased.

"Stop playing and answer me, man."

Seriously, Earl tried to search his mind for the first thing that caught his eye about her. "That big, pretty ass," he confided.

Eve feigned shock but she had known the answer. The fact that he was honest was a good start. "Did you ever think we would be hanging out again?"

"Nah, not as long as Chaka was alive."

Eve had not meant to have him invoke Chaka's name into the conversation for at least a few more questions but since he had the time had come to ask. The sign ahead said, *Rest Stop, 2 miles*. She figured she could walk two miles if he tossed her out of the car.

Earl swerved the car across two lanes without hitting a brake or even looking behind him when he heard the words. "Why did I kill Chaka?" he repeated out loud. The rest stop was less than 100 feet from them now and Earl needed to rest for this conversation. He pulled in and parked in the somewhat deserted area. "You think I had Chaka killed?" He bellowed. The incredulous look plastered on Eve's face answered for her.

Earl took a deep breath between mumbling curses and threats. "You are a crazy bitch, but here's a news flash for your ass. I never laid one hand, or commissioned anyone to kill Chaka. Chaka was probably killed by the niggas in his camp and that's just the truth."

Eve was angry that Earl had the nerve to treat her like some lame dummy. Before she could say a word, Earl continued.

"He had all y'all fooled as to what kind a person he really was but since you want to have this conversation, let's do it."

Earl stopped talking for Eve to start ranting.

"You don't have to lie to me anymore, stupid. I am here with you, regardless of the outcome."

The wicked laugh left Eve feeling threatened.

"Eve, this was never about you! You were just a carefully placed pawn in this bullshit. Chaka shocked me when he claimed you as his woman because he only started fucking with you to create a war. The moment I conceded, that ended that bullshit. I always knew what Chaka never figured out about you. You were going to run and fuck because you could. So do not even entertain the idea you were the reasons for our battles. The main reason I never bothered to go after Chaka was about Ms. Sadie. When my pops was locked down, her generosity kept me alive. For that reason alone, I didn't do any real harm to Chaka."

Eve was not convinced just yet that Earl was completely being honest but she did not protest. The silence and suspicious look in her eyes said the words she held from her mouth.

"Did it ever occur to you that Chaka never did anything to me either," he demanded.

Eve could not speak. She shook her head. The slight movement enraged him. Now that he was baring his soul, he may as well tell everything. He charged forward and told her some other things that she hadn't been privy to.

"My pops, liked Chaka. He had faith that one day Chaka would make him a rich man. But all that praise ended when my dad got knocked in the apartment with enough drugs and shit to get him sent away for a long time. Anyway, the detectives kept coming around trying to get information on my pop's connections. Since I never dealt in the business, I did not have any idea about the people involved. As a favor to my pops, Ms. Sadie made sure I went to school, was clean, and fed. Meanwhile, Chaka welcomed me to the fold.

"I was down with them, hustling a little bit, when Chaka decided that I could take over where my father left off; but I had to get the DTs off my back and quick. He hatched a plan: I would give the DTs a name and they would leave me alone. But we couldn't just choose anybody or we might be fucked in the end. So as a result, Buck got caught holding the bag."

Eve started to hyperventilate. Earl was saying Chaka had planned for Buck to go to jail.

"Yeah, the sacrificial lamb was Buck. According to Chaka — and I quote – 'nobody expected Buck to do much with his life' so he was the best choice. Besides, his big ass could probably survive prison better than any of us."

Eve was almost afraid to ask, but couldn't afford not to. "Did the others know?"

Earl did not answer her question. He just kept telling history.

"At the time, I thought they all agreed, including Buck. Later, when everyone was labeling me a snitch, I knew better. By then it was too late to tell anyone. Chaka had already ousted me from the clique. Shit, I even became the nemesis for a plan that Chaka hatched. I was afraid and alone. No friend's and no family. It might sound dumb but I trusted Chaka just like the rest of the crew. As a result, Chaka convinced me to stay away for a while and he would make sure I did not suffer too much from the drama. To survive, I got out on my own and started making a little bit of money. Nothing major, just enough to eat and pay the rent on the ragged tenement apartment. My pops had long done gone back to Jamaica but he left a few friends in the world who took me under their wings.

"When crack began to really make an appearance, I was bubbling and making money. Chaka once again came up with this plan; it was a moneymaking idea, so I ran with it. I was no longer in need of friends and my naïve state was long gone. I understood the meaning of money. Chaka's money spent like any other man's so I took it. I went from small-time hustler to supplier for Chaka and his boys."

Earl had left Eve stupefied, her mouth could have dragged the floor. By the time Earl had made all his declarations, Eve was ready to run.

"I told you Chaka was a self-serving bastard. My biggest downfall when it came to him was that I was always just a means to an end. When the drama came about because of you, Chaka had already outgrown my minor racket and was doing big things, but that was okay. I was still eating until he started eliminating all competition. He offered any local traffic a chance to live by getting down with him. That offer was never extended to me. I was the fuel that kept his crew earning like mad. They needed someone to do better than and I was it."

The tears rolled down Eve's face and angered Earl.

"If a blind woman didn't want to see, she should not have asked questions," he uttered in his native patois.

Four hours later, Earl decided he had had enough driving. It was time to find a place to lie down and contemplate his next course of action. As a peace offering, Eve clung to Earl as they watched the highway and byways interchange. Suddenly, Eve blurted the question.

"If you didn't kill him, who did?"

Earl cleared his throat. "I've had my thoughts about that for some time and each time I come back to Quinton and Buck."

Eve's laughter filled the car like music bouncing off the ceiling and floors. "Quinton would probably stab Anissa and bury her in the back yard before turning sides against Chaka. If Buck found out the chances were he could kill Chaka. But I still can't see him going through with it and not revealing something after so long."

"Financially, they both had the most to gain from the legit business to the street traffic. Besides, I always thought that Chaka was the most conniving of the group but Quinton was the smartest by far. He just let everyone think Chaka was the brains of the operation," Earl confided.

By the time they got to North Carolina they had resurrected Ms. Sadie and was blaming her for her son's death. They headed straight for the posh Marriot hotel to check in and rest before Earl went about his duties.

Pop was impulsive, irrational and greedy. He decided that waiting for the chance to get at Buck might not ever come if Earl were the reigning king. Therefore, he planned to secure a few investments of his own. The apartment in Sasha's building where he kept his stash had been vacant for days. No one had been in or out and the remaining soldiers were on the lookout for Buck, but he was ghost. The day Pop took the initiative to claim his future, all the world was on tilt. The idea was going into Bucks' apartment and steal everything not nailed down. One problem was the neighbors. The next was getting the door open. It was simple: the steel door couldn't be kicked in so that meant a locksmith. A locksmith would have too many questions. That was not an option. The only other thought was Sasha. Maybe she knew where Buck kept his spare key. If he was lucky, maybe, she had a spare. The longer Pop thought about the burglary the more elaborate his plans got. A mechanic was working on a car door when Pop decided that he might have the right tools to get inside the apartment. Greed was a character flaw in many of the people Pop chose as confidantes. He promised the bootleg mechanic a grip if he helped him get into an apartment. The man did not bat an eyelash as he offered Pop any assistance he needed. A down payment got Pop the power drill that could pop a lock out clean. The man explained, "It's a matter of applying a little pressure to the lock and you in the door." Pop was stunned at the ease it took to get in and search the place. Carefully, he searched, coming up with two portable safes: one digital and the other an old-time dial. Pop was not the least bit nervous, he was just eager to see his pockets filled to the brim and then some.

In the bedroom, there was an average-sized bed and all the furnishing of a home. But the footlocker seemed out of place. A crack head could smell his next victim long before he saw him. Well, a nigga like Pop could smell money. At first glance, there were a bunch of sweaters neatly packed inside but underneath was a mother lode of crisp, wrapped one-hundred-dollar bills. The cellophane was wrapped tight. After careful consideration, Pop took all ten wrapped packs and placed them in his waistband. Next, he hoisted the two safes into separate duffel bags and abandoned the disarray.

In Sasha's attempts to please him she had given him a key to her place, hoping he would use it. Today he had good reason to climb the steps to Sasha's apartment where he hid all his newfound fortunes, and left. She would not even know he had been there. Pop retraced his steps back to the mechanic and handed him an envelope filled with cash. The wide grin disappeared when Pop jammed the knife in his chest and turned it. Too easy, he was convinced.

Buck had another spot where he kept his fortune but he could chance that today. That posed a dilemma because there was always someone there, so he had to creep light. During his swindling, he hadn't calculated that his men were watching his every move. They wanted in on the pie and if they couldn't get some, Pop would have none. They had a meeting without him to discuss the best way to make him understand he was a movement alone but there were levels to this and the trickle-down theory applied in their case.

Pop was not a master manipulator; he was a straight hood. If he could not convince you to do things his way, then next the threats were followed by death. Those tactics were saved for lame niggas. In this case, he was one young'un in a camp of strength. They would as soon see him dead on the sidewalk then let him run rampant without repercussions. The three men were posted by the lamppost as Pop turned the corner, smiling. They greeted him with the usual dap, keeping things to a minimal. The country drawl of Patchy caught Pop's attention.

"Yo, kid, what you come off with," he questioned.

Pop was caught off guard and accepted that every man standing there wanted a cut of whatever he had.

"Not much, just two safes, that's it," he lied.

The other two guys rocked on their toes as they asked for the take.

"I couldn't walk out with it in broad daylight, so I left it at the chick's house that lives in his building."

"Alright, we want to see what we got to work with." The soldier exaggerated the words "we" to indicate this was a joint effort.

"True that," was all Pop trusted himself to say. They had come to an understanding despite their temporary leader's reluctant behavior.

Later that night, Sasha watched as Pop searched her closet and came out with the two duffel bags. She felt the urge to question when he put them there because she certainly did not intend to be the fall girl if the cops ever rolled on her. Prison separated lovers and she convinced herself she could live without his abusive ass if she had to choose between his dick and jail. If she were in prison, he could not give her any dick. Speaking out of turn left Sasha holding her face. The blood that dripped from her lip was enough to shut Sasha up until Pop left to go wherever with his bullshit. The first thought was to ask for her keys back but he would probably really kick her ass if she tried a move like that. The decision she made had to be effective or she would just be subjected to more abuse. Changing the locks was a better idea than out and out confrontation.

Pop's boys were all sitting in the apartment that Earl had given them since they had arrived. Each man was trying to find a way to crack the safes without damaging the contents. They thought up everything from liquid nitroglycerin to just straight dynamite. The laughter at the dilemma left everyone feeling better about the caper – everyone but Pop. He wanted his fortune free and clear.

Earl went to the motel just off I-95 in search of his boys, only to find police and ambulances everywhere. The place was roped off and the sheriff was questioning some of the customers who had been brave enough to stand around. Earl practically ran back to the Marriot. The truth was he was not certain of the events but he knew whatever happened; the twins probably knew he was coming.

Eve never made it back to the hotel. Danny and Dave spied her coming out of the side entrance and convinced her she would be safer with them. Eve's hesitance was short-lived when she saw the flash of Quinton's angry eyes. She climbed into the van, staring straight ahead; she wished that she could be anywhere else but t here. Danny helped Eve from the truck. He walked beside her as they entered the club through the back door. They went into the office without anyone noticing anything out of the ordinary. Eve sat opposite the desk, appearing cool as a breeze despite the hollow feeling in her stomach.

Dave grinded his teeth as he stared at her, wondering how she could have been so deceptive, pretending to mourn Chaka even after she had probably been the reason he was killed. Danny was not going to wonder about anything he just asked her in a monotone voice.

"Why would you help him after all he did to us – even you?"

Shame forced Eve to drop her head. She could have told them that Chaka was not everything they believed him to be, but she did not have any proof except Earl. She clamped down on her lips and silently prayed they would just kill her quick.

By the time Buck and Quinton came into the office, the twins were frustrated beyond repair. Eve attempted to square her shoulders and prepare herself for the worst but the false bravery was wasted. Quinton charged at her, snatching the chair from beneath her while she still sat perched in it. "Bitches belong on the floor," he spat.

While her legs went in one direction and the rest of her in another, she hissed. Too afraid not to speak and terrified of the damage if she said a word, she laid there in her own misery. Buck rescued her from the floor, returning her to the chair.

"It's this simple, nigga. I am not going to harm a hair on her head in memory of Chaka, and I can't watch you do anything dumb, either."

Buck was thinking for the later date when the misery she caused surfaced and she would have to live with it. "If she dies now, it would be too easy."

The tension in the room was on full tilt, but the twins understood Buck's reasoning and nodded in agreement. Quinton, however, felt like they were betraying Chaka.

"Let's just kill this bitch and then go get Earl's treacherous ass before he could dip."

The silent tears streamed a path down Eve's face as she listened. Quinton stood with his jaw slacked as he watched her holler over the niggas death and he was still breathing. Eve decided this was as good a time as any to shut his ass up for the good, or make him kill her. When she began speaking her voice shook with emotions but as the words flowed, she became stronger. Her only regret was that the truth would destroy Buck but she wanted to make it clear that Chaka was no saint. Dave was closest to Eve now as she spun her tail with the venom Earl spit the day before. They had all questioned Chaka reasoning for allowing Earl mercy. Eve opened her mouth and the words took form and flowed.

"Why did Chaka wage death on anybody else in his path but he allowed Earl to live? Earl created the most drama. He was always trying to find a way to get back at Chaka, using me even to make him jealous," she reasoned. "So why didn't he just rid himself of his biggest nemesis?"

They were stumped for a brief moment but Quinton was not there to debate why. He was there to fix who. The sound of Eve revealing that Buck was a pawn so that they could advance left everyone speechless. As generously as Buck had spared her, he was now ready to kill her. The weapon had been drawn from its holster and pointed at her head in a flash. Danny and Dave each stepped away from her and watched in horror as Buck's gun hand shook. Quinton reacted slowly, not wanting Buck to turn at the slightest movement and fire. He placed a hand on top of Buck's and twisted it from his hand. The gesture was not to save Eve's miserable live but done to save Buck. He knew if he allowed his friend to kill her, he would not be able to live with himself. Buck would probably become the pawn Chaka had made him out to be.

The angry tinted glow of Buck's eyes scared everyone but for fear, they all stood still. Buck went to the mahogany desk and flipped the massive furniture over. The computer and papers went flying everywhere. The noise must have alerted security because Danny saw them all heading in the direction of the office. When Buck flipped over the desk, he must have struck the remote; the closed-circuit monitors all came to life at once.

Six hulking men were standing at the door, deciding the best way to get the door to cave in. The battering ram would not work and shooting the door in might injure the wrong person. Finally, Dave opened the door and tried to squelch the situation but before he could, the security team was heading for Buck. The first body to rush in caught a quick blow to the throat. The next man ducked but was not ready for the crushing blow of Buck's knee to his face. By the time, the third man entered the room he stopped himself short, examining that his bosses were fine but the captain of the security and his lieutenant were sprawled out groaning and in pain. Immediately, man three slowed the other bouncers from entering and explained it was just all a misunderstanding.

The injured pair on the floor collected themselves and exited the club, heading straight to the hospital. The physical contact helped calm only a small part of the rage Buck felt. He really wished he could disprove the hateful things Eve had uttered. Defeated, he plopped himself into the seat and stared at Eve for any evidence that she was lying just to hurt him. Danny and Dave truly did not know what to make of the situation. Quinton, however knew Eve's words were true. He now understood why Chaka carried on the way he did when Buck shunned them. He now understood the distance Chaka had gone from friend to foe. Had Chaka not been dead and buried, Buck would have killed him slow.

After about four hours, Earl was suspicious that Eve hadn't returned. The phone startled him from his fearful thoughts. "Hello," he answered.

The caller did not introduce himself. He just started talking.

"Listen, I got your girl, I'll trade you her life for yours."

Earl's laughter could be heard clear across the room. "You can keep that bitch. I was done anyway," he confessed through fits of laughter.

Shortly after that, the line went dead.

Earl marched past the front desk, claimed his vehicle, and kept going further south. He figured that the twins would expect him to head back home to Buck and Quinton awaiting trap. They had managed to foil this plan but there were many others in the works. Earl had forgotten that in order for his ultimate goal to succeed, everything had to fall precisely in line. This was not just about the money or murder, this was about getting even. By the time Earl reached Atlanta, Georgia, he was exhausted. He did not feel like talking to anyone but decided it was in his best interests to find out how things were working back at home. The moment he spoke with Pop, the knot that had formed in the base of his neck eased. For the first time in a long time, Earl was able to sleep without constant nightmares.

The first morning light brought with it the true gravity of where his life really was. Earl primarily had lived in the gutter. It was his way of life but he always managed to climb out squeaky clean. There was a way to fix this problem and save Eve. She at least deserved the chance to change her life and become a better person. Earl feelings had changed as quickly as a good night sleep. He needed the chance to speak with someone that might lead him in the right direction.

The island dialect poured through the phone lines as if his father were sitting next to him, instead of back home in Jamaica. Earl explained the dilemma he had created and the emotions that had brought him to this point in his life.

His father listened intently; unsure at first what to say to his son. It suddenly occurred to him that Earl had called him for help. The Roots Man's voice was filled with concern as he begged his son's pardon for not being there at the most crucial times of his life. Earl accepted the apology for what it was worth and listened to the carefully chosen words from his mentor.

"Can you live with yourself if you walk away?" the Roots Man questioned.

Earl thought briefly and answered honestly.

"Yes, but if I walk, where can I go? This drama had been brewing for a long time. Chaka used me and I was dumb enough to allow it. Now they think I killed him. Eve accused me too, until I was able to explain."

The Rootsman tried to encourage his son; the confusion and bitterness he felt were more than warranted.

"You have to understand that I failed to give you the things you needed to make you stronger. From the beginning, you had to make your own way. Earl, do things the way you see fit. I promise to stand by you when it matters."

The speech hadn't cleared the fog of whether to run forward or take his chance to go backward, but Earl appreciated the fact that his father would support whatever decisions he made. The conversation ended with a promise that neither knew how to fulfill. Earl knew that he would not hide. He had to go home and deal with the mess that Chaka and he had set in motion. The determined line across his forehead was a testament to the serious thought it took to head home.

His shoulders were hunched over the steering wheel as he drove with purpose. He fought fatigue for miles as he convinced himself that he was doing the right thing. The fog began to lift as he thought the chances of Dave or Danny harming Eve was too minuscule. She was a family member. The longer he drove, the more he thought about the possibility of the real killer.

Buck, he was certain, could not have found out about the betrayal, especially since he was the only person that knew the truth. Maybe there was a time when Buck might have wanted to harm both Quinton and Chaka. Especially after Angie was killed in the accident, but he found a way to forgive. Lately, he had even been dating one woman seriously; he was improbable but not completely ruled out.

Quinton had more of a reason than anyone did. He was the true brains of the Baker Boys 5 back in the day, but more recently, he was the glue that helped the Dirty Dozen stay focused and gave them the superstar status that kept them in the millions. Yet, all the praise went to an undeserving bobble head, Earl reasoned.

The universal rule is, if you kill the head, the body must crumble. If that was true, then Chaka wasn't the head. The proof was that his death had not caused the slightest ripple in their operations. To their credit, they seemed to be doing just as well, if not better, since the tragedy. It was plausible that Quinton had finally gotten tired while everyone praised the image of Chaka's greatness. Eve had confided that Quinton had just barely missed the officers who brought the bad news. She had even remembered that he smelled like gunpowder for some reason. He never mentioned how he knew about Chaka's death and he damn sure never told anyone where he was coming from when Chaka was dying.

Earl was convincing himself that maybe he was right about Chaka's right-hand man. The words "people judge you by the company you keep" played repeatedly in his mind. The truth about Chaka was that he was definitely selfish, conniving, and his loyalty was about as strong as a thin, cheap garbage bag. None of the things he had learned about Quinton had suggested that he was like his friend. But Earl hadn't been the greatest judge of character.

There was traffic ahead, just as Earl's mind had hit a zone. Suddenly he was forced to mentally take a detour. Suppose Eve was fronting when she decided to accuse him, knowing she had been the reason for his death. Their relationship had been dysfunctional from Chaka's secret life to Eve's cheating ways. They were both selfish as hell, so he could dismiss her as the culprit. Eve had confessed that she wanted out of the relationship but lack of courage and greed kept her bound to the misery.

Anissa could not be ruled out of the equation, seeing that living with Chaka could not have been easy. Eve bragged that Quinton took his cues from Chaka on how to treat a woman. Most nights if Chaka stayed out, then Q would not come home and for a while, Anissa tried to deal with the disrespect but one night, Anissa blew up. According to Eve, Chaka was saying that he was the boss of Q and she had better fall in line or she could find herself another man. Anissa made it clear that the blatant disrespect would not continue and she did not give a shit that he was the boss. She even went so far as to point out to Chaka that he was just a conniving, selfish person that had gotten away with so much because the men around him were willing to tolerate his rude manners.

Reasoning was Anissa's strongest asset and she did not have a problem with explaining that she took care of herself so if he thought that she needed any man, he could kiss her natural fat ass. She counted down all the reason he should want his friend to be in a productive relationship, since he had not managed to maintain one with Eve. Chaka, of course, did not like that and tried to drive a wedge between the couple.

To prove her point, a week after the confrontation Anissa left Quinton, leaving behind anything he had ever given her. She applied for campus housing and decided that she would prefer to be a struggling student than tolerate more of the bullshit. Quinton got wind of all the drama going on between Anissa and Chaka when he was not home. Until she had moved out, she never told Quinton anything. Quinton pleaded with Anissa to come home. He had to make all kinds of promises and most importantly, he had to deal with Chaka.

She refused to come back until the semester ended. However, she would visit on the weekends and leave for school on Sunday night. He had been miserable without her and as a result, he made Chaka miserable. They did not agree on anything. By the time Anissa moved back, Chaka understood that there was at least one woman in the world that was not his fan. There were times he would try to cause fights between the happy couple but soon Quinton began to see the light. Anissa definitely did not have any love lost for Chaka.

The twins, Earl decided rather quickly, had no reason to kill Chaka. Going away to college had taken care of the day-to-day interaction with Chaka. So if there was any resentment, distance and time took care of that.

Earl decided that he did not have all the components regarding Chaka's murder, especially since everyone suspected him. Once again, he felt that he was a patsy for the excitement someone else had caused.

Twelve hours later, Earl was climbing the steps to his home. He did not bother to alert anyone to his presence. It was better that he rest and have a clear head for the drama that would unfold. The nagging shrill of his cell phone would not stop. It seemed suddenly everyone wanted to talk with him, yet no one left a message. He did not have a clue when darkness claimed the streets but he was wide- awake and ready to deal with the nocturnal elements.

Standing in his shower, he allowed the water to beat against his aching shoulder blades as he pondered his very first steps. Pop, he figured, was the safest route for now. Punching in the telephone number, he waited to here a familiar voice.

"Yo," was the sound he heard on the other end after several rings.

"Alright, nigga, I see you still alive," Earl, said after laughing in Pop's ear. In his lazy drawl, Pop agreed. For some reason, Earl did not feel comfortable telling Pop he was back in town so soon. Pop was giving Earl all the usual lines about everything being normal and the crew keeping low profiles. Earl interrupted his chattering.

"Alright, it's good to hear all is well, I should see you soon."

The phone line disconnected abruptly, leaving Pop to wonder if Earl was having any success in the Carolinas.

The thought flew from his head as he heard the shouting from the living room area. One of his homies had opened the digital safe. The shouting stopped the moment they stared at its contents. Inside the safe there were several stacks of money, a baggie filled with a white powder, and two large, silver handguns. The look on Pop's face was pure shock as he drooled over the purest coke he had every seen. He wondered if his crew understood the real meaning of this situation. Everyone started talking at once.

Busta, the excited exclaimer, won the battle for who would talk first.

"I heard about shit like this but I ain't never seen nothing like it — that nigga Buck gonna come back here and turn this fucking city upside down for this shit! It probably costs a fortune, and we in here laughing like we hit the jackpot. The worst thing is we do not even know how to cut this shit and make it marketable in the street. Nobody has seen that dude Quinton or Buck since Earl left this bitch so for all we know, that nigga Earl might be dead."

The mutiny was in full swing and it would not be long before every nigga broke camp to save his ass. Pop could probably hush the noise for a minute but they needed someone to confirm that this was indeed what they thought it was.

19

Family Secrets

Petra sat on the sofa staring at her daughter, wondering how one person could influence the look of someone so greatly. Chanice had her father's big head, deep-set eyes, and long curly lashes. Even her freckles were the same pattern as his. Sadly, she realized her daughter's butter complexion and quick wit were even influenced by Chaka's very existence. Chanice looked annoyed.

"You're doing it again, Mom."

Petra offered a weak apology for making her uncomfortable.

"I miss your dad so much, when I look at you it's like seeing him."

"But Mommy, I'm not Daddy – I'm Chanice," she said with a nervous smile. Earlier in the day, her grandmother explained that her father's death was sudden and it saddened her mother. The reason might have made sense to the adults but to Chanice, she only wondered whether her mom had died too. Chaka Jr. was not fazed by his mother's confusion. Fortunately, for him, he did not resemble his dad as much as his sister.

Petra's mother decided it would be best if she moved in with her daughter for a while, since she seemed to be having such a hard time.

"My grandchildren aren't going to suffer the loss of two parents because you can't function. Grieving is a process as anything else in this life, but you must remember you cannot mourn him for the rest of your life.

These babies need you," she chastised.

Petra agreed but she did not know how to put the grief in its proper place.

"Mama," she cried, "why did he have to be like that? Why he didn't just stay with me and let me love and care for him?" The unbridled tears streamed.

The elder woman wished she had the right answers to make her daughter understand that this was his choice. The soft words that left her mother's mouth frightened Petra.

"Baby, you talk like you are guilty of not protecting him from his decision to leave. Chaka was a man. He was responsible for his actions, not you."

Petra's labored breathing caught her attention and she worried that maybe she had said the wrong things. Her grief made her tell her mother everything that troubled her about Chaka. Sitting on the chair, Petra's mother tried to understand the babbling through her daughters tears.

"Mama, you don't understand. From the beginning of our relationship, we were responsible for the other. Whatever he needed I provided. When I was not taking my studies seriously before I found out I was pregnant, Chaka would threaten not to see me until I got my head back in the books. I was going to run away when I found out I was pregnant but Chaka promised that he would provide everything, so long as I stayed on course and got my degree. In return, I did not complain when he came home, because I knew he was out there working for me. I did not fight back when I discovered that Eve existed; I just accepted it. But I couldn't accept when he promised to marry her. That was more than I was willing to deal with. I worked hard to maintain a home he could be proud of and he was planning to marry her.

"A few nights before he was killed, it was Juniors' birthday. I cooked and baked a cake. We were all having a good time when the phone went off. When Chaka returned the call, I knew that he would be leaving soon. But I didn't expect to be so angry about it. I could hear the girl yelling, saying he was spending too much time out and telling him to come to her. At first, he dismissed her and we carried on like nothing until the beeping began again. Mama, I could not deal with it so I took the thing and mashed it against the wall. Chaka did not say a word. He just got up and went to bed. For the briefest of moments, I had his full attention. That night, I told him that I was angry that she was still able to create so much tension between us – I was first."

The wailing sounds of Chanice forced the woman to the living room to see the child lying on her back. The footprints on the bookshelf indicated that Chanice had tried to climb up the shelf and had fallen. Junior stood back in horror as he watched his sister lying there unable to help her. He ran the second his mother began yelling, for he would get a beating too for being in the near vicinity. Luckily, the elder woman was there or they might have been beaten something fierce. Instead, she helped Chanice to her feet checking for any serious damage, and then she turned to her eldest granddaughter.

"I bet you won't try that anymore," she said with a stern look in her eyes.

The sniffling and whimpering softened Petra's heart. Her daughter could have really been injured, all because she was crying over Chaka. The sadness turned to anger as she accepted Chaka was already alright. She needed to be sure her children would be alright. At that moment, she held Chanice in her arms, softly chastising her for trying such a stunt.

"What did you want from up there anyway," she asked.

"Daddy gave me a necklace and I remembered he put it on the top shelf. That was the day Junior and I was playing freeze tag outside. It kept getting caught in my hair."

Petra remembers the necklace but she had not seen it in a while. Slowly she began to search the top shelf until her hands felt the coarse metal.

"I got it," Petra yelled, "right here."

The comforting smile brightened up the room. Junior slid back into the room just as Chanice hugged her mom. For some unknown reason the sight and feel of the necklace left Petra feeling hollow, like there was something she should remember, but because of her new consciousness she refused to allow the matter to cloud her judgment.

The night brought on determination. She was going to do everything that she had neglected for months. As the children slept soundly, she walked about, figuring her first steps. The bedroom closet still held many of his things. After a year, she was still holding on to them as if he would return. Hoisting the sweaters from the overhead shelf, she refused to get caught up in the scent that permeated the room. She pushed her things to the side and began pulling down hangers with his pants attached. The next stop was the bureau that contained his underwear and T-shirts. Slowly she removed all the things that held her captive in her home. Her mother heard the moving about and decided that Petra needed the time alone.

By the time Petra made her way to his socks, her eyes were clouded, but the tears would not fall. She began speaking to his memory as if he were sitting at the foot of her bed.

"Chaka, there were things in our relationship that just were never going to be perfect. It did not matter that I was willing to sacrifice every-thing to make you happy. It did not matter that I accepted all the misery that was yours. That I let you come into my life and take over. You were never going to do the right thing by me. Here I was, with two children, living in this house waiting for you and you had another. She was every-thing you claimed you hated but you still were promising her things that should have been meant for me." The defeatist attitude turned into pure hatred as she continued to talk to nothingness.

"I begged you to tell me thing's that explained the reason you raced home to her. You never said a word. I wondered if she was smarter and you laughed as if I was telling jokes. I needed to know what she had that made you love her more than me and our two children."

Slowly the elderly woman climbed the steps, hoping she could get to her daughter before Petra completely lost her mind, but it was too late. Petra had been cutting item after item as she talked to him. The hatred in her eyes blazed like wildfire but there was nothing to say. Petra turned to her mother just as she entered the door. A wicked smile crossed her face as she raised the scissors and brought them down hard on the mattress she shared with Chaka. The blind fury frightened her mother. She would have never believed her child capable of such a violent display.

Slowly her mother prayed that Petra would realize the damage and calm herself. The silent prayer worked because Petra began to lose mo-mentum. The hysterics subsided and just as suddenly as the outrage started, it was ending. Like seeing for the first time, Petra surveyed the damage and instantly felt the rush of shame. Turning her back to the travesty, she lowered her body to the floor.

Fear held her mother just beyond the doorway, however, love forced her to speak.

"Petra," she called and received no response. In a more demanding voice she called again, this time getting the acknowledgement that Petra had recognized her name.

"Reasoning hasn't worked for you and allowing you to work through this have made the situation worse, so I am just going to be brutally honest with you."

Petra sat transfixed by the stern look in her mother's eyes. Nothing could have been more embarrassing than sitting on the floor in a heap of clothes, looking deranged and lost. The words made her feel like a child in need of a good scolding. Her mother refused to mince words before Petra could defend her actions her mother was telling Petra off.

"You have been behaving as if he was your entire life. Your children should be your world and that is the truth. Now I won't take away that you are angry with him for the decisions he made, but you chose to stay and accept your lot in this life. You could have left and lived a different life without him, but you would not hear any of that. Honestly, you are acting as though he is alive and he is rejecting you for some woman. Chaka is dead. He won't and can't come back so move on. Judging by this turmoil in this room, if he had chose her over you – you would have probably killed him."

The words tumbled from her lips, leaving her with a strange feeling. The chill crept up her back and stopped any further reprimand. She glanced about the room and wondered if her daughter could have done just that. Could she have killed Chaka?

The thought caused her mouth to go completely dry and her heart ached that she could have missed the evidence. Guilt was running Petra mad.

20

Face to Face

Buck was the first to express his resentment with foam collected at the corners of his mouth. His arms flailed above his head as he spewed the words.

"Eve, a bitch like you don't understand the true impact of the shit they do until they have to live through it. If I thought killing you would make me feel better, I would pump you full of so many bullets it would be like putting a 1000-piece jigsaw puzzle together. But the greatest punishment for you is survival. When the world is on your shoulders, you're going to wonder why terrible things keep happening to you and the answer is going to be all the misery you caused. I won't promise after today I'll be so generous with your life, so I strongly suggest you stay the fuck out my path." She had heard the words but couldn't believe they were going to let her live.

Earl stood at the safe in his bedroom, above the portable fireplace, questioning if there was another way to go through with his plan. A while back Buck had come to a Christmas party to bicker over Eve's virtue and had gotten the shit beaten out of him. In the process, Buck had dropped his gun. At that moment, Earl had hatched the plan to use the gun to implicate Buck in a murder. But the police had to have a way to connect Buck to the victim. Sasha was good as any choice. She was his last known steady girlfriend and if she turned up dead with a bullet in her with Buck's fingerprint on it that would seal his fate.

Sasha had mentally prepared the items she needed for her stay at her sister's house. The suitcase lay out on the bed, open for the garments of her choice. Quickly she waltzed back and forth, examining one outfit after the next before making all her selections. Finally, she had suitable clothing. Suddenly it occurred to her that she had not chosen one pair of shoes for her pilgrimage. As she contemplated the appropriate shoes for her outfits, she heard the slight knocking. The interruption made her stand still and hold her breath. She figured if she didn't respond, maybe the uninvited visitor would go away. Instead, the light taps became loud banging and she knew it was Pop. She decided she would not open the door no matter how much he banged, she would just wait him out.

Pop's patience was wearing thin as he began kicking the door and calling her name. His persistence unraveled Sasha, making her hands tremble and her body go numb. She tiptoed to the door and uttered, "I called the police. Please leave." The constant noise stopped and gave her a false sense of safety. With the speed of a cat, she slammed the case shut and forgot about any shoes. Slowly she tiptoed back to the door and listened, hoping Pop had gotten the message and gone away. As a safety precaution, she looked through the peephole and felt comforted that he was not there.

With the suitcase at her side, Sasha quietly opened her top lock and turned the knob, releasing the latch that secured her inside. When the door creaked opened slightly, Pop burst in. The heavy steel door flew into her chest, sending the suitcase flying behind her back. As she fought to maintain her balance, Pop stepped past the threshold. Sasha tried to move but shock held her down. As he advanced toward her, she backpedaled, trying to get away. Pop tired easily from the cat-and-mouse game and offered his hand to help her up from the floor. His face betrayed the threat of a serious ass kicking. Feeling cornered, Sasha allowed him to help her up.

As she stood to an erect position, Pop struck her with a right cross to her head. She went sailing across the room into the wall. The force of the blow and Sasha's feeble attempt to stand excited Pop.

He whispered in her face, "My dick is hard right now."

The next punch was timed perfectly as she struggled to raise her throbbing head, he slammed his fist into her eye. The cracking sound made Pop feel like he might cum. Her whimpering made him angrier.

"Stop crying, you fucking up my shit," he demanded. The next jab to Sasha's stomach made her double over – straight into his raised knee. Her nose made contact with his knee, forcing her to see stars and feel faint. She crumbled to the floor, unconscious. The sound of sirens stopped Pop from delivering another blow and stopped him from getting the money — his real reason for being there. Pop did not have time to look left or right, he did not even bother to close the apartment door all the way as he rushed down the steps to freedom. If he had taken a moment, he would have seen it was an ambulance and not a police car.

Pop had been sneaking with Eve for months. However, they kept their relationship a secret. The moment Pop decided to go into Sasha's apartment he knew he needed a cover incase the police arrived before he could get the money. Pop convinced Eve she had to meet him on Buck's floor to take the duffle bag before he left the building.

Waiting two floors below was an nervous and anxious Eve. Ten minutes later, she was ready to run when Pop convinced her she had to go in the apartment and get the bag out of the closet. There was no time to argue, he stated the facts and didn't give her a second to think as he pushed her up the steps. After Eve approached the door she couldn't turn back. Pretending to be visiting she called out to Sasha. After stepping through the door she saw Sasha's body lying limp between the bedroom and bathroom. Tip-toeing alone Eve got her bearing and moved along, afraid to look down or step in the blood that was all over the floor. Nervously she raffled through the closet along the floor bed and realized the bag wasn't there. As she tried the overhead shelf, she heard the squeak of the door being opened. Eve could have shit all over herself as she decided getting under the bed was the best hiding place. She tried to hold her breath but felt the slow burn of bile tickling the back of her throat.

Earl dressed with purpose: a black knit cap, black sweat pants, and matching sweat shirt. He appeared as a nondescript black man on a mission. He parked his car and walked the rest of the way. As Earl got to the parking lot, he thought he recognized Pop exiting the building.

Earl climbed the steps to Sasha's apartment without any more thought as to where Pop could have been coming from. He was the ladies' man in the crew, so it was anyone's guess which single woman had captured his attention. The moment Earl reached the door he could see it was slightly ajar. With the tip of his gloved hand, he eased it open and called out to her. Sasha groaned softly at the sound of her name. She prayed that maybe it was one of her neighbors coming to make sure she was okay. As Earl traveled in the direction of the sound, he prayed that she was not home with someone.

The slumped body lodged between the bathroom and bedroom made him feel queasy. Unable to speak for the pain, Sasha's eyes pleaded for help. Earl raised the gun, pointed, and shot her in the face. He dropped the gun to the floor, turned, and walked away. He reasoned that he had helped her from a life of suffering. Her face looked like it had been scraped with a cheese grater. The bones in her nose were twisted and her right eye was hanging out of the socket. Earl hoped he would not dream about the grotesque image tonight.

He walked back to his car and got the eerie feeling someone was watching his movements. The first phone he came to he called 911 as an anonymous caller, giving the necessary information to get a police response. Earl was convinced on his drive home that he might not live long enough to see his plan complete but Buck would definitely serve time for the murder. Earl never gave thought as to who had beaten her to a pulp. He was all too willing to accept it must have been Buck, anyway.

Buck did not have time to think about his own safety, he was too busy reliving the old feeling of resentment. Angela's death had left him angry and bitter with the two people he trusted most. Often times he believed that those two men were betraying him, but he would just as easily accept the thought was paranoia. Now he knew for sure Chaka had no real value for him or his ability to be a friend and the madness began again.

Could Q have been a part of the plan to set him up? Just as the thought rolled around in his head, he began to have trouble breathing. Quinton sat in the driver's seat while Buck, in the passenger's seat, seemed to be hyperventilating. Quinton navigated the truck to the shoulder of the road to check on his friend. As the car pulled slowly to a stop, Buck raised his head. There was no question that something was torturing Buck. His eyes were red and his chest was heaving up and down.

"You alright, man? You seemed to be having trouble over there," Q tried to make his voice light in case Buck was angry with him.

Buck turned his glare to Quinton as if he were seeing him for the very first time.

"Nah, nigga I ain't alright. You let me go to jail for some shit we were all down with. You and that sorry son of bitch used me to take the fall. I lost everything that year: my chance at life, a decent girl, my freedom, and more importantly, I destroyed my grandma's dream for me."

Q just allowed Buck to air out his anger, hoping that when it was time to defend his actions, Buck would believe him. But he lost his patience just as Buck got to Ms. Sadie.

"I wonder if she was down with the plan to fuck me, the stupid football star over because she didn't think I was worth anything."

"Yo, Jahson, you reaching now. Chaka did some fucked-up shit and I am as angry as you are because I can't help, but I wonder how else he used us all. But if you asking me whether I knew about the plan to send you up, my answer is emphatically no. I would not have gone along with that shit and I hope all these years as friends proved it. Granted, we were all guilty, but I like to think I could have dealt with my punishment had things worked out differently.

Buck lost control of his emotions. He leaped from the truck, slamming the door. The mere fact that things had not worked out differently left his heart heavy with resentment. Quinton recognized Buck's frustration but was helpless to make things better. For his fallen friend, he harbored a new sense of pity. For his broken friend, he wished he could fix the years gone by.

The sense of dread came over him as he accepted that this might be the last time they were friends. All the years the crew had been together

Buck had become his confidante, and he still believed that if he lost his brother it would be like losing half of him. The will to hold on to outdated shit in the name of Chaka lost its luster. All Quinton wanted to do now was mend the fences between he and Jahson.

Buck leaned against the truck, working out the bullshit in his head. Once he even threw up his hands, as if surrendering to some unknown thing. Quinton climbed from the truck slowly, walking toward him, hoping to make heads or tails of the faraway look in Buck's eyes. As he got closer, Buck's anger boiled over. The first punch landed square on Quinton jaw, rattling his teeth. The next was the left cross to his right eye and the last was the uppercut that landed Q on his back. The battle came so quickly that Quinton hadn't had time to recover and fight back. He could only cover up and hope the damage wouldn't continue too long. Buck's knuckles split and the shooting pain in his hand left him a little less aggressive.

Quinton rose off the grown and yelled at his attacker.

"You stupid motherfucker, you feel better now? What you want to do, kill me?"

Buck turned his back as Quinton walked toward him. The force of the blow from being rushed from behind sent Buck face first in the dirt. Two grown men, worth millions of dollars, rolled around on the side of the road like children wrestling. Finally, out of breath, Quinton went back to the car. He climbed into the driver's seat and left Buck there, sitting on the side of the road.

Twenty minutes later the truck came back up, stopping just in front of Buck. Neither man had the courage to say anything for fear they might start fighting again. The rest stops were coming fewer and fewer with each mile. Quinton decided he could not wait any longer. He pulled into a restaurant, leaving Buck sitting angry in the car. Buck's impatience got the best of him. He wandered into the diner to find Quinton sitting at seat with a menu held to his face. The aroma of grilled onions carried Buck to the booth were he claimed his own menu. The anger was still fresh as the waitress took their order and left. Buck finally spoke, despite the fact that he had caused the pain that had left Quinton battered. He was still concerned about his well-being.

"You okay?" he asked with a slight smile on his face.

"Yeah, motherfucker, in your old age you hit like a girl. All ain't forgiven though. When I get home and Anissa sees my face, I'm gonna let her beat your ass."

Buck could not laugh at the threat. Anissa had been taking karate classes for years, and even in her pregnant state, Buck feared Anissa. She was the only chick that he knew had a black belt. The expression on Buck's face made Q laugh as much as his jaw would allow him. Together the duo ate and held a new reserved silence that something had transpired in the relationship. Q prayed they had gotten over the hurdle of betrayal Chaka caused. Buck hoped Q would understand when he disappeared for a while, that there was no way to be certain that the twins and even Q hadn't been a part of the drama to let him get locked down. He needed to put some space between the things he called his life and the drama from yesteryear.

Rolling back into the city had Buck contemplating if he was even going to go back to the places that once held so much joy and pain. Anything left behind he could definitely live with out. He clicked off the things he would be leaving: money, the drugs, the women, and even the cars. The only person he owed some explanation was Angela's mother, whom he had been visiting at least twice a week since he got out of jail. She had become his surrogate mother and confidante when things seemed to have burdened him to a point of no return. He did not want her to worry about him and he needed to tell her that he loved her. The thought of leaving her behind made his heart ache but he knew he had to go or he would only lose himself in more drama.

Quinton pulled into his driveway with Buck asleep in the passenger seat. He tapped him and told him to get the hell out. Anissa was waiting in the kitchen when Q swaggered through the door. The horrified look on her face made him wince and he began talking fast.

"Nissa, I'm okay. Everything is fine. It looks worse than it really is."

Before she could form the words, a tired Buck stormed into the kitchen with mere scraped skin missing from his nose, forehead, and chin.

"You simple motherfuckers been fighting each other," Anissa yelled. "I can't believe this shit! Y'all too grown to be rolling around in dirt, acting like y'all kids. I swear I'm going to call Brenda right now and tell her."

Brenda heard the commotion and walked down the steps to the fuss. Buck was stunned to see her there. He spun around to greet her when she began her own tirade. "What the hell happened to you?"

Anissa answered, like an all-knowing guru. "Every now and again these two get into some squabble over some dumb shit, mostly shit Chaka caused before his death. And what you're seeing is how they handle it: they kick the shit out of one another."

Both Buck and Quinton starred at Anissa in amazement. The laughter that filled the walls of the kitchen left the women standing dumbfounded. She had been more accurate than they would ever tell. Damage repaired, the couples went into the living room and began talking. Guilt was riding Buck as he shared his plan to just give it all up and walk away. Quinton understood, and confessed that he felt the same way. The lost expression on Brenda's face made Buck weary that he had not told her everything.

Sasha's funeral had left everyone wondering how this could happen to such a nice person. Buck had offered the usual support to her family when the arrangements were being made. He and Quinton had purchased all of the flowers for the service, being that she had been a good friend in the troubled times with Chaka's funeral. Dana told Buck everything Sasha confided in her. She revealed the disturbing news that Sasha had been hanging out with some cat name Pop. Something made Sasha think he was trying to harm Buck and his friends. She claimed she wanted to warn you but feared what would happen if she was wrong. When Sasha realized how dangerous he was, she decided to leave her house for a while.

Buck deduced that this Pop character must have gotten wind that Sasha was putting him down and did not like the idea, so he killed her.

The room was packed with friends, family, even coworkers from Sasha's job had come to offer support. Petra walked in the room donned in a black pantsuit and dark sunglasses. Flanked at her side were two men that seem vaguely familiar to Quinton. As they recognized one another Petra nodded to Quinton and he returned the gesture. But the nagging feeling wouldn't let him go. During the service, Quinton pulled Buck's coat to the duo sitting at Petra's elbow. Buck could not place them, he was too caught in the news that Dana had just shared.

Like a flash of lightning in the middle of the service, Quinton remembered where he knew them. The smirk on the face of the man to the right let Quinton know he was on target with his remembrance. There, in the service, Quinton would have lost his ever-loving mind if Dana had not started screaming at the top of her lungs. Pop, donned in a black Italian suit and shoes, sauntered into the church and took a seat opposite the deceased family. Though Dana had never met Pop, she knew it was him based on her sister's description. The chocolate face and green eyes with his ever-present spinning waves made Dana hysterical. She called him a murderer in front of everyone in the place. Decorum ended the moment she saw his face. In three and a half inch shoes, she tackled the man she believed responsible for Sasha's death. There was not going to be anything refined about her behavior. Dana was showing out to the fullest. Pop was stomped, kicked, spit on, and beaten until he ran from the church.

For Buck, the face was familiar to him as one of the flunkies hanging with Earl. Suddenly, Buck wondered if Earl had him kill Sasha as a message to him. Was Earl really trying to start a war, which would leave a lot of people victim to the bullshit? In an instant, the battled was necessary. He had to get out of this funeral and suit up for war. Quinton had been friends with Buck long enough to know his look of war and that look suggested they were about to leap headfirst into a killing spree. The twins must have known there would not be peace in New York, because they had arrived in time to attend Sasha's funeral and claim a body or two.

The last viewing of the body before they closed the casket took a great deal of time. The row that contained Buck and his crew finally got their chance to say goodbye, but none of the men returned to their seats. They headed straight for the exit. Outside, Quinton shared that the two guys at Petra's side were the men that had killed Chaka that day in the car. Buck and the twins looked at Quinton as if he had sprouted a second head.

Quinton revealed to his brothers in the game that he had been there. He had seen the faces of the killer's seconds before they put the bullet in Chaka's chest. He confessed that he never revealed the entire truth to anyone because he felt like a coward for not saving Chaka. He had failed and shame kept him from telling them the only other person beside the killers that knew he saw their faces was Anissa. The twins began to complete the others' thought as if they were one.

"You mean to tell me that Petra had Chaka killed?" Quinton nodded in the affirmative leaving Buck confused.

"You sure? That doesn't make sense. She was in love with that nigga."

Quinton was just as dumbfounded as they were but he had to say something. "I don't know why. I guess we're going to have to ask her."

Buck shook his head. "It doesn't matter the reason by me. They did me a favor." Buck decided he wanted to hear the reason but he would not participate in the revenge, no matter how the crew felt. Chaka had betrayed him and he wouldn't help avenge his death. The truth was Buck had been confused about so much but this he was adamant about. That's one war they will fight alone. Quinton opened and closed his mouth without saying a word to Buck. However, he felt the tingle building in his core. He knew that Chaka had betrayed Buck and even understood Bucks reaction. But he wouldn't accept Buck was walking away from this fight. Unwilling, to let things rest he turned to speak just as mourners exited the church.

When Petra stepped onto the sidewalk, she was alone. Her eyes were covered by the dark shades, hiding the look of scorn in her heart. Quinton went to her side and she looped her arm through his elbow and spoke softly. Incredible he thought to himself this bitch is really playing with my intelligence. The melody of her voice could have soothed a raging bull but it was having the opposite effect on Quinton. Quinton had drawn his gun. The smooth movement didn't stop Petra from close contact. She was not afraid either. Somewhere in her mind, she wanted him to kill her. It would end the guilt and the hate. Never slowing her step she guarded her words.

"I know you recognized my brothers," Petra said as she took a step. "Now you know the truth about who killed Chaka. The only thing you aren't certain about is why."

She said the words as if they were talking about a recipe, instead of the death of her children's father. They had somehow found themselves positioned between two benches and Petra took a seat first, waiting for

Quinton to understand that she was going to tell him everything he desperately needed to know. With reluctance, he claimed the seat furthest from her. Quinton resentment left him completely unaware of Bucks presence. He was fixated on Petra and the pain she had caused.

Buck called to Petra, forcing her to acknowledge he had followed them. Petra turned to the waiting arms of the only man she considered more special than the entire crew. From the moment Buck found out about her children, he sheltered them well. Uncle Jah, as the kids screamed every time he walked through the doors, was a goodtime uncle. He played on the floor or chased them around in the yard. If there was a movie for kids, he was the first to mention it and promised to take them or buy the video. Never once in their short lives had he broken a promise to them. After Chaka's death, he became the mentor they needed to get through the pain of missing a father. Before her mother came to help her out, Buck had taken the kids off her hands, prepared their lunches for school, and even helped them with homework. No matter how things turned out, she knew Buck would care for her children until his last breath. Not just because they were Chaka's but because he loved them genuinely. Somehow, they allowed him the chance to be a kid again. Quinton watched the exchange and understood that Buck had taken his stance; he was going to be on Petra's side, no matter the outcome. Quinton finally, understood the meaning of betrayal and disloyalty. Watching Buck holding Petra left Q bitter. Petra waited for Quinton to sit and when he finally did, she began to tell him the things that led up to Chaka's death.

Pop went to survey the bruises he suffered at the funeral for Sasha. He wasn't sure he hadn't killed her but his warped sense of responsibility sent him to the funeral parlor. Pop's impulsive behavior hadn't allowed him to think that maybe her family had known about him and the things he had been doing to her. He wanted to pretend he was just as much a mystery to her friends and family as she had been to his. But the truth was revealed in a matter of seconds of him walking into the church. He often wondered had anyone found the money he had stored in the apartment,

Eve had gone upstairs like he told her but he wasn't sure if she found the money. Ironically, he trusted the woman that Earl believed belonged to him. Surprisingly, he was awe-struck by her candor and her sex. Greed was clouding his judgment but Pop wouldn't see it until it was too late.

Earl had been sitting on the couch when Pop rushed in, heading straight into the bathroom. When Pop waltzed into the living room, he was stunned.

"What truck ran into you?" Earl teased.

Pop laughed. "Nothing I can't handle." Earl's sudden awareness that Pop was dressed up made him wonder where he had been. Pop explained that he went to the funeral of a chick he had been seeing a while ago. Earl had known today was Sasha's funeral and he couldn't help but put two and two together. "You were seeing Sasha?" Earl asked.

Pop looked over his shoulder. "Yeah, we use to do a little something sometimes," he answered, as if it was obvious.

"When was the last time you saw her?" Earl asked, almost out of breath.

"A day or two before she was murdered," Pop lied without looking up.

Earl now knew that Pop had beaten Sasha but he could not reveal how he knew just yet.

"Earl what's with all the questions?" Pop demanded.

"You saw Sasha the day she was killed. I know that for sure but what I ain't sure about is — did you kill her?"

Pop's wide eyes confirmed what Earl knew: Pop had beaten her, but why, he wondered. Earl was asking the questions he knew the answers. He watched for his reactions and barely listened to the answers.

Before Pop could recuperate, Earl asked why. Pop confessed without much prodding.

"I beat that ass for trying to diss me but I left her alive when I heard the police sirens."

There it was. Everything was clicking in place. Reasoning with himself, he realized Pop had been the nigga he saw leaving the building minutes before he entered.

Earl leaped from the couch.

"Nigga, you just too smart for your own good! There are too many bitches in the world to be sour because she ain't want your ass no more.

Now look, that bitch dead, Buck probably gunning for your ass, and I got drama of my own to fix. Not to mention the cops is probably after you too."

The yelling and disrespect was too much for Pop to accept. He began defending the nonsense he created.

"First off, nigga, I ain't giving a fuck about that broad. She gave up the information I needed to hit one of Buck's stash houses. Secondly, I put the shit in her apartment and when I went back to get it, she had changed her locks and was acting like she wasn't gonna let a nigga in to get his shit. Lastly, nigga, I am smart."

Pop moved the couch and revealed a trap door used to hide drugs and guns in the apartment. He hoisted both safes from the space and revealed the things he had stolen. In total, there were six neatly wrapped packages of brown coke and two guns. Pop was proud of his little caper.

Earl saw the look on Pop's face and went bananas.

"Nigga, do you realize that they are going to kill you slow when they track your ass down? Do you understand that these niggas might appear soft as butter but they were living this life long before you were a speck in your father's eye? A man that can afford to house all this pure shit could rid the world of your entire family," he hollered.

Pop was not respecting anything Earl was spitting. Instead, he spewed some shit of his own.

"Earl, you just jealous because I accomplished some shit you could only dream about."

The hysterical laughter that left Earl made Pop look curiously at his new nemesis.

"I didn't survive in this game by being disrespectful, or even impulsive. I have my share of bullshit and downfalls but more importantly, I am living. I wish you all the best but I am warning you, take your goodies and run."

The tables had turned and Pop was laughing.

"I ain't going no fucking where. If those niggas want me, I'm right here waiting. Me and my homies will clear out this whole motherfucking town if need be. That's the reason Ian sent us up here, anyway."

Earl smiled. "Okay young'un, do your thing."

As he left the apartment, he asked, "Have you seen any of your partners today?"

Earl did not wait for an answer, he just kept moving. Pop did not bother to read anything into the last remark. He knew them niggas were earners and were probably out chasing paper.

Petra debated on the best place to start.

"I met Chaka hanging out with Sasha at school, my second semester. We hit it off and before long we were spending a lot of time together. Despite the fact that he had business in the streets and I was supposed to be in class. I do not know what did it for me but I was in love. The first thing Chaka forced me to accept was that school had to be my first priority, especially when my grades came in and my average had dropped a whole grade point. He stayed away for a while and made me promise that I would do the right thing while he was gone. When he came back, everything was back to normal for us, except I was more in love for his sacrifice. The first year we were together, I got pregnant but I didn't have a clue as to how was I going to raise a child on a student's salary, let alone go to school. Chaka convinced me that he would do whatever it took to make life easy for me in order to continue with my education. Never once did he offer me marriage or a serious commitment, he just promised to provide. That was enough back then but as time went on, still there were no promises of commitment.

Junior was on the way and suddenly this bitch Eve becomes a real factor in my relationship. I mean, she was claiming my place in his life."

Quinton was hearing the bullshit but it didn't make much sense. He didn't give a fuck about the way they met or why they were together and the more she talked the more his anger mounted.

"Chaka was coming to me complaining that he wish he had done things differently, but he had to live with the shit he created. Then she claimed that she was pregnant or some shit. Things were only getting worst for us to be happy. They were living together and the last straw was hearing him tell her he would come home to her forever after that night." The fire in her eyes matched Quinton's as she barked.

"Hell no! I had played mistress long enough. I was either going to be the woman he would spend the rest of his life with or I would see him buried in the ground."

As the words left her mouth, spit followed.

"I didn't have the courage at first to see him dead but then he did the unthinkable. He had brought Eve a platinum chain with a medallion that declared her his baby girl. Well, that night I forced him to give it to Chanice and tossed his sorry ass out of my house. I was not going to step away from the pain he caused anymore." The transformation of the woman Petra had always appeared to be to the monster that had created this drama stunned Q and Buck.

"I could not smother the feeling of betrayal, hatred, or even jealousy! This woman had claimed the heart of the one man I would have died for."

Calmly, she told them exactly what she had done.

"That night, I put my children to sleep and we followed his cocky ass to the gas station where, at gunpoint, my brothers waited. . I knew that if I did not cast some shadows somewhere, you would have turned the world upside down trying to find the killers. But thank God, you didn't get caught up. By the time you arrived, you only saw the end results of the pain that motherfucker caused.

"My only regret is that I still feel the effects of his blatant disregard for the woman I was to him."

Quinton arm shook as he felt the weight of the gun in his sweating palm. Is this bitch serious he wondered mentally? She killed Chaka because he was having an affair the snort that left his nostrils stopped Petra for a brief second. Finally, she had a reaction now she would tell him everything.

"He cried to me at night about the lives he ruined. Because of it, I became his cheerleader, encouraging him to do the best things for the family. He confided in me about causing Buck to be locked up. He told me all his little insecurities and I held it all to my chest like a fucking therapist when the reality was, I was his woman, the mother of his children, and I was not good enough still."

As Petra spoke, the raw hurt was in her voice. It seemed to build into hate without a second beat.

"One of us had to go! Since she was just as much a victim as I was, he was the only solution."

Quinton sat speechless as Petra held her head ramrod straight. He attempted several times to speak but the words were stuck in his throat.

"Every now and again I wondered how I would have to tell you both before an innocent person suffered as a result of the murder. Nothing came to mind except hoping you would recognize my brothers if you saw them. The guilt has been riding me lately and this is my solution to ridding me of that useless feeling."

The tears stung the back of his eyes. The gun in his hand shook. Quinton found the words but did not know exactly how to make them come from his mouth. Buck moved first to embrace Petra and offer his support to her pain. She returned the gesture. Quinton was not forgiving. He chastised her for taking the most brutal course of action, when she could have just left him and moved on.

"You had other choices, Petra. Now look: your children will have to live without their father."

The feeling of betrayal took on a life of its own. He had respected her, even placed her on a pedestal. He was going to loose it. Buck had not seen the gun in Q's palm.

She cut Quinton off.

"And you will have to live without a friend, is that it? Chaka was going to have to make a decision soon enough about my children and that bitch. Well, I made the decision for us all. Don't expect me to apologize because I would do it again if given the chance."

The raise of her head and the strength of her words were stronger than Quinton could stand. Her voice hadn't waiver and his anger turned to blind rage. He imaged the shot before he heard it. He saw her face explode before he felt the warmth of the blood splatter all over him. He heard Buck cry out seconds before he felt the sting in his back. Silently he prayed before he accepted his decision. He wouldn't live with regrets or the disloyalty, he was going to take action and fuck the rest.

He could not fathom the words; he tried to understand how the love he witnessed between her and Chaka had been a smoldering inferno. His mind told him to run but the heavy burden in his heart kept him rooted to the bench. The confusion lifted and a trail of anger stood in its wake.

"How could you do something so wrong," he asked sounding like a deranged man.

The thread of sanity was unraveling in front of Bucks eyes. He leaned forward and stared at Quinton. The look was an attempt to make him surrender but the rushing tears and the empty stare made Buck and Petra nervous.

This is that moment the trio had lived to realize. Quinton raised the gun to her side. Through blurry tears, he waited for her to move or even scream, instead, she smiled.

Danny noticed a tall lanky man standing off to the distance. He looked out of place, not staring at anything in particular. Dave moved like a panther stalking its prey. The twins knew they had come this far they had to go forward. Buck was with Quinton they would kill anything in their path that posed a threat. However, the lanky character stood just far enough not to be noticed. He allowed his vision to concentrate on something else as not to give the victim a chance to see him coming.

Petra was daring Quinton to pull the trigger.

"Buck might have suffered jail, but Quinton you were supposed to pay the ultimate price," she spewed.

Quinton wanted to shut her up and the only way to do it was to shoot her. Buck listened as she weaved a tale for them both.

"Chaka was convinced Quinton wanted his position but lacked the courage it took to take it. Eventually, he reasoned Anissa would either take you away all together or force you to take the lead. He could not allow that to happen. The plan was to kill you but he did not have the heart."

A loud shot rang out, putting everyone on alert. The people still waiting out in front of the church ran back inside. There was a series of shots, fired in a rapid succession and a cloud of gray smoke. The acrid smell of gunpowder permeated the grounds. Buck, Petra, and Quinton sat stone still. Petra opened her mouth in horror as the sound escaped from her lungs. The rapid beat of her heart began to slow as she watched the blood leaking. Water slid from her eyes as she realized the pain was greater than any she had ever felt. Her head dropped forward as her eyes stared straight ahead. Suddenly the sound ended.

Nightfall had found each man alone with his private thoughts, wondering if going after Earl and his henchmen was even worth the bullets it would take to kill them.

Buck was ready to throw in the towel and move on from the drama when he saw the broad shoulders and wide-open strides marching toward him. Oblivious to the eyes that followed him, he watched the movement of his prey. Judging from the way he held his head, down to the lazy way his arms swung back and forth. Pop wasn't prepared for an attack. Finding Pop was easy especially after Buck realized Eve was up to her old tricks. Trading in or up, whichever suited her need. The truth was becoming clearer as he sat knowing the time had come to kill Pop. Too many things were left to chance. They had allowed their own loyalty, fears, and even greed to make them patsy's in another man's twisted war. From Chaka to Earl they were still running and gunning after the illusion of freedom. Realizing this only made Buck more determined to pull together any strings that threatened to rise up.

Some men were born to the paths they had chosen. Buck however, had decided he was forced on this path and he would die trying to destroy it. He promised himself that after he killed Pop, Earl was next. The thought was as simple as waking up the next morning. Finally, he decided that killing Eve was a string that had dangled long enough. The evil had awakened in Buck and he was making no effort to quiet it. He was feeding it as he imaged himself luring Pop toward his car.

Pop saw the movement and got suspicious tilting his head downward he recognized the imposing figure. Fear creped up Pops back as he accepted Earl was right. Backing out of the block was his only option. Pop was quickly assessing his chances. Buck leaped from the vehicle with death and destruction on his mind. Pop reasoned he could probably out run the burly bastard so he set out on his trek. Buck was on his heels, running low with his weapons drawn and ready to fire. Pop's arrogance had once again placed him in a lurch. He wished he had a better hold on his surrounding but decided he had one shot at living. Surprise was the only element he had left.

Buck had always been a smart killer. He knew that darkness covered his tracks but the sound of one wasted shot could claim a life that he had not aimed for. Pop was not nearly as savvy. He tugged at his weapon, hoping to slow his stalker down. The first shot rang out and told Buck exactly where Pop was heading. Buck marveled at how easy this would be. As Pop ran, he lost his bearings and instead of taking the ramp that led him to the alley, he was trapped off in the yard that led to a dead end.

Pop realized too late, that he was cornered. In an attempt to come down the ramp, he fired several shots. Buck was certain of his position but he was not sure if he could let himself relax before he killed his prey. No more shots rang out for too long. There it was; Pop's head slid from around the brick wall. Buck was elated. "Easy," Buck declared to himself seconds before he opened fire. The beast had come face to face with the lamb. Taking a deep breath, he leveled his gun at the sparkle of his gold rope chain and fired one shot.

Pop's body slumped against the wall with the impact of the first shot. The very words that Earl uttered haunted him as he took his last breath.

"Take your goodies and run."

Buck whispered in Pop's ear, "I know you stole from me and now I'm getting even with you for killing a friend."

The last shot was in Pops face to ensure a closed casket.

The last gasp was clear when Pop leaned awkwardly against the bricks. Buck did not look back. He sauntered away through the alleyway Pop had managed to miss, walking out on the other side as if he had not just been involved in the racket outside. The two cannon like sounds from Bucks gun had rattled windows and set off almost every car alarm on the block. Yet, he still calmly walked away as if out for a stroll. Time would not take care of the pain Earl caused. Buck had to see him and pass judgment on Earl's soul. The thought that Earl was a victim never occurred to Buck and he refused to let go of the hatred he harbored now that he was forced to face the next truth. Earl and Chaka had set him up from the word go.

Earl had witnessed the entire ordeal unfolding from a distance, but nothing compelled him to move to help Pop. The will to be great without work and effort had made Pop think he was invincible. The thought that he could waltz in and steal somebody's hard-earned fortune and cause tragedy in their lives, was enough for Earl to allow Pop his opportunity to rise or fall. He secretly wished that Pop had the balls it took to rise but seeing Buck coming out of the space unharmed, confirmed that Earl had backed the wrong horse once again.

Earls convinced himself he could kill Buck as he raised the gun at

Buck back. Sweat fell in his eyes as he tried desperately to take aim. Unconsciously he held his breath and placed his finger on the trigger. Fear gripped him as he dropped the gun in his lap. Frustration made him realized he still had too much loyalty to a false memory. The memory of teenage boys talking about girls, sharing Right On magazine or claiming the fly cars as they drove through the block. Sitting alone with his thoughts forced him to accept his convictions to this game. The last few weeks, Earl had to deal with the man he was and not the man he wished to be. He had set out to do so many great things now that Chaka was dead, but the ugly truth was that he lacked the ruthless manner it took to be The Man.

As for Eve, he was convinced that it did not matter where she was in life; she would always manage to go where the money was. The thought of Eve brought Earl to his knees. He wondered how one man could be so weak for a woman who did not have the least bit of concern for him.

The constant ringing of her phone made Eve angry. She hoped that whoever called had something important to say other than, "What you doing?" From "Hello" and hearing the husky baritone voice, Eve sat straight up in bed. He did not ask her to get up, he demanded that she get up and open the door. He would be there in ten minutes.

Eve leaped from her platform bed, scrambling about trying to bring order to her space. Quickly she changed from the ordinary T-shirt and sweatpants to his favorite teddy. She lit candles and sprayed herself with her favorite scent. To no avail, an hour had gone by and he did not show up.

Two hours into her dream the doorbell's annoying buzz woke her. She was really pissed that he could make her wait this long. She contemplated not letting him in at all. She thought that would make him think twice about keeping her waiting around. Slowly she opened the door without asking any questions and was astonished to find Earl on the other side. He pushed past her and strolled in as if he had been invited. *The nerve*, she thought and took her frustration to him vigorously.

"What do you want, Earl?" she asked with more attitude than called for.

Earl waited for Eve to look in his direction before he spoke to her. "How long did you think he was going to be your secret? Did you really think I wouldn't figure out that you were fucking him too?" he yelled at the top of his lungs.

Eve tried her best to look bored by his one-man act but she feared that he might really know her secret. Eve had become good at bluffing but decided Earl did not matter anymore. Folding her arms she began slow and exaggerated,

"You come up in here, yelling about the man I'm fucking but the truth is it isn't any of your business."

As long as Earl was not interrupting, Eve thought she was telling him how it was going down.

"You have always been second fiddle. It shouldn't bother you now. Why are you angry? Is it because Pop is a soldier in the General's army?"

There he had suspected the truth. Eve was indeed fucking Pop and she was proud of her affair. Earl felt the anger boil over inside him and felt helpless to stop it.

Eve saw the change in Earl's demeanor and had the right sense to be afraid. Inches from her, he wrapped his hands around her neck, squeezing until he felt her going limp. She clawed at his hands, hoping they would let up and give her some air. No relief came—Eve was giving up when Earl heard the slight whimper and let her go. She dropped to the floor on all fours like a sack, coughing and trying to catch her breath. With the immediate intake of oxygen, Eve had began to change back to her normal rosy coloring.

She crawled away from the door over to an overstuffed chair and climbed into the seat, curled up in a ball. Earl did not leave. He sat across from her and delivered the news of Pop's demise. She refused to believe him at first, but something in his smirk told her all she needed to know. Although he released her, she still felt as if she was strangling. The pasty look returned to her face and Earl laughed.

"Don't look so happy to be stuck with me," he taunted.

Eve whispered the words "Fuck you" despite the burning in her throat and lowered her head to cry.

"Why did you kill him over me? Shit, you left me for dead in North Carolina. Why did you do this?" She pleaded with him for answers.

"First, you simple bitch, I didn't do shit to him. Buck got hold of him for stealing some valuables from his home, not to mention Pop killed Sasha," Earl gloated.

Eve's emotions were all over the place. She could not accept that yet another man that promised to be there for her had been killed.

"Earl, you're going to get yours! That I am sure of. No way are the twins, Quinton, and Buck going to let you walk away from the shit you set in motion. If, by some sheer miracle, they let your ass live, Ian is going to come for you with both barrels."

Earl had long ago accepted his fate in the hotel room, but he would not allow her to see his fear.

"Besides, you simple bastard, I know for a fact it wasn't Pop that killed Sasha."

Earl felt like ice water had been poured in his veins. His hands were clammy and his eyes glazed over. He slowly spun back to her with fire in his eyes, asking her to repeat what she said. The look on Eve's face said she knew that he actually shot Sasha.

"Pop may have beaten her near death, but it was someone else that put the bullet in her skull."

Nonchalantly, Earl spoke. "Whatever you think you know, bitch, you better keep to yourself. It don't much matter anyway, 'cause I figured your ass is about dead too." He leaned close to her and slapped her in the mouth as a warning. Earl left the house without a backward glance at the imp that still seemed to be the cause of most of his drama.

"You like hitting women, you bitch, but I didn't see you hitting them niggas when they were herbin' you. Now you a fucking tough guy! I wish I could be there when they catch up with you – you punk-ass motherfucker!"

The first law of nature was self-preservation. There was no way in hell Earl was going to lay down and die. He felt like a predator in the middle of an unknown land, waiting for someone to pick him off. As he hiked away from Eve's door, his mind raced over all the time he wasted. His heart pounded with each step alerting him that danger was definitely in the air. If the twins were waiting for him to return, right now he was a sitting duck. Vulnerable in every sense of the word, Earl palmed his .44 magnum and prayed that the police were not on the prowl. A cat leaped from a nearby porch, almost making Earl jump off the ground. Seconds before he fired a shot he realized it was just a feline scurrying across his path. That had triggered something in him. He was done being afraid. The night's air had made him brave. He reasoned that if he died tonight, it would not matter to anyone, so he might as well fight to live.

The Black Lincoln sat four houses away from his home. He recognized every car on the block; except it. That, he figured, was where the twins must have sat. He did not slow his strides. Using all his senses, he marched at an angle to the car to see the twins sleeping. The headlights just inches away turned on startling Earl from any further action. The beams did not move the occupants of the Lincoln, but it forced Earl to his home.

Pacing back and forth, Earl chastised himself for not taking Buck's life when he had the chance, and now he was even angrier that he could have made a big mistake by trying to kill the twins in front of his home. He knew he had better get his priorities straight or he would perish and die. Lying in the darkness, Earl realized his memories and loyalty were a major hindrance to his next breath. The proof that he was a target sat just inches from his home. Only strength could get him to the next level of this game. Out numbered, Earl cleared his mind and made a plan. Peering through the blinds he noticed the car was no longer there. More brazen he opened the window for a better glimpse at the area. The twins had gone he reasoned as he began the next phase of his plan.

The dawning of a new day brought on new convictions. The facts were that Earl could eliminate his mishaps by getting rid of some dead weight. Three of the six men Ian had sent to New York were still alive and Earl did not want to be responsible for their well-being. They were the first order of business. It was time to send them home. Next, he planned to deal with Ian and his unreal demands on an unseen fortune. The best way to deal with the likes of a man like Ian was make them offers that they could not refuse. Earl had intended to do just that in person. Next, he was going to see the twins wherever they were and either he was going to buy his freedom from this nasty business or he was going to blast his way from the bullshit. He would be free from running or he would be dead.

Lastly, he had to deal with Eve. She had become a problem and her breathing might cause him his life, if he managed to get out from under all the rest of his circumstances. He could not have her blackmailing him over Sasha's murder.

Three men marched in the airport at La Guardia, looking fashionable in their NY clothes, pseudo-NY swagger and richer than when they arrived. They were heading home with laced pockets and lies to tell about the Big Apple. Earl, however, decided he was going to drive to see his favorite cousin. Six hours after he hit the highway Earl pulled up in Ian's circular driveway. It had been his safe haven since Ian starting putting up million-dollar numbers. Earl actually believed Ian had bigger ideas of grandeur than he did, but none of that mattered. Ian's girlfriend opened the door and headed to her car as Earl walked up to knock. She pointed in the house and said, "He's in the basement — go on in." Earl looked around to discover Ian was alone in the house. That made for a better discussion.

Although, Pop stole the product from Buck, Earl was going to use it to his advantage. Four of the six bundles were in a duffle bag he found as he sauntered through the house. Earl had come ready for battle. Hidden underneath the colorful sweater was a bulletproof vest, and the two Magnums holstered at his side barely hidden by the short leather jacket. Ian was watching television when he noticed Earl coming down the steps. The fake smile made Earl angry. Instead of warm greetings, Earl got down to the reason he was there.

"As payment for your loan, I personally came here to give you this. It should settle our debt but if it doesn't, we can talk." Earl slid the duffel bag across the floor at his cousin. The smile on Ian's face broadened; he could barely contain his excitement. Desperately he tried to control the muscles in his face, but to no avail. His eyes danced and he nodded along with his laughter. By the time, he finished drooling, Earl had slid both guns into his palms with both hands behind his back.

Ian looked from Earl to the contents in the bag. With a serious face, he told Earl, "Bring me four or five more packs like this, and were even."

The devil emerged from Earl as he spoke.

"Cousin, I'm really sorry you said that because what you have there is all I'm offering."

The wide grin slowly faded from Ian's face as he stared, confused. Suddenly the light had gone on. Ian stood up from the chair only to come face to face with Earl's midnight black firepower.

Ian quickly reclaimed his seat and started talking. The stuttering was enough to make Earl cry with laughter but the nervous twitch in his lips and the constant blinking of his eyes confirmed that Ian was still playing baller and shot caller.

"This is good enough, don't worry. This'll do."

Earl knew that Ian had probably shit his drawers but he understood now that Earl was not to be fucked with. Going home would be the hardest thing he had done but he had to face the pressure he had left behind.

The ride home was more about Earl's unwillingness to let go of a vendetta that made no sense. It was about getting even with the ghost of Chaka and accepting he could never get even with Chaka. For two states, Earl tried to answer was it all worth it? Finally, just outside of the toll to New York he decided it had been. The money was worth it, the countless women that existed for his pleasure. The chance at succeeding at the one thing he never dreamed he wanted to do was worth the drama that unfolded. A wide grin etched across his face as he decided he could rise above the Baker Boys 5. All needed was the right amount of money. He would rock them to sleep. Pay for his freedom, make them believe they had won and then kill them all.

The tenants in Earl's building had moved without much prompting. The first signs of the coming demolition work convinced them that the absentee landlord was a snake. He hadn't given them any notice on his intentions to tear down the property. For months, the rent had gone un-collected but the tenants didn't complain. Earl was known for his disap-pearances. However, he would come back expecting every nickel owed from the time he was gone.

The boards had been in place for weeks. The windows were re-moved from the frames. The decorative doors where replaced with steel and a replica of the chains the Marshals used to evict occupants. Furnish-ings were tossed in the rented dumpster as the fake construction crew cleared out the place. The neighbors passing didn't give a second glance to the crew knowing that the owner of the place hadn't been around for months. They figured either he'd sold the property or the city had condemned it.

Buck watched from the concrete mixing machine. Laughing at his own genius until his sides hurt. The plan was to level Earl's home but instead they were illegally, confiscating it and leveling him with the bare shell. The floors had been ripped up and the walls were nothing but exposed beams and hollow brick. All the clothes that had been discovered were neatly collected and delivered anonymously to the local thrift store. The gators, the fine watches, nice minks, silk shirt, and tailored suits were going to grace the backs of those in need. The pennies they would pay to look good made Buck feel like he was giving back to the community on Earl's dime. The Italian couch was sitting along the curb when some local crackheads picked it up and carted it off. The sight of the huge couch on two shopping carts rolling down the hill would have caused someone to talk shit but this was the 'hood.

Lounging back in the cut the crew laughed as they watched the crackheads stop passerbys trying to sell the treasure they had just acquired. Tears sprang from Dave and Danny's eyes as they marveled at Buck's commitment at getting even. Each man would pay to see Earl's face the moment he realized what had happened to his home.

The heat had forced people outside. Kids were running about laughing and having a good time when they saw the car. The black Jaguar rolled into the block as if it were apart of the street. Its dark tint hid the driver but the loud bass of the music caught their attention. The slow roll of the chrome rims were shining against the smooth tires. Earl had brought the car as his coming home gift to himself. During his absence, he'd missed the comforts of his luxuries and the Jag put him in the right frame of mind. Short of yelling, *I'm back motherfuckers,* he sat back and grinned at the success he achieved in such small time. Pulling into the first empty parking space, he sat bobbing his head to the sounds of Wu-tang. He wasn't paying attention to his surrounding, he was too busy living in the moment of his achievement.

Finally, after a few moments the neighbors recognized Earl. "Astounding," Ms. Harding laughed as she watched the slow fluid motion of the young man she had thought was dead. The people sitting in front of her door playing cards and dominoes were just as shocked to see him come out of the car.

Earl knew that the car would cause whispers but the angry glares he received were uncalled for he thought. Still he hadn't noticed that his home was merely a structure. Instead of allowing the jealous faces of his neighbors to bother him, he raised his hand in an attempt to say hello. He walked past all the homes he had been passing for years before he realized the beautiful home he had remodel and invested in was gone. "What the fuck," he whispered as he looked at the two homes that sat on either side of his property. The look on his face was confusion and then turned into angry frustration.

The bellow that escaped his voice left the neighbors snickering. "Yeah, they thought your shit was repossessed by the city," one of the card players whispered. Earl turned toward the stoop where the people were sitting and headed in their direction. Mr. Harding stepped off the stoop just as Earl stomped on the pavement.

"What the fuck," he demanded as if they owed him an explanation. Mr. Harding shrugged his shoulders and offered what he knew. Earl couldn't believe this shit. He had come home to a shell of what he called home. Tracing his steps back to his structure, he lost his mind. "I'm gonna kill them bitches," he yelled. As he sat in the car, he didn't feel the same pride for the vehicle as he banged on the steering wheel and allowed his tears to flow. Tears of anger and frustration clouded his judgment as he tried to make sense of the bullshit. Buck, Dave, Danny, and Quinton were walking corpses he thought. Recklessly, he pulled away from the curb heading toward the real estate agency that had been apart of the Baker Boys 5 portfolio.

The neighbors watched in amusement as the Jaguar left the block. They laughed and told jokes all night thinking that Earl was crazy for coming back here knowing he was a wanted man.

Dusk was setting in as he waited, hoping one of them would come out of the agency. So far he had been there for more than two hours and the door hadn't even opened let alone for him to know who was inside. Earl pulled his gun from beneath the hidden compartment in the door panel and leaped out. Stomping across traffic he had decided he was going to wait to get at these niggas. Either they would die or he would but he was prepared.

The door swung open as Earl raised the gun at the pretty young woman sitting at the receptionist desk.

"Shshsh," he whispered as she began, "May I help you."

"There is no money here on the premises. The safe is lock and I just work here. Please don't kill me," she begged.

"Are they here," he demanded.

"Yes, Mr. Holding is here in his office," she answered nervously.

Earl placed the gun to the forehead of the reception and ordered her to get up. Just as she stood her bladder gave up. She walked toward the office silently praying that the stranger wouldn't kill her.

Buck was sitting at his desk when he heard the knock. Slowly he turned as the door opened. The fear in the receptionist wide eyes was a testament to her fate. *Poof, Poof,* was barely a whisper as the bullets entered through her back and she fell forward. Earl was just inches from being inside Buck's office when the young woman hit the floor. The hate in Buck's eyes radiated as the contempt oozed from Earl's eyes. Earl wanted to see fear. He reasoned he wanted Buck to beg for his life especially see his ass was as good as dead anyway. The *Poof* hissed again from the gun just as Buck fell backwards with his hand covering his stomach. In Earl's excitement or confusion he didn't fire a second shot. He turned and walked away. Back in the safety of his car he laughed.

"I killed you – you stupid motherfucker! After all this time, I finally killed your slow ass. Yes," he hollered as he pumped his fist in the air.

Buck growled as he felt the pain in the pit of his stomach. He had to trip the alarm and alert the alarm company he needed an ambulance before he passed out again. Struggling to get to his feet was harder than it looked. Slowly he crawled until he was able to pull the handle of the hidden safe beneath his desk.

The silent alarm had done its job but Buck wasn't sure he would live to receive the help that they were sending. The room spun around him as he lay motionless on the floor. The darkness took over as his eyes drifted closed and he struggled to catch his breath. He desperately tried to hear the sounds of the ambulance, but instead he heard the sounds of his ragged breathing.

Fifteen minutes later the police arrived and found the reception faced down in blood covering the plush carpet. The attendants from the ambulance found Buck lying face up in blood just inches from the woman.

The EMT yelled, "This one is breathing," as he alerted his partner that was standing back with the small defibrillator in his hand....

Melodrama's Upcoming Catalog

OCTOBER 15, 2007
LIEF AFTER WIFEY By **KIKI SWINSON**

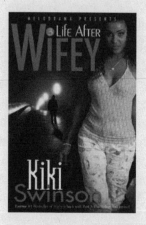

DECEMBER 15, 2007
24/7 HISTRESS By **CRYSTAL LACEY WINSLOW**

UNCORRECTED PROOF
OCTOBER 1, 2007
A novel by
JACKI SIMMONS
THE MADAM

Guess who's inside of her little black book...

Chapter 1

The Problem

Jade wondered if the fall from the fifth-floor window would be enough to kill her.

As she glanced across the street and watched the early afternoon sun glint off the Metro-Life building, the wheels of her mind turned faster and faster, hoping she could think her way out of this one. Nervously, she crossed and uncrossed her legs, aware that he was watching every move she made. This had to be some kind of a joke. Any minute now, Ashton was going to come out and tell her she'd been *Punk'd*.

She drew her face away from the window and focused on the gun aimed at her head. Reality had sunk in long ago and despite all they had been through, she knew he wouldn't hesitate to pull the trigger. Her mind was made of mush and all thoughts had fled her mind except that of her own survival. She figured sprinting to the door was out of the question because a bullet could definitely travel faster than she could. So fear kept her in the seat, hoping that this wouldn't take a turn for the worse.

Clearing her throat, Jade said, "This was not what I had in mind when you said you wanted to talk."

"You know, one of the reasons I hired you is because of how you think. You're hardheaded, Jade. You don't like to take no for an answer.

You do only what benefits you in the end. Well, this is a different type of situation. I need you to do something that will benefit me. I knew this was the only way to get your attention." The loaded .45 in her face had most definitely captured her attention.

Alphonse Stanley, like Jade, was not used to hearing the word "no." He had pulled himself up by the bootstraps to become a driving force in the world of entertainment. He and his partner, Tony Vice, had been struggling to book major acts for popular venues. They began to push the envelope in order to get appearances for musicians in places that were unheard of. Stanley and Vice had been one of the first to book a rap artist in Japan. Now, almost thirty years later, Vice having died of cancer nearly ten years earlier, the empire was untouchable.

They dominated the industry, supplying agents for every form of entertainment; literary, sports, music, acting, comedy; it was a one-stop shop for every celebrity looking for an agent. Stanley had purchased the Greenway Building on 32nd Street to house his fleet. Each division had its own floor and about ten agents; Stanley occupied the top floor, along with the sports agents. Jade herself had been with the company's music division for the past five years and had quite a few celebs under her belt. She was, in fact, the top agent at Stanley and Vice, bringing in more money than the two bottom agents put together. And now that the shit Stanley put up with over the years had piled up and was hitting the fan, he wanted Jade to clean it up.

The office wall behind her was made of glass, reminding everyone that the boss was always watching. Usually, the floor was abuzz with action but not a soul had passed by in the half hour she'd been here. Jade shifted her eyes from the gun to his face and back to the gun. She spoke to the weapon.

"Is this at all necessary? Aren't you being a little irrational?"

"I'm not being irrational. You need to understand, Jade, that this is strictly business. I take my business very seriously."

She folded her hands, determined to keep her cool. "I noticed. You're threatening to kill me."

"I didn't threaten you. I gave you a business proposition. Which will not be turned down."

His exact words were, "Do it or I'll kill you." That surely sounded like a threat to her.

"A business proposition has two ends. Apparently, I have no say in this matter. And why—"

"Questioning my decision is only going to make his harder for the both of us. I need this money. The company needs this money. You're the best agent I have. You're smart, beautiful, business-minded. I can't afford to have you say no, and I can't afford to have to look for anyone else who can do this."

Jade sighed and studied her fingernails. "What happened to downsizing? What's wrong with that? We can afford to drop the dead weight."

Stanley appeared to be comfortable with the conversation at hand as he shifted in his seat, the gun still trained on Jade. "That's where you're wrong. We *can't* afford to drop any dead weight. If anyone else leaves and takes their multi-million-dollar wallets with them, we'll be too far under to dig ourselves out."

"You want me to perform an illegal service if I value my life. You want me to run a whorehouse."

"You're putting words in my mouth."

"Am I?"

"When did you hear the words 'whorehouse' leave my lips?"

Was he kidding? This *had* to be a joke. Jade was tempted to stand up and slap him. The gun made the thought remain a temptation, not an action.

"I can't do that."

"I didn't ask you whether or not you could do it. I gave you an either or. *Either* you do *or* you die."

"You're going to kill me if you don't get your way? This is outrageous. Blackmail is above you."

He laughed, a rumbling sound that rose from deep in his chest. He waved the gun. "I like how you put that. Blackmail. Well, for lack of a better term, yes."

Jade shook her head and stood to leave, straightening her suit.

The gun followed her. "One more step and I will level you, Jade. Aren't we supposed to be a team? There's no 'I' in team. I can't do this alone."

Jade shook her head again, slinging her purse over her shoulder. "Well, there ain't no 'we', either. I'm not doing this."

"We can drag this out as long as you'd like. But the only way you leave this room is working overtime for me," he cocked the gun, "or dead. Your choice."

"You're threatening to kill me for something I have nothing to do with. I'm not getting my hands tied up in this," Jade shouted. "This is your shit, you got yourself into it, and you need to get yourself out!" She turned her back and swung the door open.

Stanley stood up. "I am very serious about this. I can't bail without you."

She knew he was. Her eyes closed and she bowed her head, biting down on her bottom lip. Silently, Jade laid her cards out on the table. Stanley had no problem killing her. As tempting as the offer was, she wondered if it was worth the risks. Before she opened her eyes she made a fly-by-the-pants decision, regretting it instantly but knowing it would save her life.

Jade took a deep breath before opening her eyes and turning back around to face him. "Would it be too much to ask that you not point that gun at me?"

"Do we have a deal?"

"Would you lower the gun?"

"Do we have a deal?"

The air was thick with silence and neither of them blinked during the battle of wills. He was going to get what he wanted whether she liked it or not.

"Yes."

He lowered the gun, not before gesturing with it. "Sit down."

Jade shut the door and sat back down, crossing her legs again and folding her hands. She felt completely helpless. In any other situation she was behind the desk pointing the figurative gun, making the threats. Now the tables were turned and he had her trapped in a vise grip. She hated not being the one with power.

Stanley kicked his feet up, sliding a cherrywood box closer to himself. He lifted out a cigar and put it under his nose, savoring the aroma. Producing a cutter from inside his jacket, he clipped the end and lit it. Taking a few deep puffs, he blew the smoke in her direction. She turned her head away and the smoke curled toward the ceiling.

"Now, in your rush to turn me down, we never got to discuss the perks."

She snorted. "I wasn't sure there were any."

"For starters, a salary increase."

"How high?"

"Double; maybe triple, in time."

She raised an eyebrow. She was already bringing home numbers high in the six-figure bracket; a couple of extra dollars wouldn't hurt. "And legalities?"

He turned up his face and waved the cigar, the smoke dancing away. "Don't worry about that."

"I am worried about it."

"Don't be."

She exhaled quietly, knowing she would have time to weigh pros and cons later. "Well, then, we need to talk numbers. Exactly how many people need to be involved?"

"Six, maybe seven. If it works out as well as I'm anticipating, you can expand."

He had the entire thing thought out before she even came in the room. She was a pawn in a chess game he had already figured out how to win. "What's your part in this?"

"They take a third and I take the rest, to be put into the company." He clasped his hands together and aimed them at her. "You get to live."

"So let me get this straight. These girls are going to make money on my watch, which you take and use to save yourself from going under?"

"You pick up quick."

Her head was spinning. She rubbed her temples. This was outrageous. "And that's all?"

"That's all."

It was a long while before she answered. "Fine."

"Good. And before you go, stop making it sound like I'm doing this for myself. It's for the best. For everyone. You work here, don't you? You like what you do, right? So, think of it as taking one for the team." He batted at an imaginary pitch.

Jade stared at him blankly.

"I'm glad we could work this out. You'll be hearing from me." Standing, Stanley waited for Jade to do the same. He stretched his arm out in front of him, indicating her dismissal. He was smiling as if nothing had ever happened.

Jade pulled the door shut behind her. She nodded and smiled casually as she passed her coworkers in the hall, very aware that Stanley was still watching her through the glass walls of his office. At the elevator, she chanced a glance backwards. As she expected, he was watching her. Like fucking Santa Claus. *He sees you when you're sleeping, he knows when you're awake.* Exiting the building through the downstairs garage, Jade was fuming as she started up her car. She flashed her ID and drove outside, where it was five lights later that her heart finally slowed to a normal pace. Her fingers were shaking as she handled the steering wheel.

She needed to talk to someone who would understand what was going on, and more importantly, help her get herself together. The only way she could turn down the proposition Stanley had made would be to leave the country and disappear. Since she wasn't planning on giving up her entire life at the drop of a dime, she knew that her only option was to go along with this outrageous idea.

Even as the words ran through her brain, Jade was having a hard time convincing herself. Jade had stumbled into something that was much bigger than she. But the go-getter inside her was determined to make it work to her advantage.

The purse skidded across the hall table and hit the floor when it left Jade's hands. She sucked her teeth and locked her door behind her. She kicked the purse as she walked past, letting her hair down with a flick of her wrist. Kicking off her heels, she shrugged out of her suit jacket and laid it on the table, promising herself to come back for it and the purse later. Right now she needed to think. Quitting smoking five months earlier was a decision that returned to bite her in the ass, now that she needed a cigarette. A relaxing drink was the next best step.

"Baby?"

Jade jumped out of her skin and whirled around, ready to fight. She caught sight of the speaker and her heart fell back into its place.

"What the hell are you doing here? You scared the shit out of me."

Cameron noticed. He hadn't seen her in over week and this was not the response he was expecting. He saw how tight her body was and immediately responded to his woman's needs. His big hands made their way to her shoulders. "What happened?"

She didn't skip a beat as she replied, "Long day."

His fingers worked a kink out of her neck. "Oh yeah? Tell me about it."

Her eyes opened slowly. Was that a question or a statement? She went with the most vague answer she could find. "I'm just glad I'm home."

Cameron seemed satisfied as he walked her into the living room. He and Jade had been together for seven years and Jade felt as though he was her soulmate. He was her equivalent, only in the male form. They had been engaged since Christmas and no other man had ever made her happier. Though her schedule as an agent and his as an A-List event planner kept them apart sometimes weeks at a time, they spoke every day.

"You want to talk about it?" He laid her down on the couch and slid her stockings off.

Sure, why not? Let's see, where do I begin? Well, my boss threatened to kill me today after blackmailing me into helping him get the company out of debt. I have no choice but to do what he says or else you'll never see me again. Ain't that something? "Not really," she answered.

"Stay there. I'll be right back." She didn't nod, just watched through half-open eyes as he jogged into the kitchen. He was a good man, a man that didn't deserve the hailstorm of shit that was about to come crashing down on his head. Her eyes were closed when he returned. Something cold touched her hand.

"Chardonnay. Relax." He put the bottle on the floor next to the couch.

Jade thanked him and lifted the drink to her lips. She didn't open her eyes, only slowly sipped her wine and thought.

He threatened her life. She wasn't able to move past that point, it was stuck in her mind and every time she thought she could let it go, it popped back up. He was serious about this.

Of course, she could go to the police. But she knew the outcome. He wasn't treating this like a game and she didn't expect him to. There were serious decisions to make here, decisions to be weighed out.

One massive pro was the money. It wasn't that she really needed it; her salary gave her plenty of flexibility and comfort, but she was not going to shake a stick at a little more.

If she looked on the bright side of this thing, she'd be rich and she'd be in. Not that she didn't also have status but much like the money, a little more couldn't hurt. For a few minutes, the plan was perfect. As the liquor opened her up and mellowed her out, and Cameron's hands continued to work their magic, her mind wandered into the specifics: namely, the cons.

What he was asking her to do was enough for a lengthy prison sentence. It wasn't her conscience that was bothering her; it was her logic. She saw right through him. He was a moneymaker and he was using her as an amenity. He expected her to keep his clients happy. He didn't care how she did it, only that it got done. The offer wasn't anything to turn her nose up at but the severance package left much to be desired.

What if the money wasn't what he told her it would be? What if she couldn't build up a client list? Who could she trust beside herself? What if it all fell apart? The biggest "what if" was rubbing her feet at that very moment.

She loved Cameron with all she had. They had been together since the day she graduated college. He wanted her to be his wife, she knew, and he would do anything she asked. She also knew if she did this, she would be putting him through hell, but she didn't have much of a choice. It was either that or he could kiss his woman goodbye.

She knew her man. If she told Cam that she had been threatened, he'd be on the next thing smoking to the police station. She didn't want to hurt him. Yet at the same time, she figured that what he didn't know wouldn't kill him.

"You sure you don't want to talk about it?"

Jade opened her eyes. He had interrupted her train of thought. "What?"

He pointed at her. "Whatever you're thinking about is tearing up your face."

Because I'm contemplating life and death, baby. She lifted a hand to her cheek.

"That bad? I must be tired."

"You look it."

She playfully kicked him. "Oh thanks. I feel so much better."

He smiled at her and caught her foot. "You're sexy anyway," he said, one hand traveling up her leg.

She smiled when he said that. He returned the sentiment and took it as a sign. Jade sat her glass on the floor and lifted her hips. Cam pulled down her skirt and panties in one motion. Flipping her hair over her shoulder she unbuttoned her shirt. He was already undressed by the time she did so. She tossed her clothes on the floor and climbed onto his lap, biting hard on her lip as she lowered herself onto him.

Jade scratched his chest with one hand, the other softly holding the back of his head. Cam held on to her hips as she rose and fell on top of him. "I missed you baby," he breathed into her ear. "I missed you so much." He licked her ear then, sending a chill up her spine. Jade moaned softly, biting his neck as gently as she could.

Cameron lifted his hands from her hips and unsnapped her bra. Jade leaned back and slid it off her arms without breaking the rhythm. She kept up the ride as he took one of her small breasts into his mouth. While he massaged and sucked, she continued to moan, digging her nails into his shoulders. Every move they both made turned each other on more and more until both of them were a melted, sweaty mess in the middle of the couch.

Jade climbed off Cam and lay back, panting hard. He was breathing hard as well, legs sticky from their exertion. He looked over at Jade and smiled. She returned the smile. They smiled at each other for a long while.

Some inside joke brought on by their eye contact caused them to both laugh aloud. He reached down and grabbed the bottle of wine. Jade held out her glass for a refill. Just when she needed him, he always delivered. She loved her some Cam.

That was all she wanted, just to forget every other moment. After the day she had, nothing felt better than to clear her mind of everything except her own pleasure.

Two hours later found Jade sitting back on the couch, brooding, Cameron's head in her lap. They'd made love again, on the floor this time, long and slow. He'd been sleeping like a baby since. Since Jade couldn't remember the last time she felt so good, she put off thinking about her situation until just now.

She looked down and rubbed his cheek. He didn't stir so she lifted his head and replaced her lap with a pillow. Tip-toeing away, she lifted the phone out of the cradle and went into her bedroom with it, shutting the door behind her.

"*You have reached Marcella Jenkins. I'm either on the phone or away from my desk. Please leave a detailed message and I will return your call as soon as possible. Thank you.*"

Jade rolled her eyes and left her message. "Call me. It's important." She clicked off and let the phone fall back to the bed, knowing it would be a matter of seconds before Marcella called her back. She was right.

"What happened?"

"I have a problem."

In her office across town, the late afternoon sun streamed through her windows and bathed her office a bright red. Marcella leaned back and lifted her feet onto her desk. She and Jade had been best friends since high school. Marcella was co-owner of Shooting Stars, an agency for aspiring models. "Yeah?"

"Well, apparently he's seconds away from filing chapter eleven. The company is in serious debt."

"How much?"

"Three-and-a-half million dollars."

Marcella's feet fell off the desk. "*What*? What's going on over there?"

"We need to upgrade. He said his artists are leaving and taking their money with them. So he wants me to persuade them to stick around."

"And how do you plan to do that?"

"I don't. He planned it already."

"What's on his mind?"

Jade repeated the conversation she'd had with Stanley earlier in the day. Marcella listened closely, stopping Jade every so often to make sure she understood. Marcella shook her head in disbelief when it was over. She herself knew Stanley had been bleeding money, but to use Jade as a bandage was unthinkable.

"So what are you going to do?"

The line was silent for a while. Marcella thought she'd hung up.

"Jade?"

"I'm here."

"What are you going to do?" she repeated.

Another long silence. Then she heard Jade sigh.

"I don't have much of a choice."

He saw her coming from down the hall. As she stormed in his direction, her full-length suede coat billowed around her and her matching boots stamped out an angry rhythm. If he squinted one eye and gave her white hair, she really could have passed for Storm of the *X-Men*. He smiled at the look on her face, amused by her anger. He already knew why she was here; he was well aware of how close she was with Jade. Their conversation had undoubtedly made its way to Marcella's ears.

Marcella flung his door open and filled the room with her presence. He had to hand it to her. The woman knew how to make an entrance. And she was such a beautiful vision, such a lady, so classy—

"You filthy piece of shit," she spat.

He pretended to be unfazed. "Good morning, Ms. Jenkins. It's lovely to see you again."

Marcella pointed at him. "Don't play games with me, you son of a bitch. You know why I'm here."

"I'm quite sure I don't."

"I know what's going on. You know you're a dog for what you're doing to her."

He clasped his hands together and pointed both indexes back at her. "I don't think that's any of your business."

"It damn well is. She is my business."

A nasty visual crossed his mind. He brushed it away. "Are you here to threaten me? Because I'm not moved."

"I'm not here to threaten you. I'm here to get all in your ass. I got my eyes on you, you bastard."

He shifted in his seat and looked past her, out the glass wall. "Marcella, if we're quite finished here, I think you should leave."

She narrowed her eyes to snakelike slits and breathed venom into her next words. "You better kill me if you want me to keep my mouth shut. Because there is no way in red hell you're going to make her go through with this." She turned to exit in a blaze of anger. As her hand touched the door, he called out to her.

"Ah, Marcella."

She turned.

"You had better keep your mouth shut."

She snickered. "For what?"

"Because if you don't, I *will* kill you."

UNCORRECTED PROOF
DECEMBER 1, 2007
A novel by
ENDY
IN MY HOOD II
THE SAGA CONTINUES

1

The night wind whipped in circles as paper blew about the street. A can rolled back and forth as if in the middle of a tug of war with the wind. The street lights had been broken out by the drug runners in an attempt to keep darkness over the area. The area being the corners of Isabella Ave and Grove Terrace in Newark, NJ.

It was 4 am and the night was cold. Jack Frost had definitely reared his ugly head on this night. A lone car cruised up the block of Isabella almost crawling. The two occupants of the old worn out Toyota Camry both looked in the direction of the apartment building that occupied the corner. A figure emerged from the darkness of the apartment's doorway and stepped out into the moons light. The car stopped and pulled over to corner. The young man who had emerged from the building, glided over to the old worn out Camry.

The young man was dressed in a pair of Paco jeans three sizes too big, swallowing his narrow body. Charcoal gray Timberlands swallowed his feet as he bopped along the sidewalk clumping his feet to the pavement. His gray Ecko goose coat hung to his body like a sleeping bag. The black hoody that he wore underneath was pulled tight around his head.

"What up?" he ask the passenger of the car as he stood 2 feet from the vehicle.

"Let me get two and two?" The male passenger said stretching his eyes.

The young man then turned towards the entrance from which he had come and held up two fingers on his right hand and then two fingers of his left. He then turned back to the passenger and grabbed the two twenty dollar bills that he held out the window. After taking the money the young hustla' walked away from the car and headed towards the building. As he approach another young man emerged from the building wearing almost the identical ensemble but in blue. They by passed each other as if they didn't know one another. The young man in blue clunked over to the car and tossed the drug purchase into the passenger's hand. And just as quickly as he appeared he disappeared even quicker.

The car drove off and rounded the corner faster then which it had approached leaving a trail of polluted smoke.

"Damn it's cold out this bitch!" The young man in the gray whose name was Day-Day proclaimed.

"Yo man I'm bout to bounced to the crib. It's slow as hell out t'night any way," the young man dressed in blue whose name was Unique said.

"Word I'm with you. Yo come to my crib so I can finish whopping yo ass in NBA basketball on Playstation," Day-Day said.

"Nigga please and then you woke up!"

The two stood in the deep doorway of the apartment building. Because of the darkness of the street without the lights, you would not be able to see them standing there. They huddled there in an attempt to escape the harsh winds that blew about the streets.

"What time is it?" Unique asked.

Day-Day reached into his pocket and pulled out his cell phone.

"It's 4:20. Yo at 5 that's a wrap."

"Cool, I'm wit' that," Unique agreed.

"Yo kid did you ever fuck that girl we met outside the strip joint the other night?"

"Naw son, when I was talking to shorty I saw she had a blister in the corner of her mouth. That shit turned my stomach. I wasn't sticking my dick in her mouth or her pussy," Unique said frowning up his face.

"Ill that shit is nasty. Shorty was fire too. That trick had a fat ass man," Day-Day said.

"Yeah I know but, that bitch was burning and I wasn't with that shit, condom or no condom. You smell me?" Unique said firing up an already rolled blunt he retrieved from his top pocket,

"No doubt B, no doubt."

The two young man stood there in the doorway of the apartment building passing the blunt back and forth between the two of them. Unique began to pull knot after knot of money from the different pockets of his coat. He began to arrange the loose money merging it into the stacks he already had neatly in order. He passed Day-Day five bundles to hold.

"What's that right there?" Unique asked.

"That's five yards. I got about two and a half right here."

"Yo, let's bounce, its five minutes to five," Unique said looking at his cell phone.

"Aight hold up," Day-Day said while he continued to put the money in order and place it back in his pockets. "Let me get the stash out the hallway and we out." He turned and went into the buildings hallway.

Unique jumped up and down in an attempt to heat up his body. He poked his head from the entrance looking up and down the street. Up the block he could see someone moving towards the building. He watched as the figure moved from side to side in a drunken stupor. He rubbed his hands together and put them to his mouth blowing warm air into them never taking his eyes off of the figure approaching. As the figure came into a closer view, Unique could see it was a man who appeared to be completely inebriated.

The man stood about 6'2. He was wearing a trench wool over coat, a black scully on his head pulled down to his eyes and a winter scarf tied around the lower half of his face creating a mummy look. A cigarette dangled between his fingers as he stumbled almost falling to the ground. He landed on a nearby parked car and rested there for a moment.

Day-Day came through the apartment buildings door holding a brown paper bag. He began to roll the bag up when he noticed his friend was staring at something.

"What's up man?" he asked.

"Look at this mutha-fucka right here," Unique pointed towards the drunk.

"Damn that nigga out on his feet."

They both watched as the man made several attempts to push himself off of the car finally falling to his knees. They both chuckled as the man had difficulty getting his bearings together. Finally he was able to regain his balance and continued to stumble towards the apartment building.

"Yo you ready?"

"Yeah let's roll," Day-Day said.

The two teens stepped down off the step and hunched their shoulders as an attempt to block the oncoming wind. They walked beside each other heading towards the drunk.

"This mutha-fucka is twisted," Unique said.

Just as they where about to walk past the drunk, he stumbled and bumped hard into Unique. Unique was then knocked into Day-Day and he spilled to the ground.

"Damn nigga, what the fuck is wrong with yo drunk ass?" Unique announced.

Day-Day scurried to his feet. "Mutha-fucka I should split your skull for that bullshit," he yelled reaching for his concealed weapon located down the front waistband of his jeans.

Before he could remove his gun the drunk retrieved a 357 magnum from the inside of his coat and blew a gaping hole through Day-Day's neck. The blast from the cannon sent him flying into the alleyway of the side of the building. Unique was in such a stake of shock, that he failed to reach for his own weapon before the .357 was then turned on him.

"Run ya shit," the drunk said with a raspy voice.

"Yo man here just take the shit and let me live." Unique reached into his pocket and threw the knots to the ground.

The gunman stood there staring at the young boy. Unique then reached into another coat pocket and threw the rolled up paper bag to the ground. The gunman then unloaded a round to his knee, nearly severing the leg. He fell to the ground eyes wide in a state of shock. No sound came from his mouth do to the numbing pain. The gunman walked into the alley and removed the money from Day-Day's pocket. He then turned and walked out of the alley while reaching for his .40 caliber from the waist of his jeans. Never breaking his strike he popped Unique in the head twice as he stepped over him and proceeded down the street.

UNCORRECTED PROOF
DECEMBER 15, 2007
A novel by
STORM
DEN OF SIN
What happens in the DEN, stays in the DEN...

1

"Like A Boss" – Slim Thug

"Tell me you love me, Des." I was saying this shit for his benefit. Hell, he could've been making Confession; I really could have cared less. I was here for one purpose and one purpose only. I was here to bust a nut on his tongue and drench his hands in pussy juice. The best part? He was going to waltz his dripping ass out of here without even washing his face or hands. I don't care what I had to do. He would go out to meet them with Pussy Juices a la Nadia dripping off his hands and facial hair.

"I love you, Nadia." Des was so pathetic. One minute he was looking at me with unabashed lust in his eyes. The next, he was looking around fearfully as if the door wasn't locked. He really needed to calm the fuck down. Nobody was coming in here 'til I was done; especially not her. "You know I love you, Nadia. I want to make love to you all night, every night. I can't get enough of your sexy body, your beautiful face; this gorgeous hair."

Yeah, yeah, I'm thinking; *just get on your knees.* I licked my lips and smeared spit on his before I eased him to the floor with one hand. With my other, I was pulling down my zipper of my Paper Denim jeans and dropped into a high-backed chair in red velvet. I was about to unleash the beast and let the fun begin. My clit was hard and ready long before his tongue disappeared into my slit. It was on now.

"Crawl over here, Des." I was ready to bust! Just knowing that his wife, the Deaconess, was somewhere on the other side of the locked door was utterly orgasmic. His pitiful ass crawled toward me. My jeans were down to my knees, my thong pushed to the side. When his lips were in striking distance, I snatched him into my bush and closed my eyes. One hand on each ear, I rubbed my clit up and down his forehead.

"Just let me put it in, Nadia, please. Just a little bit. I won't come in you, I promise. I love you, Nadia. Don't do this to me." *Yeah, yeah*, I'm thinking; *not today. And you'd better not stop*. My abs were getting a hell of a workout. I left a li'l juice on his earlobe.

"Oh, you love me? How much, Desmond? Tell me how much you want to be inside this tight, hot pussy that ain't been stretched out by four babies, like hers." The Deaconess could move a small South American village into her snatch and have plenty room for more. Babies, my ass. She could have that shit. I had my legs up in the air, his wet sloppy tongue slurping my pussy like a starved dog.

"Nadia, I…" He never got to finish that sentence. His lying-ass words disappeared into the bush. He was always about to leave her. Later. Next week. *Yeah, yeah, Des,* I'm thinking; *just keep licking*. I was jerking his head up and down. He looked like a bobblehead doll.

"What, Des? What where you saying? You love me? How much do you love this? All I want to hear is that you're leaving her and are finally come home to Nadia. Don't I deserve it? Don't you deserve me?" I was getting my shit off, knowing I was about to send his pussy-smelling, cheating ass right out to her. Next week, I would fuck him in her Lexus SUV and leave a little Nadia Juice on the plush leather.

"Nadia, I…" His words got cut off in the bush and drowned out by my moans. My hips were up in the air, his tongue stabbing my asshole, then sucking my pussy lips like a homeless man on his first meal. I was not hearing his lies today.

"You ready to move into this pussy for good? Put your hands in it. You feel all this? All this wetness is for you, Des. You did this to me." Three fingers from each hand parted my nether lips and dove in. Regardless of how much of a terrible, married liar he was, the sex was vigorous and juicy. But he wouldn't get his married dick in my Pussy a

La Mode today. I gripped the back of the chair, using the last of the strength in my legs to cum in his face and burn my scent into his facial pores. I couldn't control what he did away from me but damn it, I would have a say in how shit went down on this day.

"Deacon Desmond, are you ready? The morning service has started." The male voice boomed, the rattle of the handle and knock at the locked door pushed my orgasm over the edge. My head thrown back in reckless abandon, trembling legs vise-gripped around his head, liquid Scent eau de Nadia broke through like my pussy was a New Orleans levee.

"I'll be just a minute…" Des was stuttering. I was steady milking his tongue with my pussy muscles. In and out. Up and down. Harder and softer. Harder and harder. His struggles to pull free intensified my orgasm and another levee broke.

"I'm not done, Des," I whispered. "Make them wait." My legs burned in secret delight. I squeezed harder. I came harder.

"Nadia, the congregation…" Des was whispering. I tuned him out. I thought my femurs would snap, literally break to the shape of his head and yet, I couldn't stop. I squeezed harder. And released everything I had. Silence from behind the locked door. Struggling for breath, Des wheezed, coughed, moaned and swallowed my cum.

Oh well. I was done. All Hell could break loose now.

"Desmond, you open this door right now!" A female voice now. It was the Venezuelan tribe keeper at the door. I could tell it was her by the nasally, I-don't-put-dick-in-my-mouth whine. It was the same voice on the telephone when I called their house to fuck with her.

"Nadia, I got to get out of here. I have to wash, to freshen up before I walk out there." Des struggled to his feet and suddenly looked older than his 39 years. His face was shiny with perspiration and slick with pussy juice. His skin was glistening what he couldn't or didn't swallow. His neck probably hurt, too.

"You don't have time to wash, Des. You've got to get out there. They're waiting for you." I reached up to stroke his face. "Take me with you."

"Nadia, are you crazy? I have to meet with the congregation. I have to shake hands, hold hands, pray with people." His pale face deepened with color as he wiped his slick hands on his robes. "I can't go out there like this."

"Take me with you, Des." I repeated. "I can't go out there and stand with you as your wife, your woman. I can't hold my head up in society with the man I love. I can't proudly walk the streets with the man I want to spend the rest of my life with because society frowns upon divorce in the church." I hung my head low. "I couldn't take their parents from your children." I think a tear escaped.

"Nadia. Please sweetheart." He was weakening. So utterly predictable. "You know I love you. If only things were different with her. Maybe next year, when the kids are a little older."

I reached up to kiss him, licking his cheeks and goatee.

"Desmond." The Brazilian tribal hunter was beckoning again. The door handle shook fiercely and the whine took on a hint of concern. "Desmond?"

"Des, you have to go. Promise me you'll think of me when you dance to the Patron Saints of Fertility and Monogamy." I wiped a smudge of cream off his eyebrow. "I love you, Desmond. Go to her. Do the right thing."

I pushed him toward the door. The Columbian tribal dancer was about to bust open the hinges. I watched him slowly turn and walk to the door. I had to stifle my laughter. It was a damned shame. If he was about to go out that door and into the sanctuary during Sunday morning service smelling like Eau de Toilette de Nadia's Pussy, I was going to pass out. Oh God, Stacey, where are you when I need you? She was never going to believe this shit. I circled the pastor's desk and stood behind the door as he turned the lock and opened it and stood to greet his wife, Maria, the Chilean tribal witch doctor. His hand reached behind the door like he needed strength to go out the door smelling like Perfume de Pussy Nadia. I grabbed his hand for moral support. If he actually pulled this off, I was bottling up a supply of Limited Nadia's Ass and putting it on the market first thing Monday morning!

"Desmond, what were you doing? Where have you been? We've been looking everywhere for you." That whine, coupled with the nasal effect, had me wanting to spring from behind the door, fists first. "Service has started without you."

"Please, Maria, don't start. I was praying."

ORDER FORM
(PHOTO COPY)
MELODRAMA PUBLISHING
P. O. BOX 522
BELLPORT, NY 11713-0522
(646) 879-6315
www.melodramapublishing.com
melodramapub@aol.com
Please send me the following book(s):
LIFE, LOVE & LONELINESS ISBN: 0-9717021-0-1
THE CRISS CROSS ISBN: 0-9717021-2-8
WIFEY ISBN: 0-9717021-3-6
I'M STILL WIFEY ISBN: 0-9717021-5-2
A TWISTED TALE OF KARMA ISBN: 0-9717021-4-4
MENACE II SOCIETY ISBN: 0-9717021-7-9
SEX, SIN & BROOKLYN ISBN: 0-9717021-6-0
CROSS ROADS ISBN: 0-9717021-8-7
IN MY HOOD ISBN: 0-9717021-9-5
STRIPPED ISBN: 1-934157-00-7
EVA FIRST LADY OF SIN ISBN: 1-934157-01-5
THE CANDY SHOP ISBN: 1-934157-02-3
24/7 HISTRESS ISBN: 1-934157-03-1
LIFE AFTER WIFEY ISBN: 1-934157-04-X
THE MADAME ISBN: 1-934157-05-8
IN MY HOOD II ISBN: 1-934157-06-6
JEALOUSY ISBN: 1-934157-07-4
DEN OF SIN ISBN: 1-934157-08-2
ALL ABOVE BOOKS ARE PRICED AT **$15.00**
UP CLOSE AND PERSONAL ISBN: 0-9717021-1-X
THE POETRY BOOK IS PRICED AT $9.95

@ 15.00 (U.S.) = _____

QUANTITY

Shipping/Handling* = _____

Total Enclosed = _____

PLEASE ATTACH, NAME, ADDRESS, TELEPHONE NUMBER(for emergencies)
_____

*Please enclose $4.60 FOR PRIORITY SHIPPING MAXIMUM 2 UNITS.

*Please enclose $3.50 for STANDARD SHIPPING/FIRST UNIT
(.50 CENTS FOR EACH ADDITIONAL UNIT.)

FOR BULK ORDERS PLEASE CALL THE PUBLISHER.
To pay by check or money order, please make it payable to Melodrama Publishing.

Send your payment with the order form to the above address, or order on the web.
Prices subject to change without notice. Please allow 2-3 weeks for delivery.

WWW.MELODRAMAPUBLISHING.COM